MISSION IN HARLON COUNTY

Gift to board Ersland

C Rud
6-7-2022

Mission In Harlon County

BOOK TWO
THE PURSUERS SERIES

Charles Paul Reed Jr.

Storybook Adventures LLC

Dedication and Acknowledgements

This novel is dedicated to my sweet, artistic wife, Dona Lee Reed, the most interesting person I know, and who blesses me every moment I have in her presence.

Cover Art by Bryant Hastie
with all rights to Charles Paul Reed Jr. Storybook Adventures LLC

Cover design by Pepper Reed

I very much appreciate the following individuals who read and provided valuable input in every aspect of this novel
(In alphabetical order)
Gary Buscombe
Mark Church
Martha Weatherl

Copyright

Also, by Charles Paul Reed Jr.

Trouble in Harlon County – First novel in the *Pursuers Series.*

Justice in Harlon County – Third Novel in the *Pursuers Series*

Tracks to Harlon County *Twenty-one Tales of Life and Adventure*
in the Pursuers Series.

The Long Caper, A time-travel novel to 1865 Harlon County.

1

"I should have plugged you when I had the chance!" John Coates looked over his shoulder toward the old man as he descended the steps toward the alley behind Miss Emmy's house. John's heavily bearded jaw knotted. His black, deeply recessed eyes above a hawkish nose flitted about the alley, searching for a means of escape, while he tried to think of a way to distract Pappy. While the War of Secession raged, John had never fit in with an official Confederate unit. Instead, he rode with an assortment of well juiced "leaders" whose primary goals were self-aggrandizement and well-lined pockets. Although the war was officially over for almost a month, such units, being more attuned to outlawry than soldiering, kept up their raids with little regard for their victims' political convictions. John Coates' recent attempt to lead his own gang had not ended well. Nor had his attempt this day for revenge.

Pappy Jordon, spry for a man of sixty-seven years, followed his charge off Miss Emmy's back porch toward the sheriff's office with a forty-four-revolver pointed squarely at his prisoner's back. Pappy's thin face was deeply tanned and creased from a long life as a farmer exposed to northwestern Georgia's hot, moist climate. Now his lips were taut with concentration; his eyebrows, sparse and cotton white, pulled close together. He ran his forefinger across his thin mustache. He knew that the swarthy, slouch-hatted man six feet in front of him to be a shrewd, sometimes crazed, cold-blooded killer.

Pappy's red-rimmed eyes spied his revolver lying in the dust. He had been forced to relinquish it when Coates had the drop on him a few minutes earlier. The killer had intended to murder Pappy's young friend, Bronco Brumley. But, with a surge of courage, Pappy's niece, Sarah Jordan, had helped the old man turn the tables on Coates.

Pappy stooped down to retrieve the old revolver. His middle-distance vision was such that it had taken him four shots from the saddle to dispense with a timber rattler in the road the previous day. He grunted with the effort of straightening up. He hid his vision impairment and made it a point to complain out loud as little as possible about his back. He was not wearing his holster. He hefted his weapon and tucked Coates' six-gun down the front of his britches. He aimed to herd the lanky outlaw a few blocks to the sheriff's office.

Coates slowed his pace. His hands were trussed behind his back, bound at the wrists with the strings from an old, threadbare apron Pappy had spied on the back of a chair in Miss Emmy's kitchen.

"All right, no lollygagging. Keep walking." Pappy waved the gun, and they continued across the alley, on the shortest route to the jail. "I have got a happy notion that between the sheriff's charges for murder, and the army's charges for horse stealing and attempted payroll robbery, you will be spending a lot of time behind bars somewhere. That is unless you get the rope."

Coates spat in the dust. "Beckett's jail can't hold me," he growled. John was a skinny, greasy bearded, six-footer who towered over the older man. His thin lips pulled back when he talked to reveal horse teeth unevenly stained from chewing tobacco. For all of his bluster, he knew very well the old man was right about prison. In fact, the old farmer didn't know the half of it. When all of his most recent killings came to light, a stiff rope was more likely his end than not. But that possibility was only in play if he remained a captive. As they proceeded down the alley, he eyed the stolen Union horse he had tied to a nearby bush and calculated how many steps it would take to get to it. Much would depend on how good the old man was with a six-shooter. Of course, the short distance between them would not require accuracy. As they dodged around abandoned crates and clusters of weeds, Coates held one conviction; he wasn't going to be satisfied with just getting away. Revenge was always high on his list of priorities.

At present, he directed all of his ire toward the old farmer who had him in tow, but his ultimate target was Bronco Brumley, the young Union soldier he had just attempted to bring into his sights back in Miss Emmy's parlor. Next in line were Bronco's two Union soldier companions. John Coates would never forgive or forget the humiliations he had suffered at the Yankees' hands. In the larger scheme of things, this old Georgia farmer would be way down the list. But at the moment, he was John's most urgent problem.

Walking toward a jail cell was a guaranteed stress builder. John Coates often lost control of himself under stress. He could feel the inner tension building as they proceeded down the alley. Beyond the stolen horse and the backside of several buildings, they crossed Belmont, a side street, and then Avon. It seemed peculiar to Coates that their small two-man parade seemed to attract no attention at those crossings. That was an unexpected blessing. The fewer gawkers, curious children, and kibitzers there were around, the more likely his escape attempt would be successful.

Coates knew it was better to make his play on the street than trying to dream up a scheme to break out of jail. They were a block from the back door of the Lucky Star Tavern, owned and operated by Miss Emmy and a favorite hangout for Pappy. Coates wondered if the old man would parade him inside in search of assistance. If not, it was only half a block more to the sheriff's office. So as they passed the last building before reaching the back entrance of the Star, the lanky man knew his time to make his play was running out.

A volunteer hackberry tree had sprouted close to the back wall of the hardware store. It was grown enough now to partially obstruct the alley. Several of the scraggly limbs drooped low and encroached on John's path. He eyed it as they approached and formed his plan on the fly. Instead of walking around the growth or ducking under it as he would usually do, Coates stayed upright on its fringe, so the rough branches brushed across his face and left shoulder. John's momentum carried several branches with him. He caught a small limb in his teeth as it swept past. The bark and leaves felt sharp and trashy in his mouth. He dragged it forward for a couple of steps. The old man continued to follow close behind him, oblivious to the possible implications of his actions.

Coates felt the tension build in the captured branch as it and those interlocked with it pulled back harshly against his direction of travel. It was a living spring that grew taunter with each step. The rough surfaces stretched painfully against the edge of his mouth. After just a few steps, the tension built so that they threatened to lacerate his lips. He tolerated the discomfort until he estimated that Pappy was in the most vulnerable position along the branch's recovery path. He released the limbs with a swift bobbing motion and a twist of his neck. The wash of branches brushed off his hat and scratched his cheek. Simultaneously, John jerked against his bindings with all the strength he could muster. The apron strings were old, and years of repeated washings had weakened the fabric. He could feel the individual threads tear a little. In desperation, he redoubled his effort and felt them rip apart thread by thread, until the separation was complete with a sudden snap. His hands were free! Coates spun around, eager to go on the attack as the limbs whipped back into the older man's face.

"Dammit." Pappy raised both hands to ward off the stinging assault. His immediate reflex overrode his sense of an even more potent danger.

2

Mrs. Sarah Jordon stood immobile on her Aunt Emmy's small front porch. The swing's four supporting ropes vibrated as the light contraption swung through a ragged, disjointed arc, evidence that the two young people had hastily vacated it. Sarah watched in silence for a moment as the tall, young, ex-Union infantryman, Bronco Brumley, swiftly descended the front steps. His distressed blue eyes looked back toward Sarah just once as he stepped down to the walk. They were darker and more resolved now. The pain that she had engendered only a few minutes before was brutally evident by the set of his jaw. The breeze teased at the brown curly locks that escaped the confinement of his Union army cap. Now his pace did not falter. Instead, his scuffed army shoes sent up tiny whiffs of dust as he strode away.

Sarah reached back to catch one of the swing's supporting ropes and steadied it before she dropped down hard into her previously abandoned seat. Her heart was raw, but her beautiful green eyes no longer held tears. They followed the handsome Bronco Brumley in his rapid progress down the street. He had always seemed, so light-hearted during their previous encounters. His harsh response during their just-ended confrontation stung her. They had first met during her husband Jimmy Jordon's prolonged absence amid stories from returning soldiers that the young soldier had been killed.

Now, she felt her affection for Bronco swell, even as she sent him away. Regardless of the difficulty, she knew it was the right thing to do. She and Bronco had become more than casual friends. The lack of any word from her Confederate husband for many months had made it possible for the young Union soldier to soften her heart. She acknowledged her own culpability even as she recognized that the young Yankee had asked too much of her. Everything changed with the receipt of a letter from Jimmy. He was alive and coming home!

Bronco had made a mistake in letting his desire for Sarah turn the possibility of her widowhood into a certainty in his mind. So, he had recklessly unleashed his fanciful regard for her, even as she good-naturedly discouraged him. But now, with the receipt of Jimmy's letter, Sarah's many previous efforts toward discouragement seemed trivial and inadequate to her.

Sarah's momentary introspection was interrupted by a familiar sight on the small-town avenue. A horse and wagon were approaching. But it was not just any horse and conveyance. She recognized the blaze between the horse's eyes. Her father-in-law's horse, Moon, pulled the wagon. Sarah stiffened and leaned forward. "Jimmy?" She had a moment of apprehension. From his just received letter, she knew that Jimmy's arrival was the conclusion of a four hundred-mile walk from a prisoner of war camp far to the north.

A new apprehension seized Sarah. Would her young ex-Confederate husband now approaching in the wagon and the ex-Union soldier stalking away on the walk somehow sense their shared affection for her? She held her breath. Her hands clenched. She resumed her breathing as they passed each other without so much as a glance. At that moment, just after the two men passed, the young man at the reins spotted her on the porch. He grabbed his hat and swung his arms in an exaggerated, hailing motion. His big winsome smile spread across his face, and the light brown hair blew forward across his sunburned forehead.

"Jimmy?" Sarah repeated his name as she slowly rose to her feet. Her heart leaped. For months she had feared that her young husband was dead. Now her prospective widowhood vanished. Suddenly, she felt her anxiety rise for another reason. Her young husband was too spare. His suit hung as limp on him as on a coat hanger. As he grew nearer, such was her astonishment that she was scarcely aware of a muffled gunshot far off in the distance. Standing in the wagon's box, holding his hat aloft in one hand and the reins in the other, was the young man she had prayed that God would return to her. Despite his undernourished appearance, the young man was still grinning when he pulled up in front of the house. Jimmy jumped out of the wagon with a show of bravado and grimaced for a second as his sore feet struck the hard ground. The war was over, and he had walked for almost a whole month, urging himself forward on weary limbs and blistered feet. Jimmy had defeated his pain with the only incentive he had; the promise of this moment. Then he grinned again and dodged around the hitching post, and a redheaded man on the walk and bounded up the steps. Finally, he reached down to take her into his arms.

This reunion was the idyllic moment he had long promised himself. The vision of Sarah's beautiful face had been the beacon he had held before him as he trudged the many lonely miles home. After their initial embrace, he drew back and took off his hat and coat and placed them on the end of the swing. He rubbed his face with both hands. "I can't stop smiling!"

"Neither can I!" Her eyes were warm. They glistened a little as everything else in her world faded from her thoughts. She sat and pulled Jimmy down to the seat in close beside her. Her small hands settled into his big ones.

There was an unseen audience to the activity on Miss Emmy's front porch. Mister Elwood Clemens leaned back in a cane-bottomed chair in front of the dress shop across the street and watched the little drama between Sarah and first the Union soldier and then the returning Confederate. Elwood was wearing his going-to-town trousers and a threadbare blue long-sleeved cotton shirt. He was sitting in a shady spot with a clear view of the proceedings along Pepper Street. His vista was interrupted from time to time by the occasional passing of a wagon or horse and rider. He did not hide his admiration of the young lady, for she was a pretty little thing!

Elwood was a big man. He was six-two with too much gut for a man of twenty-seven years. His clothes were clean today, though a bit ragged. His nose tipped a little to the left from a bar fight, now long forgotten. The bent nose was an odd memento given the minimal time he could afford to hang out in bars. A track of wart-like growths graced the left side of his neck and continued up under the dark beard in front and back of his ear. As Elwood's financial circumstances deteriorated, the time elapsing between shaves had lengthened, and shaving was no longer even a monthly decision. His small eyes were unusually dark and held a poorly hidden potential for hostility. The nose was prominent, the brows thick. The dark interior of those eyes surrounded by watery pink eyelids gave him a feral, swinish appearance.

Elwood had been allowed to attend school off and on for several years and then pulled out in sixth grade. He was subject to occasional angry outbursts, and the other children learned to give him a wide latitude when he appeared to be brooding. Finally, his old man said he could cipher well enough, and there was work to be done on the farm. Once the old man died, Elwood could come to town every two or three weeks and hang out at the Lucky Star to nurse a cup of coffee or sit outside any of several saloons and stores and watch the doings as he was just now.

Like many young men, Elwood had taken a liking to Miss Sarah when she started rounding out. Once she graduated from school and started working full-time at the Star, he tried to flirt with her some. He was a bit clumsy with it. It took a while for her to figure out what he was doing. He was too old to be a part of her social circle. Once she did catch on, he realized that she was avoiding him when she could. She wasn't unpleasant about it, but he could tell. That withdrawal intrigued him rather than angered him.

While he sat across the street and observed, she and the tall Yankee feller were having a tiff. What had first caught his attention was the young Bronco Brumley pushing on the front door as if briefly blocked in some way. Elwood concluded that the young woman was holding the door closed. He thought that maybe he should intervene, but her obstruction was brief. She threw it open sudden like and after a few minutes inside, they both came back out and sat in the swing, jawing. It looked like she was doing most of the talking as women are prone to do. Then the Yankee jawed some back and jumped up and hightailed it down the street.

Bronco's swift departure brought a surge of glee to Elwood. He leaned forward and peered around the post, half expecting the young Yankee to turn back. She was such a purdy thing that it was hard to picture a man just walking off. Sometimes people could change their minds. But no minds altered this time. For Elwood, watching from afar, the whole episode struck him unseemly, seeing as how she was married, and Brumley was a Yankee. Elwood could not abide Yankees. Observing their over-familiarity with southern gals put him on edge.

Then no sooner did the Yankee leave than Sarah's husband, Jimmy Jordon, showed up! Dammit, the word about town was that he was dead! Now what? For just a moment there, he thought there would be a small crack in her social life, and he might try again to slide into that vacancy. But Jimmy's surprise arrival blew that idea to hell. It was pretty disheartening to sit and watch anymore, but there was a pile of work staring back at him if he went home. So, he sat. He watched with both hands resting on the top of his paunch a few inches above the buckle of his gun belt.

3

Bronco strode from the porch down Pepper Street to the corner, turned onto Main, and increased his pace. Several blocks along, he spotted his horse alone at the hitching post outside the Lucky Star. Several missing horses revealed that his friends had already left for the Jones' farm about thirty minutes out of town. Earlier, he had been with the Jones brothers and his friend, Preacher, as they celebrated the elder brother, Tom's release from jail. His disastrous encounter with Sarah had been so brief that he was pretty sure that the men could not be too far ahead. He pondered how quickly everything could change. Bronco's anticipation of marrying Sarah premised on his contention that Jimmy Jordon would not return from the war had turned to ashes. He was ready to concede that she had given him ample reminders of her hopes for her husband's return. But Bronco had chosen to ignore her cautions. His friends had also counseled him that he was moving too swiftly with the relationship. Now it was all crashing to earth. He did not totally blame her. He just did not entirely blame himself. He wondered absently if this was what Preacher meant by fate; some things are meant to be, and others are not.

He reached the Lucky Star, tugged the pinto's reins from the hitching post, and with the squeak of saddle leather, swung quickly into the saddle. So preoccupied was he with his loss that he gave no thought at all to Pappy or John Coates and their journey toward the jail. He flicked the reins against the big horse's rump and galloped down the street.

With the wind in his face and his Union cap pulled down to rest tightly just above his eyebrows, he turned toward the Jones farm. After only a few moments, he had been transformed from a man with a full-fledged plan for his future to a man facing an empty horizon.

As he cleared the edge of town and the first farm lane went by in a blur, he spotted three horses and riders far ahead. His friends appeared to have stopped at Crow Creek. Preacher was a short, robust tree trunk of a man with beefy arms and muscular legs. His head was big and square-cornered, reminding Bronco of an anvil. When amused, Preacher smiled wide with a gap between the front teeth. Bronco watched that barrel-chested man replace the cap on his canteen and remount his horse from his distant vantage point. Bronco's other friend, Sarge, sat straight in the saddle. You had to know him well to catch any hint of amusement revealed by a slight uplifting of the corners of his mouth. Tom, Sarge's brother, was a thinner, taller, older version of Sarge. A wounded Confederate Major, Tom had lost his right arm at the elbow late in the war.

Bronco reached them at a gallop and reined his horse to a stop. His mouth was dry, and his lips were grim. He was suddenly very thirsty. He didn't look directly at the three men. Instead, he leaped from his horse, swept off his blue Union cap, dropped to his knees, and used both hands to throw water on his head and face. He dipped his head beneath the surface. His splashing about reminded him of something, and a slow smile teased the corners of his mouth. Then the memory of his encounter with Sarah erased the expression so that when he surfaced, his face was grave. He quickly sat back on his haunches, placed the cap back on his head, and took in his friend's actions in his peripheral vision. As he rose, he reached for his forty-four. He whipped around and brought the revolver to bear on the two men who were more than half out of their saddles.

"Don't even think about it!"

Preacher laughed and slapped his leg. Sarge nodded at Preacher, and in mock surrender, they settled back into their saddles and held up their hands.

Tom looked confused by this display of bogus antagonism. He was not privy to the inside joke. Tom had not been present when the two men had dunked Bronco once before at a similar stream while drinking just this same way. Nor was Tom in the mood for such hilarity now. After two weeks in jail, he wanted to be home.

"So...?" Preacher started to speak.

"Women!" Bronco holstered his revolver. "That's all I have to say."

His friends exchanged glances and shrugged. Their experiences had taught them to wait some things out.

Pappy Jordon's surprise was total as the freed branch whiplashed into his face and knocked him off balance. Coates, with hands now unfettered, was on him in an instant. A quick blow to the side of his head sent the old man tumbling. Coates grasped Pappy's gun hand before he hit the ground. As he twisted the weapon away, a snarl escaped his thin lips. John spit the remnants of dusty hackberry leaves and green bark out of his mouth. He swept up his hat from the ground with a glance around and turned the gun on Pappy. Coates felt a jolt of pleasure run through him as he slowly, almost offhandedly, squeezed the trigger.

The weapon bucked in John Coates' hand. The old man's brittle body jerked as it absorbed the impact. He fell back and lay as if pinned to the ground, then with immense effort, he rose on one elbow. John brought his weapon to bear on the fallen man again. He savored the moment until he was interrupted by a commotion down the alley. Someone struggled to open the stubborn back door of the Lucky Star. Pappy's ancient eyes stared up at him as he took in the situation. His breath was labored as his free hand clutched his side. There was blood seeping between his fingers. The old farmer fell back, his eyes stared unblinking into the distant skyline, and then he was still. Satisfied, Coates retrieved his weapon from Pappy's belt. There was a little blood on the grip. He quickly swiped the fresh blood on Pappy's pants' leg and slipped his own gun into its holster. "Feels fine," he murmured. His black eyes flashed as he savored the elation that washed over him. "Feels plumb fine!"

The back door of the Star creaked half open, and the first man in line swore in frustration. Coates pushed aside his pleasure and looked around again. He instantly realized that his priority was to retrieve his stolen horse. So he ran awkwardly down the alley in his oversized snakeskin boots back the way he and Pappy had come.

In a matter of moments, he stumbled back into the area behind Miss Emmy's porch and grabbed the horse's reins. He tugged the big stolen kladruber stallion into motion and led it through the narrow space between Emmy's house and the one adjacent. He heard a commotion behind him and turned to look over the horse's rump to see a group of men running toward him well down the alley. The men were gaining, and the man in the lead had his gun drawn. Coates moved into the narrow passage between the houses and out of their line of sight and headed for Pepper Street that fronted Miss Emmy's house. He reached the front corner of the building. He hesitated as he surveyed the avenue. The young couple sitting in the swing on Emmy's porch was too self-absorbed to notice him. He could see the back of the pretty girl's head leaning against the young man's shoulder. Bronco! Coates felt his blood boil again. Here was the man who he had unsuccessfully tried to kill just a few minutes earlier. He was elated to have a second chance at him. But this was no time for finesse.

Coates moved stealthily up to the couple from behind. At that moment, as his hatred of Bronco grew white-hot, he lost awareness of everything else. With deadly focus, John Coates jabbed the muzzle of Pappy's six-gun against the young man's head and pulled the trigger. This explosion under the porch's roof was more deafening than the earlier one in the alley. The bullet entered at the base of Jimmy Jordon's skull. The young man lurched forward as the smoke rose from the gun's barrel in a swirl. Death was instantaneous. The girl screamed and shied away. She turned her stunned, contorted face toward John Coates. Sarah stared into his euphoric pin-pointed pupils as he placed the muzzle against her forehead. She closed her eyes, and her shoulder rose in a useless defensive motion. He squeezed the trigger again.

The hammer descended. There was only a click. John grunted and pulled the trigger twice more. He looked at the gun dumbfounded before he remembered that it was Pappy Jordon's weapon. The sound of running feet and muffled voices from the passage between the houses grew more pronounced, and his attention centered on the weapon wavered. Hurriedly, he threw down Pappy's useless gun and mounted the horse. He spurred it down the street as several men appeared with guns drawn. They fired two shots after the retreating figure. Then in response to the girl's screams, the men crowded up to the porch.

4

Preacher and Sarge were sitting with Tom Jones around his kitchen table, sipping their coffee. Sarge was leaning back in his chair, his gangly legs outstretched. Bronco had headed straight to his room and left the men to speculate among themselves about the status of his love life. It was pretty clear that things had fundamentally changed, but the details remained a bit of a mystery.

"He'll tell us when he's ready." Preacher said.

"That's so." Sarge agreed.

"Are you still planning to head out tomorrow?" Tom had little patience for idle curiosity about the young man's romances. Now physically recovered from the loss of his arm and with his head clearer in the aftermath of his temporary dependence on laudanum, Tom was doubly aware of his farm's condition and the rapid passing of the opportunity to get crops planted. He had spent some time walking around, noting the state of his property and own limitations. During the war with men away from home, many farms converted cropland to vegetable gardens managed by wives and children. Tom had no family. His three slaves had disappeared the same day he joined his regiment of Georgia volunteers. He ruminated on the fact that he had fed and clothed them for years, and the minute he turned his back, they lit out on him! He was also behind on his taxes! It crossed his mind that these three able-bodied men could make much progress, setting things right.

Sarge and Preacher nodded in the affirmative to his question. The kitchen conversation was at a lull when they heard a ruckus in the front courtyard.

The frantic pounding on the door brought all the men to their feet. Tom led the way to the front. One of Sheriff Beckett's deputies stood on the porch. Another was rocking restlessly forward and back in his saddle.

"Beckett sent us out." The man seemed hesitant to speak further.

"Oh?" Tom looked from one man to the other. Still sour from the tour of his farm, he was ready with a comeback. "Has someone come up with a reason to throw me in jail again?" Tom did not disguise his distaste for law enforcement, even when the law enforcement officers were friends of thirty years.

"Huh? No, Tom, nothing like that." The man seemed at a loss to say more as the remark had thrown him off track.

"John Coates has wounded Pappy Jordon and shot Jimmy Jordon dead." The man on the horse barked.

"What? When?" The men looked at each other in disbelief.

"We were just in town just an hour ago!" Tom said.

"Yeah, well, it just happened." The deputy on the porch found his voice. "He put a slug in Pappy Jordon in the alley behind the Lucky Star. He snuck up on Jimmy Jordon and shot him in the back of the head. The sheriff is putting together a posse, and since you've had your troubles with Coates yourself, he thought maybe you'd want to ride along."

Sarge looked around at Preacher and realized that Bronco had joined them in time to hear the news. Both men looked stunned but were shaking their heads in the affirmative. "We're in!" Sarge said.

"Sheriff Beckett is trying to get together all the information he can. We're supposed to meet at the jail as soon as we can get there," the deputy said.

"All right. We'll get organized and head that way. Don't wait on us. We'll be a bit." Sarge said.

The deputy remounted his horse as Sarge, Preacher and Bronco headed to the back of the house to gather their belongings. Tom was standing in the parlor when they returned.

"You're not just going to take off now, are you?" Tom lamented the news, for he reckoned correctly that his earlier imagining of the men sticking around to help set things in order was a pipe dream. Sarge looked at him in surprise.

"We were leaving tomorrow, anyway." He was holding a deerskin pouch the size of a shoe. He hefted it once and handed it to his brother, who accepted it with his good left hand. The unexpected weight of the pouch caught him by surprise and bore his arm downward. In his weakened condition, it was a bit of a strain for him to pull it back up.

"We recovered the gold father left me. There is enough gold in there to get you on your feet. I did not forget that I spoiled your plans to sell off Brownie when I rode north with him years ago. I just couldn't let you do that. Seeing him yesterday made me proud that I helped him escape. I'd be lying if I said I'm sorry." He nodded at the pouch. "This is part of my inheritance. I'm giving it to you. So, now we're square plus some." He looked into his older brother's shocked eyes and patted his shoulder. "Good luck, Tom. I wish you well." He held out his hand. Tom set the pouch down on a table, and Sarge accepted his brother's left-handed handshake, as did Bronco and Preacher before the three men filed out the front door. They stored their loose items in their saddlebags.

Tom lifted the pouch and followed them across the porch. He eyed the deerskin bag suspiciously. Inheritance? Where did Madison get gold? Then it came back to him. He did remember his father doing some prospecting when they were young. Tom hefted the pouch. It seemed almost magical for this to appear now when he so desperately needed it. He hefted the pouch again and waved his stump absentmindedly at the retreating men. The three men mounted, reined their horses around, and headed for town. Tom watched them as far as the front gate. When he turned back inside, his elation subsided a little. The pouch didn't seem as heavy now as it had at first. He couldn't help wondering if the gold he held in his hand was a fair share.

One thing was certain; Tom had no desire to go with them. He was eager to be a farmer again. The gold, even a small amount, opened a door Tom had feared closed forever. He thought highly of Cal Jordon and Jimmy. At one time, when Tom was whole, he would have joined the posse. He brought his right arm up and touched the pouch with his stump. His gun-toting, soldiering days were past. He went to the kitchen to inspect the deerskin pouch's contents and work on a plan. Suddenly, he had a lot to do.

5

A good-sized crowd of riders had assembled outside the jail when Bronco, Sarge, and Preacher arrived. Onlookers on foot stood together in small groups talking among themselves. The rapid twenty-minute ride had not given any of the three time to fully assimilate the reality of Pappy's shooting or Jimmy's death. Sarge looked over at Bronco and Preacher several times in route. The young man's face was drawn and angry. Preacher's face was resolute when he exchanged glances with Sarge, but the pace of their horses did not invite discussion. Then, just as they arrived at the jail, the sheriff came out and closed the office door to address the group. He looked harried. His graying hair and mustache placed his age as middle fifties though he was half a decade younger. He took off his hat and ran a hand from his forehead down to his chin.

"John Coates is a killer." Sheriff Beckett looked out at the crowd of riders. "A couple of you boys saw him leaving the place where he shot Pappy Jordon over behind the Lucky Star." Beckett's face worked for a minute. Then he continued. "And he shot Jimmy Jordon dead while he was sitting on Miss Emmy's front porch."

A rumble rose from the crowd. "Jimmy made it back?" The question came from one of two men who had just ridden into town and were attracted by the commotion.

"We heard he was kilt six months ago," his companion spoke up.

"He made it back today." The sheriff held up his hand and motioned toward a large man with a florid face contorted with pain. "You got anything you want to say, Cal?" The sheriff 'asked. Cal Jordon, Jimmy's father, looked around the group. His voice was low, and the horsemen leaned forward in their saddles to make out his words.

"Jimmy got back today. He was alright. He was thin and tired and hungry, but he was alright." He swiped his hand across his eyes. "He was a good son." His voice grew louder as he spoke. "He was a man who stood up for his town against the likes of them!" He pointed toward Sarge, Preacher, and Bronco.

The crowd growled and looked at the three men wearing Union caps. Bronco's full blue Union uniform seemed to glow bluer with the attention. He scowled and looked down at the crowd.

"Hold on, boys." The sheriff waved for attention. "We understand how Cal feels, but these boys have had nothing but trouble from John Coates themselves."

"No!" Cal Jordon raised his chin. "No one can begin to understand what I'm feeling right now! I had an uncle dropped in his tracks by this killer: A good man, a friend to every one of you. I had a son home from the war! He was a boy who was smart and strong and honest and true, and that damned John Coates cut him down. Cut him down while he was peacefully sitting on the porch in the swing with his little wife! And I can't figure out why!"

The crowd stirred again. Every man in the crowd had lost a friend, a son, a father, or a brother in the war. They had all grieved, and most of them thought they had recovered some. But, hearing Cal Jordon's words brought all the raw pain back to the surface. The men were nearing the boiling point.

"I'm sorry, Cal." Sheriff Beckett looked to be very upset himself. "I'm sorry, but this is not the time to be looking for a handy target among ourselves. These men had nothing to do with Jimmy and Pappy getting shot. Now is the time for us to serve justice and unite to track that mongrel down."

"We don't need them!" A small man stood up in his stirrups and looked around at the group. "We got everyone we need to get the job done. We don't need any Yankees' help."

"Yeah." A bearded man hit his companion on the shoulder with the back of his hand. "We got all the help we need right here." There was a round of agreement.

Beckett nodded. He could sense the mood. He looked hard at Sarge, Preacher, and finally, Bronco as he spoke. "I can see how you boys are feeling. I can't disagree. I asked these boys to ride with us, but maybe I was wrong. Madison Jones grew up here and is far from being a Yankee. We all know he just pulled Tom Jones' irons out of the fire with the Union soldier boys. I'm sure they'll understand if you men want to keep the group local." He looked at Sarge and raised his eyebrows a little.

Sarge sat straight in the saddle and looked toward Beckett, "Sheriff, we were headed out of town tomorrow anyway." He turned and looked around at the men. "I spent a good chunk of my life with some of you. Pappy was a friend of mine too, but if you don't need us, we're satisfied to leave it with you." He glanced at Preacher and Bronco. Preacher nodded his head in the affirmative. Bronco just looked away. "So, good luck!" Sarge reined his horse away from the jail.

"That's fine," Beckett said. "See, boys, we're all of one mind. Our job is to catch John Coates and bring him to justice. Our job is to track down his ass, and we need to get started. Now, if you don't have your provisions yet, you need to get to the store and stock up. Let's say half an hour back here? Alright, let's get after it."

He clapped his hands as a signal for everyone to get cracking." He turned half away, looked over his shoulder, and caught Sarge's eye. Then he jerked his head toward the alley beside the jail.

6

Preacher dismounted first at the back of the jail. He held the door open for his companions and followed them inside. The sheriff was sitting on a bunk in an empty cell. He seemed wrung out, and sweat beaded his forehead.

"Thanks for coming in, boys." He rose and leaned against the bars."I'm sorry I pulled you in for the welcoming you got. It's kind of predictable, I guess, but I miscalculated."

Sarge looked at his companions and smiled a trifle. "Don't worry about it," he growled. "Just because we aren't riding with you doesn't mean we can't ride. We might get lucky on our own"

Preacher nodded. "We will be fine. You can't fault a man who has lost the most important thing in his life. Can you tell us what happened?"

"Well, it's real hazy. We don't know why Pappy was in the alley with Coates. We don't know what set Coates off to shoot the old man. Right now, Pappy is unconscious down at Docs. He's lost a lot of blood. As far as Jimmy is concerned…." His voice trailed off, and he heaved a sigh, then blurted out the truth, "We don't know nothing." He looked toward the front office, where they heard muffled voices. "We don't have any idea where Coates might head now. Two old boys brought in the bodies of Coates' Uncle Jonas and his son, Dooley, earlier today. They found them half-buried at the old man's farm. So maybe his killing spree started there. Maybe he's gone plumb loco." He stopped to collect his thoughts.

"Coates has always been plumb loco," Sarge said.

"That is so," Preacher said. "He's had a fondness for killing well before we had our first run-in with him and that bedraggled captain he was running with over in Alabama."

Beckett eyed them. "So, any ideas about where he might head out to?" There was no response. He shook his head as he looked around his vacant cells. "One of them boys he was running with out at Carson's Junction might have known something, but the major's troops hauled them off before any of this happened. I hate to head out with a posse with no idea which way to ride."

"I'm guessing that Coates is broke," Preacher said. "That being the case, he could be looking for easy money pretty quick. Coates is real partial to easy money."

"That's true." Sarge nodded. "He could be leaving a trail. Your delay in getting this mob started could be a blessing. If you're looking for ideas, I'd suggest splitting your riders into three or four recon groups and heading them out in different directions. If they come on news of a sighting or a farm robbed, they can send someone back with the news. Keep some men here to hightail it out to the other groups if an actual clue comes in."

Bronco had been uncharacteristically silent. He listened with his head down. His scowl deepened. "What did Miss Sarah say?" He looked with dead eyes at Sheriff Beckett.

"Well, nothing really. Aside from verifying Coates as Jimmy's killer, she was totally in shock and grief-stricken. All we can surmise from what little she and Cal say is that Jimmy drove their wagon into town to surprise her. The two of them were sitting on Miss Emmy's front porch when Coates came up behind and shot Jimmy dead right in front of her." Beckett put his hand up and rubbed his forehead. He looked at Sarge. "I like your idea about splitting up the posse, though." He turned and started to walk back to the office and stopped. "Thanks for showing up. Sorry I brought you in for nothing." He walked back a couple of steps to shake their hands. "Good luck to you." Sarge and Preacher wished him luck as well. Beckett nodded in response to Bronco's scowl and walked purposely through the office door and disappeared.

"Well, we have the same dilemma, don't we?" Sarge looked at his companions, and his eyes settled on Bronco, who was fiddling with his cap.

"Not really." Preacher smiled. "John Coates had an itch to see New Orleans." Sarge and Bronco looked at him open-mouthed. "He did?" Sarge said.

"He did." Preacher's smile deepened. "Of course, at the time, he pictured himself going down there with a pile of payroll money."

"Instead of broke," Sarge grunted. "You didn't tell the sheriff this because?"

"Because I was afraid the information might get us invited back into the posse."

"You think so? Would that be so bad?"

"Yeah. Look, this crowd of farmers is all hot to trot right now, but I'd bet a shot of sarsaparilla that, after a little time on the wild goose chase the sheriff has in mind, most of them will be ready to call it quits before the day is over. So eventually, we'd be on our own anyway. This way, we skip all the dirty looks, petty snipping, and bellyaching."

"All good points." Sarge looked at Bronco. "Any thoughts?"

"Sounds good to me."

"What part?"

"The part where we track down Coates."

"I know you are fond of Pappy, Bronco," Preacher said. "But we have two advantages over the others. First, we know he wants to go to New Orleans, and we are headed that way anyway. So if they don't get him, we will."

Bronco looked up. "Yeah, we'll get him, but that won't be enough. No matter what happens, that won't be enough."

Sarge and Preacher exchanged a glance. "It's never enough, but I get the idea you mean something more." Preacher said.

"Yeah," Bronco said. His voice wavered a bit with tension. "Because I got Pappy shot. As sure as if I put a bullet in him myself, I got him shot. What if he doesn't make it?" He wiped the back of his hand across his brow. "And, I'd bet the farm if I had one that I'm responsible for Coates killing that Jimmy Jordon fella too."

Sarge and Preacher leaned in. "How's that, son?" Preacher put his hand on the younger man's shoulder. The return and fate of Sarah's young husband was not by itself an explanation for Bronco's comment.

And then Bronco told them everything. He told them about his close call with John Coates and the near-shootout in Miss Emmy's parlor. He finished with how Miss Sarah used the door like a battering ram into John Coates' face so Pappy could get the drop on him. "If Pappy dies, I'm the one responsible. I let him walk out of there knowing he was old and feeble and that Coates has more tricks than a card shark." The men watched his face twist with the memory. "I was in such a rush to get Miss Sarah alone and propose that I let myself believe he'd be okay to walk that low-life killer to the sheriff's office by himself. How could I be so stupid?"

"I can see why you think that," Sarge said.

Bronco looked up as Preacher dropped his hand from his shoulder. Bronco swiped his hand across his eyes again.

"Yeah, I do, too," Preacher said. "There were a series of events. And you made some unfortunate decisions along the way, and there was a bad result, so you're ready to take the blame."

Preacher squared around to face the younger man. "But you didn't have complete charge of events. None of us ever do. You didn't personally pull the trigger. You didn't put the gun in Coates' hand. You didn't do anything to make Coates the killer he is."

Sarge said, "Look at it this way. How do you suppose an officer must feel when he sends tens or hundreds or thousands of men into combat? Are all of them perfectly trained? Did all of them clean their weapons the night before? Do all of them even have the will to fight? The answer is, he can't know. He can't know all those things and a thousand more."

Preacher leaned forward. "Pappy walked out of there with his gun on Coates. He was a grown man with as much experience as the three of us combined. Hell, he fought in the Mexican War. The same result could have happened with any of us. If you had gone instead of Pappy, it could have been you shot. We'll never know all the possible outcomes. All we can do is catch the maggot and get Pappy some justice."

"Are you prepared for that?" Sarge said.

"I guess so." Bronco straightened.

"While we're on the subject, do you want to drop in and check on Mrs. Jordon?" Preacher asked.

Sarge raised his eyebrows and watched Bronco's face.

"No," Bronco said. "She told me her decision about us already." He paused. "I'm probably the last fella she wants to see right now."

"Maybe," Preacher said. "Even if that wasn't the case, this is probably a bad time to knock on that door."

"Let's get to the general store and see if the farmers left us any vittles to buy," Sarge said.

They walked their horses around the side of the jail to Main Street in time to see two men on horseback join the groups of riders ready to head out of town. They took off in different directions. The third group, including Jimmy Jordon's father, was pulling up outside Doctor Jenkins' office. Sarge considered stopping in too, but it looked crowded, and there was nothing they could do.

7

Mister Elwood Clemens watched the developments with the posse from a bench across the street from the jailhouse. He scratched his heavy black beard and combed his fingers through his dark stringy hair while he considered the recent events. His dark, brooding eyes, below thick eyebrows, were thoughtful. After the fuss on Emmy's front porch subsided, he had moved to take up his new observation post. From Elwood's perspective, neither Jimmy nor Pappy Jordon was a great loss. The Jordon clan was a bit too conventional and respectable for his taste. Now, listening to Cal Jordon carrying on about his boy kind of put him on edge. He had no notion of joining in. Clearly, ample resources were ganged up to take on John Coates if they could find him.

Clemens ignored the redheaded man sitting on the other end of the bench as he looked around for Sarah, but she was not in evidence. He could understand that she'd be upset. It had been a sight to see. John had appeared out of nowhere and just walked up and plugged Jimmy. Damn! That was cold! Elwood had to admit that he was as startled as the girl when that six-gun spit fire into the back of the young man's head. Once, early in the war, Elwood had caught a couple of rebels trying to take one of his sows. He plugged them both before burying their remains behind the barn. They hadn't been locals, and no one had ever come around looking for them. But they had at least been facing him when he put them down. No doubt about it, John was a cold, hard man. As far as hunting him down, Elwood had other fish to fry. He wouldn't be surprised if John was already out of the county, given the head start his neighbors were giving him.

Mrs. Sarah Jordon lay on her side with a pillow over her head. Her extended weeping had subsided from pure exhaustion. There were only so many tears. The hurt in her stomach from the sobbing and retching could not be compared with the injury to her heart. Pain from the latter threatened to be a permanent condition. Her Aunt Emmy came in quietly to report that almost every man in the immediate area with a horse to ride was out looking for John Coates. She lay a gentle hand on Sarah's shoulder, but the girl was unresponsive.

Sarah kept running the brief script through her mind. Once she learned of Pappy Jordon's fate, it was not hard to connect the faint gun report she had heard while sitting on the porch to his injury. Sarah could now trace every moment from that shot in the distance to the explosion of a six-gun inches from her head. She relived the hideous series of emotions she had watched cross John Coates's face, from glee after the bullet entered Jimmy to anticipation as he held the barrel of his handgun to her head. Finally, she had seen dismay replaced by panic as the six-gun failed to fire and the townsmen approached.

One thing was sure. Sarah felt changed forever. She held guilt from which she was sure there could be no cleansing. There was no doubt John Coates had intended to kill Bronco Brumley. That she was responsible for her husband's death was assured. If she had not responded to Bronco's boyish charm and instead hidden behind her widow's dignity, John Coates would not have come looking for the young man on her front porch. Pappy Jordon would not have marched the killer to jail and been shot en route. If Pappy died, she'd have two deaths on her account.

She lifted the second pillow and rolled over to face the wall. She tucked it to her bosom. Except for her, sweet Jimmy would still be alive. The thought made her gag again. She sat up and faced the bucket beside the bed, but all she could manage were a few more dry heaves. Her stomach was empty, as was her heart. Her life itself seemed pointless. She swung back on the bed. She pulled up the pillow, and though she prayed to avoid it, she began tracing the script of her guilt over again until a blanket of sleep enveloped her.

Sarge, Preacher, and Bronco purchased and loaded their supplies as quickly as they could. Then, with a pouch of pure gold in his saddlebags, Bronco briefly lost his inhibition about spending his dwindling army pay and grabbed up a civilian shirt, pants and hat. He put them on in the back of the store and presented himself to his companions without comment. Five horses were tied up outside Doctor Jenkins' office as they rode out of town. Word in the store was that Pappy was still unconscious. The only activity on the street was a deputy and two other men sitting on the front porch of the sheriff's office. Their horses were tied out front, ready to ride if they heard about John Coates' whereabouts. Despite Sheriff Beckett's words, they eyed the three Union men suspiciously.

"Reckon they will have any luck tracking Coates?" Preacher muttered.

"Maybe, if he does something stupid before he leaves the state," Sarge said. "Without a new move from him, I doubt the posse will get more than a day's ride out of town. It's hard to stay focused when you're swimming upstream blind." He reined his horse down the south road. "Of course, they could get lucky."

"We think we know where he's headed, and we will still need a boatload of luck," Preacher said.

Bronco looked in the window of the Lucky Star from habit as they rode by. He didn't spot anyone he knew inside. He looked around the town. He remembered his many walks to Miss Emmy's house. Two blocks to the right, the spire on the Baptist church Preacher was fond of rose over the nearer buildings. He looked at the stocky man's demeanor. The big square army cap-covered head was pointed straight to the front. Bronco wondered if he was the only one who rued their time here. He clicked his tongue at his horse to catch up. He had arrived with little and was departing with a large pouch of gold, so he should be happy. He wasn't. Say what they would, his friends could not talk him free from his guilt. Catching John Coates was the only possible salve for his conscience, and it was a weak tonic at that. He pulled his new hat down more snuggly as they passed the last store, and before long, the last trace of Titustown faded behind them.

8

John Coates was hungry. Twelve hours had passed since his last meal. He had no provisions and precious little currency on him. He wanted to pass through this country with as little fanfare as possible. The fewer people he encountered, the better. He was experiencing a reoccurring image of a heavy knotted rope around his neck. When he caught the smell of smoke drifting toward him, his first instinct was to ride on. But his stomach growled ominously just then, so he nudged the horse in that direction. If things didn't look right, he could keep going.

As he approached, he knew that it was a Romani camp. The one wagon was covered with colorful astrology symbols, and an old woman stirred a pot on a campfire. The large spoon stopped in mid-stir when she saw him. A small towheaded boy of about ten carried in an armload of deadfall kindling from the surrounding forest. He stood stock-still, almost mid-step.

"Howdy, ma'am." Coates pitched his voice half an octave up the scale to what he imaged to be a friendly tone. Anyone who knew him well would expect a lie to follow, but these people were strangers. He sat straight on his horse and cast his eyes around, looking for any other members of the group. He was startled when off in the middle distance, he heard the report of a rifle. Coates reached for his handgun.

Fear registered on the old woman's face as she jumped up and waved at him to leave it be. "It's all right, Mister! My son is hunting our dinna." Her piercing eyes took him in from the fully bearded face to the fancy boots he had taken off a dead renegade captain two weeks earlier. Her facial expression revealed little, but the eyes exposed her tension.

"Young Roma, take the man's horse over to the stream."

The boy dropped the dry branches within her reach and moved to stand in front of Coates' horse, waiting for the man to dismount.

Coates put his hands on his hips and slowly stretched his back while he coolly peered around again. The prospect of food in his belly was very tempting. So since there seemed to be no one else around, he threw the boy the reins and climbed down.

"You're riding a fine Yankee horse." The old woman pointed at the star on the saddle blanket as the animal walked toward the stream. Her slumped shoulders, arthritic hands, and gray-streaked hair betrayed her age.

Her disabilities brought back his memory of old Pappy Jordon lying still on the ground only hours earlier. A shiver of pleasure went through John.

She continued, "Seen too many of those around here lately. You should flip that blanket." She removed a plug of tobacco from her jaw. "Too many soldiers around from both sides," she suggested meaningfully. "It's been hard to hang on to our horse. Rebels and Yankees both have tried to walk off with it. We had to steal it back just last night." She motioned toward the small gray mare tied up near the stream. Coates wondered if her comment was an effort to create some sense of unity between them.

"I 'spec they was right surprised when they woke up this morning shy their stolen horse?" Coates asked. The corners of his lips curled upward in just a hint of a smile. His voice stayed high in his wheedling tone when he spoke.

John sensed that his words did not reassure her. She pretended to laugh, displaying a gap between her lower front teeth. She threw some sticks in the fire. They heard the rustling sounds of steps in the short underbrush, and a middle-aged dark-haired man emerged from the forest. He was carrying a rifle and a highly decorated game-bag over his shoulder. Coates tensed, and his hand touched the grip of his handgun, but the man largely ignored him except to nod and silently slid his rifle into the back of the wagon. The man glanced briefly at the old woman, who did not react. Then, he proceeded a bit downstream. He pulled a long knife from his boot and cleaned three rabbits in a couple of minutes. Only upon his return did he acknowledge Coates' presence.

"Yes, sir?" He hitched up his pants with one hand and touched his chest with his thumb. "Roma," he said. He gave Coates a thorough once-over through wary eyes. The old woman had a thick green branch ready for him to use as a spit. He threaded on the three rabbits and placed the spit above the growing fire. He addressed the old woman

"We need to leave here early in the morning. The further southwest we get, the less likely the Yankees will come on to us again."

"Yes." She turned from him and addressed Coates, "This is my son, Old Roma." She waved toward the boy. "This is my grandson Young Roma." She poured off the liquid in the cup and peered intently inside. She glanced from Old Roma and Young Roma back to Coates. "The tea leaves say men are coming this way."

"From which direction?" Coates glanced back over his shoulder as if the suggested riders were imminent.

"The east. Trouble comes from the east. But it will not arrive here for a little while. The rabbit will be ready soon."

Coates was too canny to be fooled. He sensed that she was looking for his reaction to this news. Strangely, it did not perturb him, perhaps because the chill down his spine was mollified by her bit of showmanship. Since the rifle was in the wagon and his six-gun was on his hip, he did not feel that these people were an imminent threat. Whoever was coming was undoubtedly a good distance away.

"Sit by the fire?" Roma motioned indifferently. "We welcome everyone to our camp who isn't after our horse."

Coates realized that the old woman was peering into a cup of tea leaves again. She searched Coates' face until his intense eyes met hers. "You may be coming into our camp in peace, but you did not leave peace behind you."

"Eh." Coates looked away but felt his gaze drawn to her again. Their eyes locked. She tipped the cup toward him.

"The leaves say you are on the run."

Roma smiled. "As does the condition of your horse." He motioned toward Coates' lathered horse.

The adults were not talkative, and the boy remained subdued. Roma did not ask questions, and Coates did not offer hints concerning the "trouble" behind him. Instead, he asked about their origins and destination, but their answers were short.

"We were in a settlement outside Atlanta until Sherman's men were almost upon us. We have been visiting small towns selling trinkets since. We will probably continue as far as Mississippi." Roma said.

"The tea leaves suggested it." The old woman emptied the cup. Old Roma considered her words and smiled a little. Then, with the rabbit cooked, Roma divided one between the old woman and the boy and handed one to Coates. Even the old woman seemed to have nothing to add, and they ate in near silence. John considered gypsies only half a peg higher than a slave. He had observed a good many freed slaves passing through Titustown since his return from Alabama. They seemed to gather in the town, looking for direction. Were they there to work or steal? He had seen none today during his brief visit. When he finished, Coates walked to the stream to rinse his hands. He dried them on his pants legs, gathered up the horse's reins, and walked back to join the family.

"Well, I need to get a move on. Appreciate the vittles." He casually pulled his revolver. "Now, before I leave, I'll need the money you keep in the box."

Roma stood, his face perplexed. "What money? What box?"

"Come on! I know you gypsies always have a box, and it always has money in it."

"We have no such box." Roma reached into his pocket and pulled out a greenback and some Confederate dollars. "I can give you this."

Coates smirked. He turned his gaze to the young boy. "That's a fine-looking young' un you got there. It'd be a shame if he got winged, wouldn't it?" His thumb rested on the hammer of his forty-four.

Cold fear swept across the faces of the two adults. Then, quickly, the old woman jumped up and pulled the boy behind her. "No!"

Old Roma started to speak, but she cut him off. "Young Roma, go get the green box."

The boy looked toward his father for guidance. Stricken, Roma nodded his permission. The boy disappeared into the wagon. A cabinet door slammed. A moment later, Young Roma reappeared with a small green box. He handed it to his father. Old Roma took two strides and thrust it into Coates' stomach. His hands clenched in frustration. "Take it and go."

Coates waved the man away and slid his gun back into its holster. He flipped open the lid and inspected the contents, consisting mainly of Confederate money. There were two greenbacks and a few coins mixed in with the Confederate bills. He tossed the worthless Rebel paper over his shoulder. He reached back, opened his saddlebag, and dumped the small change inside. He dropped the box.

"Begone." Roma's face was ashen, his fists clenched.

Coates felt his ire rise for an unidentifiable reason. He automatically touched the butt of his revolver but let his hand fall away.

The old woman looked in the cup meaningfully. "Time is not your friend."

Coates involuntarily looked eastward. "That's so." He reined the horse around, and in a moment, he had regained the road and was moving smartly west toward Alabama.

Only then did Roma call over his son and hug him tightly to his chest. "A black cloud departs."

The old woman pulled her shawl closer around her shoulders. "Yes. We are spared great evil." She motioned for the boy to pick up the box and the Confederate bills scattered about the yard. A small smile played around her mouth. "But he did not get the red box where we keep most of our money."

9

Preacher rode out of Titustown with a double sense of loss. First, he mourned the wounding of Pappy Jordon. The old man had been a friend to all of them. That he was still unconscious did not bode well. Second, Preacher remembered the loss of Lieutenant Adams from their recent soldiering days. A high percentage of wounded men died from blood loss, poor doctoring, or runaway infection. He realized they would likely never know the eventual body count of Pappy's set-to with John Coates after leaving town. He looked at Bronco. He wondered if Sarge's pep talk earlier in the day helped the young man. He seemed a little less hang-dogged, but the sparkle had not returned to his eyes. Of course, the recent loss of Mrs. Jordon could account for that all by itself.

He glanced over at his other friend. Sarge was Sarge, quiet, resolute. They had traveled and fought together for two years. Sarge was in the army for four years before the war started and eight years in total. He joined when military service was an honored tradition in the south. When war came, he kept his pledge to defend the constitution when men of much higher rank and similar backgrounds had opted for the confederacy. It seemed somehow ironic that John Coates' trail would lead them to the destination that Sarge had already set for himself. Bronco and Preacher had less clear ideas about where they wanted to go, so they were along for the ride as far as the New Orleans destination was concerned.

Preacher considered the church spire as he watched it slide by over the rooftops in his peripheral vision. The nice lady he met playing the piano, Miss Maggie Taylor, mentioned the lack of a preacher. He wondered if that conversation was a message from God. He searched his heart. Since losing his church in Missouri, he ached to receive a call to a new mission. Was this vacant pulpit calling him? He felt a universal kinship for every church he encountered. He wondered how he would recognize the right one. No, it didn't feel like this was heavenly inspired just now. Even considering the subject had built-in barriers. He was a Yankee soldier. He was vehemently opposed to slavery. He let it go. He was confident that God had a plan for him to be revealed in good time.

The following two hours provided the men with little diversion. Each was unyielding concerning their mission. Knowing Coates was headed to New Orleans did not guarantee they would catch him along the way. A hundred options were available to him in the form of forks in the road, sidetracks, and run-ins with other people. Unless they came on the man the first couple of days, a reasonable expectation was that they had little chance to see him again until they reached their mutual destination, if then. They were only a few miles west of the hamlet of Turkey Creek when aroused from their semi-slumber.

"I smell smoke." Bronco tilted his head up. They pulled up and sniffed. The scent was faint but distinct.

"Reckon it's Coates?" Bronco eyed his friends. It seemed to him that it would be more than their share of good luck to catch the man so quickly.

"I expect we'd better act like it is just to be on the safe side," Sarge said.

"I doubt he'll be sitting and grinning at us like he was in Titus-town a week ago," Preacher said.

Sarge turned to Bronco. "Reckon you could slip ahead through the brush and take a look-see?" He looked at Preacher and back to the younger man. "You are quite a bit lighter of foot than Preacher, and I are." The corners of his lips turned up a bit.

Bronco nodded. He alighted and pulled his Henry rifle from its scabbard. He was a sure shot with it, and his hunting excursions usually provided the game on their travels.

"We'll give you a five-minute head start and then continue slowly down the road." Sarge looked at Preacher for confirmation.

"Good idea." Preacher dismounted and walked his horse over to the side of the road so it could graze. "We're still a good way off." Bronco threw his reins over a limb and took a drink from his canteen.

"Ready," he said.

"Be cautious. If you come on Coates, hightail it back to the road and let us know," Sarge said.

"Okay." Bronco slipped into the trees and took in the lay of the land. Once away from the road, the trees were old-growth, and the high canopy created a deep shade. It was pretty easy to silently wind his way through the stunted underbrush and fallen timber. He kept himself about thirty feet from the edge of the road. It was quiet in the forest, and the stillness comforted him. He wondered how Pappy was doing. It took a few minutes for him to move forward enough to catch the sound of a squeezebox. He hastened his pace. He was pretty sure Coates didn't play a musical instrument, and if he did, he would be smart enough not to play it while on the run. The evening breeze shifted, and the familiar smell of a campfire and cooked rabbit grew stronger. He peered ahead and, through a break in the trees, caught sight of a young boy dancing to a lively tune.

"Lift your feet higher." A husky voice rang out. "Higher still!" A deep laugh followed the advice.

Bronco moved a bit right and left to take in the entirety of the camp through the foliage. There seemed to be only the man, the boy, and an older woman. He decided on the direct approach and stamped his feet in pine straw and jiggled a pine sapling. The music stopped. Bronco gave a greeting and made his appearance. "Hello!" He emerged from the low brush and stood with his rifle raised over his head. "I heard the music."

The man leaped to his feet at the sight of another intruder. He grabbed the boy and pulled him close.

The old woman waved a tin cup. "We've been expecting you," she said. The man glanced at her. She nodded back and turned her eyes on Bronco. "We've been expecting you ever since your friend left out of here about an hour ago."

Bronco walked a couple of paces closer. "If the man you are speaking of is who I think he is, he's not our friend." He pointed toward the road. "I do have a couple of friends with me who will be here in a few minutes." He made a hand motion indicating he wanted to fetch them and hurried down the short lane to the road.

Sarge and Preacher caught sight of Bronco from about a hundred yards away. Both hefted their six guns but put them away when they saw that he seemed untroubled.

"It's a gypsy camp," Bronco explained when they were close enough to converse. "Just a man, an old woman, and a boy."

"Ah," Preacher grunted. The men dismounted and led the horses to follow Bronco back to the fire.

"Hello," Sarge said. He held up his empty hand as a sign of peace. "They call me Sarge. This is Preacher."

"And I'm Bronco." The younger man tipped his hat at the old lady.

The man released the boy. The new arrival's Union uniforms were enough to set him on edge. "I am Roma. This is my mother, Sarna, and my son, Young Roma." He glanced toward the gray mare, munching grass a few paces away.

Sarge saw his look and grinned. "No, we aren't after the army horse you have tethered over there. We are looking for a man who may have passed this way earlier."

"I forgot to tell you." Bronco slapped his forehead. "They say Coates left here only an hour ago."

Roma and Sarna nodded their heads in agreement. "Barely an hour," Roma said. "Why are you after him?"

Preacher took off his cap and rubbed the back of his neck. "Well, that is a long list. Murder, attempted murder, attempted robbery, horse theft." He looked at his friends. "Did I leave anything out?"

"That about covers it," Sarge said. "Let's just say he is on the run on the heels of several deaths." He looked around. "You never know what will set him off. So I'd say you're right lucky to be rid of him."

"He is a black cloud," Sarna said. "It was a great relief when he left."

"Yes, he is." Sarge turned to his companions. "He has a shorter lead than I expected. It's almost dark. We need to come up with a plan."

"We're unlikely to tree him at night unless he's foolish enough to start a fire," Preacher said.

"Let's ride a little further," Bronco pressed.

"Alright." Sarge looked over at the three campers. "Thanks for the information. We'll be leaving. We'd like to get closer to him before we camp for the night." He handed Bronco the reins to his Pinto, and they all mounted.

Bronco tipped his hat to the lady, and they started away, then stopped when Roma next spoke. "One more thing, sirs." he stepped closer. "He knows you are coming."

"Oh?" Sarge glanced at his companions.

"Yes, my mother told him before he left."

Sarna nodded and held up her tin cup. "The tea leaves never lie."

10

John Coates felt a sense of relief to know that he was in Alabama. The rough dirt road did not change in texture, condition, or width, nor did the number of travelers he encountered increase. There was just a lessening of tension across his shoulders. The reduced ache in the pit of his stomach might have been due to the newly consumed rabbit, but his crafty brain added everything up and concluded that he was now across the state line. All during his flight, he had promised himself that state lines and long days in the saddle would make him safe. And even now, he stayed in the saddle long after he would have liked to dismount and build a fire. The gypsy woman's warning of men headed toward them from the east was a little spooky. It did concern him that he failed to finish off the gypsies before he left. Only the presence of the boy had stayed his hand. Coates had been a defenseless boy once. He had endured beatings regularly. Though he held no tenderness toward adults, his history had affected his harshness toward children just a bit. Alive, the gypsies were free to tell others about him. But he reminded himself that it was less important, now that he was across the state line. He meditated on these things as he continued to ride, and the darkness settled over the countryside.

Eventually, his horse decided that they had reached their destination for him by stopping dead in his tracks in the middle of the road. The lather was thick. The big strong stallion was done. Coates examined his surroundings. On the right, through a break in the trees in the moon's quarter-light, he glimpsed a body of water. He remembered seeing a map indicating a small lake just a few miles over the Georgia/Alabama line. That cinched it. He climbed off the horse and walked it until he found a game trail leading through the pine forest toward the water. The lake was a good omen, he thought. It would provide fresh water for himself and his horse. And as a possible bonus, a place to fish for his breakfast in the morning. He was dead tired. If it weren't for the danger the old woman predicted, he would be tempted to linger here for a few days. He doubted a posse would cross a state line. But, since Pappy was one of his victims, the Jordan family might have enough political influence to get the sheriff to stretch beyond his jurisdiction a bit. Still, he decided to set that decision aside until the next morning. He could barely make out his own feet as he negotiated the last steps down to the shoreline. He unsaddled his horse, and it dropped its head to drink. It was a warm evening. The air was still. The sky was clear; stars had begun to blaze overhead. An owl hooted in the distance as he knelt and washed his thickly bearded face. A fish splashed loudly nearby. A promising sign, he thought. He spread the blanket in the thick pine straw and lay back on it, fully dressed. He was too tired to start a fire. He had nothing to heat or cook and doubted he would be awake long enough to care. It was too much trouble even to kick off his big boots. He dozed off, remembering the expression on Pappy Jordan's face when he took his gun away from him. Then there was that last moment with Bronco sitting in the porch swing when he pulled the trigger. The flash from the muzzle had singed the hair. He sipped a little air through his nostrils and imagined he could smell a tinge of it still. He breathed deeply, and the fresh Alabama air displaced the singed smell. A smile flickered at the corners of his mouth. It felt good.

Sheriff Beckett's scouting party was getting restive. One by one, each man looked longingly behind them for a rider bringing news of a Coates sighting. They had accepted the elder sheriff's plan to split up and do their searches in small groups when he explained it at the jail. In the beginning, some had even nodded their heads at the old man's wisdom in organizing everything.

The group Beckett was leading stopped everyone they encountered. They rode into farmyards and questioned farmers while wives stood nearby, and passels of children hid behind the door or their mother's skirt and listened. There weren't many farms in the forested northwest Georgia area, and some of the farmhouses set back up to a quarter of a mile from the road. This day being early in the week, there weren't many people traveling the road either. At each stop, they cautioned the farmer about the danger John Coates presented and encouraged each of them to get word back to the sheriff's office if they spotted anyone they thought could be him. As the hours slipped by with no word from town and no sightings to validate their direction of travel, the men started to question both the plan and the planner.

"We've been out here riding around for four hours, Sheriff." The small man stood in the saddle and stretched his legs. "If someone did spot Coates, we're so far out now that they'd have a heck of a time catching up to tell us about it."

"It'll be getting dark soon," another man lamented.

A couple of the other men nodded. Beckett could tell that they thought maybe it was time to head back and find out if anyone had news. The lawman looked around the group and shared their concern. Without confirmation that they were headed in the right direction, spending much more time could turn his organized plan into a wild goose chase.

"Alright, boys, let's head back. No one out this way has seen a sign of Coates. So if someone has news and is riding our way to tell us about it, heading back puts us just that much closer to getting on his trail." There was a murmur of agreement.

11

Pappy stirred for the first time, and the movement sent pain shooting through his brain. It was dark behind his eyelids, for they felt glued shut, and he fought against their unresponsiveness until he managed to force them open and was able to stare at the unfamiliar ceiling. The doctor's infirmary was empty, and the room was quiet. He had visited the office some years before when his son, Howie, was injured. He brought his hand up to his forehead and then down to his face. He estimated the elapse of time by the feel of the gray stubble on his chin. He determined from its length that it was well along in the afternoon. He rotated his head very slowly and took in the room.

The shelves on his near side held boxes and bottles. A small table sat close by to his right. The bed he was lying on was harder and higher than his bed at home. There was persistent discomfort. He moved a hand and touched his side. Gauze bandages covered his ribs. It was very tender under his fingers. He made a motion to sit up, and pain shot through him again. *Damn!* He lay back. He wondered what had happened. Then in bits and pieces, he recalled lying on the ground. He felt again the stunning impact of the bullet passing through his side.

In his mind's eye, he looked up once again at his assailant from a perspective on the ground that he, in his advanced age, had almost forgotten existed. And he remembered John Coates standing over him and moving the six-shooter in his direction for a kill shot. He had realized that he had only one card to play. At the last instant, he decided to play possum, falling back pretending to be dead. Then a funny thing happened, real darkness had descended. He grimaced. That was as far back as his memory would take him. He heard the noise of a chair scraping across the front office floor on the other side of the paneled door. Then the door to the infirmary opened.

"You're awake?" Doctor Jenkins went to the bedside and put his cool hand on Pappy's forehead. "Not bad. I don't think you have a fever."

"John Coates shot me," Pappy said. His voice was weak, and he tried to clear his throat.

"We were pretty sure of that, but it is good to know for sure since the sheriff is out looking for him with a bunch of men in what could turn into a necktie party," Doc said.

"Serve him right even if he didn't kill me." Pappy touched his bandages gingerly. "What's the damage."

"Well, the slug separated two of your lower ribs, missed your lung, and came out in the back. If you don't get gangrene, you'll survive. The fact you are awake right now is a good sign. Like I said, no temperature. If you are still for a few more days, you may be able to get out of here alive."

Pappy nodded. He smiled a little. "Think they'll really string him up?"

"Sheriff Beckett and the boys have been out ever since it happened."

Pappy thought of his son. "Does Howie know?"

"Yes, he got fetched right away. He's been sitting right here all afternoon. He's over at the Star, having supper."

Pappy closed his eyes. The doorknob turned. Howie came in and halted when he saw his father's eyes reopen.

"Dad!" He limped to Pappy's bedside on his bad leg. "I've been worried about you." He put his hand on the old man's arm. He was taller than his father and more substantial too. His face was square, while Pappy's seemed more triangular with his pointed chin. "Doc said you'd pull through if you ever woke up, so I guess you're out of the woods now?" He looked at Doc for confirmation.

Doc smiled, shrugged, and spread his hands. "I've done all I can do. Now it's up to your old man and the good Lord. If he takes care of himself and stays in this bed the way I say, he could be back to his normal ornery self in a week or so."

Howie's smile faded. "Course, cousin Cal is terrible broke up."

"He is?" Pappy looked perplexed. "Why he knows what a tough old buzzard I am. He's the same way hisself. It takes a shot to the gut, the head, or the heart to kill a Jordon!" He smiled. "I'm surprised he'd fret a minute over a little hole in my short-ribs." He looked over at Doc, who was suddenly very long-faced. Howie shifted around and put his hand on his father's shoulder.

"Cal is broken up about Jimmy, Dad. John Coates shot Jimmy dead on Miss Emmy's porch." Seeing the shock on his father's face, Howie told him the whole sordid story: Jimmy's casual killing, the attempted murder of Sarah, and the mystery of why. "You know Cal, Dad. He was resigned that Jimmy might not come back from the war, but when he did and was in one piece and had a future again, this senseless killing was too much. Cal is sick, trying to understand why. And well, we all are."

Pappy closed his eyes. He shuddered. The rest of the story came back to him. He knew the reason why he was in the alley with Coates. Instantly he knew who Coates thought he was shooting on Emmy's front porch. He knew who was to blame for Coates being free. He remembered what he had just said about it taking a bullet to the gut, head, or heart to kill a Jordan. Howie's words had hit all three. His head dropped back, and he closed his eyes. A new blackness descended. By that time, he had already decided that he didn't care to live anymore.

12

It was late afternoon. Elwood Clemens caught sight of Mrs. Jordon going into the doctor's office and sauntered across the way to take a seat on the step and wait for her to come out. He had kept an eye out for her since her aunt came running down the walk to lead her, still sobbing, into the house. Both women were beside themselves. With the door open, he could hear their cries across the street. Several men had toted Jimmy off the porch and out of sight of the front windows while waiting for the sheriff. Now, as he leaned against the post on the doctor's front step, Elwood fiddled with a piece of stout cord, tying first one kind of knot and then another. He was fascinated by knots and considered himself an expert. He had come across a book on tying sailors' knots many years before. And, of course, being mainly a picture book, it had been more interesting than regular books with page after page of words. He had picked up on other knots as the years passed. He was especially fond of the hangman's knot, although he knew other more intricate ones very well. The hangman's knot was so bulky and heavy and ominous with its foreboding implications compared to others that it fascinated him. He sometimes would sit and tie and retie the hangman's knot for an hour at a time.

He was so involved with this enterprise that Sarah was out of the doctor's door and starting away when his attention shifted. He jumped to his feet and stuck the cord into his pocket.

"Howdy, ma'am. I'm Elwood Clemens." She glanced up at him and nodded her acknowledgment. "I was wondering how Pappy is doing?" Elwood took a step too close and peered down at her.

Sarah stepped back a pace, and her head snapped back into a near military posture to look up at him. She could see his thin lips forming a crooked smile over yellowed teeth. Aside from his caterpillar eyebrows, his abundant whiskers made little of his other features visible.

"Thank you, Mister Clemens. Well, he's awake, and Doctor Jenkins says he's going to be okay if he behaves himself." She could not bring herself to smile. She was unaware that Elwood and Pappy had more than a nodding acquaintanceship, so she didn't go into detail. Instead, she ducked her head as if to continue on her way.

"Well, that's real good." Elwood moved to fill the gap created by her retreat. "He's a tough old bird. I've been pulling for him." He was now squarely in her path. She was startled enough to look more closely at his face and then away.

"Thank you. You're not with the posse?" She asked the question while edging around on the street side of the walk. It was only a step up from the street, but she caught the edge with her shoe and started to lose her balance.

Elwood grabbed her by her shoulders and brought her back upright and in close. He pulled her closer than necessary. "Careful there," he said. He could see that her eyes were swollen some, and feeling the softness of her shoulders, he gave in to the impulse to draw her even closer. Maybe he thought to console her. Perhaps he had no thought at all.

Sarah stepped around him and drew away with a frown. Her mind was distracted enough with concerns over the death of Jimmy, and Pappy's condition, and even Bronco, who was probably gone forever. She couldn't even focus enough to decipher what was happening. Finally, she gathered herself and hurried on down the walk.

Cal Jordan was impatient with the pace of the search. He tried to move things along at every opportunity. Each farm stop lasted longer than Cal thought necessary. Deputy Sheriff Shires had taken his instructions seriously, and he covered each point with every farmer they encountered. *Too much chitchat.* Cal thought to himself. He tilted his head down and quit listening. The big florid-faced man carried a dread that he would eventually find that he had chosen wrong. He could have ridden with any of the three recon groups. He had decided based on which road he thought held the most promise for Coates' escape. From the beginning, it seemed like a toss-up between two routes. There were four roads out of the Titustown area. The one southeast toward Atlanta seemed iffy to him because that was sure to be a hotbed of Yankees, and Coates would likely try to avoid any Union authorities if he could.

The road northwest toward Huntsville seemed a possibility. It was further to the state line via that road, but it was the quickest way to put both the Alabama and Mississippi state boundary lines between Coates and Titustown. That road divided a mile outside of town at a junction. One road went northwest toward the Alabama state line and the other northeast into another hotbed of Yankees around their regimental headquarters at Winston. The final possibility was southwest toward Birmingham, Alabama. He had heard that there was still strong secessionist sentiment there, and it was the closest route to the Alabama state line.

So, that was the scouting group he chose, and now he was headed southwest with three long-time friends and the young deputy. They made inquiries for several hours along the way, and no one they questioned knew who John Coates was nor had any information about strangers. Cal's hopes dwindled with each failed stop until he found himself staring down in resignation at the loops of rope tied to his saddle. His big ruddy face scowled as he went over and over the tragic series of events. Why shoot Pappy? Why kill Jimmy? The more he asked himself that question, the more worked up he got. He had not been prepared to lose a son even for a cause, but the senseless of this ate him up. As far as he knew, neither Pappy nor Jimmy had ever even crossed paths with John Coates before. What in the man's nature could lead him to shoot people just for the pleasure of watching them die?

Only a few hours earlier, Cal had galloped home in answer to the big bell on his back porch. Going into his kitchen, he had found his son standing straight and strong. It was a heart-stopping moment. In his mind's eye, he remembered grabbing his boy and swinging him around in a circle, even though the young man's frame was as big as his own. But he had been terribly thin. Great joy replaced the dread he had carried for almost a year. Now his heart hardened in his misery. He motioned to his friends and rode toward the front gate before the deputy finished with his interview. The young man saw the movement, asked a few more questions, listened intently, and reined his horse around to follow.

Deputy Shires caught up with the four riders just outside the gate. "Mister Jordan, you know Sheriff Beckett said we should have folks on the lookout and give them instructions for what to do if they spot Coates."

"Well, that sounds fine until you realize that if Coates is hightailing it down this way, every stop we make puts him further ahead of us," Cal said. "He had what, almost a two-hour lead on us when we started? Well, now he has at least a five-hour head start!"

"Well, maybe, but that farmer just said that he remembered three men traveling by here three hours ago. Two of them were wearing blue Union caps."

Cal stiffened. "You're saying maybe Coates is riding with Union troops?"

"Well, no. Maybe those men were Madison Jones with his two Yankee friends."

Cal's face went blank. The men with Jones had made no impression on him beyond the full Yankee uniform on the youngest. "You think they're after Coates too?"

"No way to know except they did volunteer for the posse." Shires smiled. "They were a fair piece off, but that farmer says two of them was for sure sporting blue caps."

"So, how does that help us?"

"It means this direction is covered. Whether those Yankees intend to find Coates or not, we know that if they run upon him, they will try to ride him down."

"I still don't see how that helps."

"If we ride back to town and none of the other groups have sent in a runner, we'll know this is the most likely direction."

Cal hung his head. He knew that the deputy was crossways with his thinking. Just because the other groups were unsuccessful didn't mean anything at all. How many people had they come across who hadn't seen Coates? Not seeing Coates meant nothing. He suspected that the deputy and his friends were already feeling that this was a hopeless cause. They just wanted to go home. Maybe Beckett would read this the same way the deputy did and head the entire posse this way, but he doubted it. People would come to Jimmy's funeral. They might even shed a few tears, but when push came to shove, they were done. He was on his own. He tried to hold down his anger. He was too hurt to loosen his disappointment at these men. His rage toward John Coates overwhelmed all other emotions.

13

Sarge pulled up. "It should be dark in half an hour, and given his success so far, I doubt Coates will want to ride all night or even into the dark."

"His horse is bound to be worn out," Bronco said. He patted the neck of his pinto. "Mine is."

"Assuming, which is always dangerous, that he is still an hour ahead of us, it seems like a good time to stop and have some grub." Preacher unscrewed the cap of his canteen and took a swig.

"I think you're right," Sarge dismounted and led his horse to the left off the road toward a grassy area. The others followed. They could hear the music of falling water across the rocks in a stream nearby. The fresh water inspired Bronco, and he strode ahead toward the swift-flowing source of the sound and uncinched his saddle. He slipped it off and let the horse free. The pinto ambled forward and drank deeply. It raised its head and snorted and then went back for more.

The men started a small fire as the last light dissipated and pulled out some of their provisions.

"So, what do we do next?" Bronco looked at his friends through the rising smoke.

"Darn, good question," Sarge said. "As I see it, we are something like an hour to an hour and a half behind Coates. Not knowing where he is, all we can do is keep following the road hoping to get him in sight."

Preacher looked out toward the road. "That is true. But even if our pace is somewhat faster than his, it will take us a good long time to catch him. The state line is nearby, either ahead or behind us, and as we come out of these hills, he will have more options with the roads. If he zigs and we zag, the game is probably up until we get to New Orleans."

"You make a good point, Preacher. Clearly, our chances of corralling Coates on the road get slimmer the longer this chase lasts. Unless we get lucky and run into someone else ahead who has seen him, we'll be up a creek pretty soon."

"What if we get an early start in the morning and try to get ahead of him?" Bronco said. "We ride for a couple of hours and set up an ambush. He might ride right into us."

Preacher was sitting cross-legged with his elbows resting on his knees. He stroked his whiskers under his big jaw. "I don't know about your idea, Bronco. If he is further ahead than we estimate, and we set up an ambush behind him, we could wait around for two or three hours and never know where he is. At least knowing we are behind him gives us something to work with." His voice trailed off.

Sarge grimaced and clicked his tongue as he thought. "The thing is, we could be in front of him right now," Sarge said. "He could have pulled off the road a while back, and we've already trotted right by him."

"Dang!" Bronco looked from one man to the other. "That could have happened. We've been riding for two hours since the gypsy camp. He was an hour ahead of us. If he rode for an hour, he could be camped out across the road for all we know!" The men involuntarily looked out into the darkness and then back at each other.

Preacher grinned. "Feels kind of like searching for a ghost, don't it?"

Sarge lay back against his saddle and pursed his lips. He made the clicking sound out of one side of his mouth again and sat up.

"Is there any advantage to combining the ideas?"

"What do you mean?" Bronco fanned some smoke out of his eyes.

"How about this," Sarge said. "Before daybreak, two of us ride ahead for two hours. Then, we set up for an ambush. One of us waits here for a couple of hours and then heads up the road. If Coates is behind us right now, he'll likely ride by, and the fella who waits here can just follow him, keeping himself out of sight. But, if he is still ahead of us, he will ride into our ambush on his own, and the sweep-up man will just be late for the party."

"But if Coates is up early as well and stays ahead of our early risers, won't the ambush still be set up behind him?" Preacher asked. He was enjoying his role as devil's advocate.

"Dang." Bronco looked from Preacher to Sarge and waited.

"Boys, there comes the point where you just have to quit 'ifing' and make a decision. He shoved another stick into the fire. "You ever play poker, Bronco?"

"Some." Bronco looked surprised at the question.

"Well, one thing you know is that you can't win if you don't at least ante-up. Will you fellas anti-up with me on this? If, as Preacher says, Coates gets started early, he will be ahead of all of us. If Preacher catches up with us without spotting Coates, we'll at least be pretty sure he is still ahead of us."

The men took a second to let the pros and cons sink in, then nodded their heads in the affirmative.

"Good. Preacher, how about you riding drag on this operation? Bronco, you and I will get up two hours before daylight, and we'll see how things go."

The other men nodded, and each being aware of how soon they'd have to wake up, settled in for the night.

They woke Preacher just before mounting their horses.

"Preacher, best you be alert. Don't forget; there is still a possibility that Coates is somewhere behind us." Sarge stage whispered.

"Humm." Preacher set up and looked into the darkness. It was black except for the soft glow of the dying coals of the fire. "Why are we whispering?" He whispered back.

"I don't know," Sarge said in a more normal voice. "It's just that voices carry a long way at night."

"Yeah, they do. I can hear you fine." Preacher stretched. He reached over and picked up the coffee pot they had added to their gear at the general store. There were dregs at the bottom. He poured in a cup of water from his canteen and put it in the dying coals. He lay back down to wait for the few minutes it would take for it to heat up. "I'm up." He scratched his chest. "You, boys, be careful. I expect you have more chance of running into Coates than I do."

14

John Coates slept. He thought he could hear a horse's hooves above beyond the trees. The horse was going lickety-split down the road. Then it was quiet. Then it came back. His heart started to race. The Union payroll boys were checking out the road! He couldn't have that! His plans! His ingenious plans! All his plans could go up in smoke. Sweat popped out on his forehead. His breath came in rapid gasps. No! This nightmare couldn't be happening! He had to get up there!

Coates struggled to sit up in the darkness. He threw off his saddle blanket, twisted upright, and lunged to his feet. John gasped for air. His vision could not penetrate the damn darkness. Above, through the canopy, an abundance of stars winked between branches but provided little light below. Twenty feet away, the lake reflected a waxing crescent half-moon near a distant shore, visible through the light cloud cover. He put his palm on his forehead and willed his eyes to adjust. Finally, with a gasp, he realized that he had just awakened from a dream. His breathing slowed. The horse galloping off and returning; the memory of disaster at Carson's Junction was just a dream! It was based on his memory of his payroll robbery attempt, but now that was over. Now he camped down the slope from the road he was taking to New Orleans. He had a good head start and was safe. They would never catch him. When he got to New Orleans, he'd be safe forever from the long arm of the law. His rapid heartbeat slowed to close to normal. He pulled the blanket back up over his shoulders and sat once more where his body had warmed the ground a little, but the shivering didn't stop once the damp was on him. The matted pine straw he gathered for his bed was packed down enough to bring him fully awake. John was suddenly sufficiently conscious enough to ask an important question. *Where is my horse?* He stiffened again and pivoted his head from right to left and back. He could see nothing. Was his horse gone?

Now Coates was truly in a panic. He struggled back to his feet and walked the immediate area, trying to pierce the darkness. Hadn't he hobbled the horse before lying down? John was sure he had. He meant to. But he had been so tired. He tried calling, but he had not given the stolen horse a name. How could he call a horse that had no name? His dilemma confounded him. He walked up to a thick, moss-covered log and peed. Relieving himself was calming. He refastened his pants, returned to his blanket, picked it up, and draped it around his shoulders. He was in a fix. He wondered if his dream was triggered by the sound of his horse climbing up to the road and trotting off. His plan of starting a fire and doing some fishing seemed irrelevant now. Anger boiled up like oil. He had trusted that damned horse! Trust? He knew better than to trust! Damned horse!

There was the faintest light in the east. Maybe the horse had not strayed far? There was pretty good grass along the road. Perhaps it was just looking for better grazing! He left the saddle and gear and struggled up the slight incline to the road. It wasn't as dark there out from under the canopy. He scanned the road's near horizon, both east and west but could see nothing. West, he could see that the road rolled up and down a series of ever-higher knolls until it disappeared about two miles away. A light fog blanketed the trees on either side. "Damn it! Damn it to hell!" He jerked out his revolver and swore he'd shoot the damn horse if he could find it!

The birds fluttered noisily in the growing light. They flitted from tree to tree, oblivious to the angry man weaving in circles and waving his gun. Finally, Coates got hold of himself and started to walk west, then reversed and returned to his saddle. John had been without a horse before. He knew how to get another horse. Maybe if he continued west, he would come onto the stupid animal. John was confident of one thing; he was not going east back into the arms of the law. He calmed himself with the thought that another horse would eventually come down this way. He grabbed his saddlebag and rifle and climbed back to the road. He set out walking, aware that it wouldn't be long before his feet would be blistered. He was hungry again. It seemed like he was always hungry. John promised himself that when he got to New Orleans, he would be sure he was never hungry again.

Sarge and Bronco set out at a steady pace. It was no use trying to ride quietly. Their horses' hooves seemed overly loud in the stillness. They experimented with riding slower and faster. Regardless of their pace, the sound of the hooves seemed to ring out in the night. Eventually, Bronco couldn't stand it anymore. He spurred his horse forward at a good clip, then turned and rode back. The moonlight caught the gleam from his grinning face. Sarge gritted his teeth. He would have preferred that his friend stopped his shenanigans, but he understood the impulse. A bit further on, Bronco pulled up.

"Someone's following us," he said quietly. The two men looked back but could see nothing.

"You sure?" Sarge listened intently. About that time, his horse nickered. Then, about fifty yards behind them, another horse nickered back.

"Yep, I'm sure." Bronco chuckled. They waited with hands on their pistols. Just a trace of light in the east revealed the silhouette of a lone horse approaching them. "Is that Coates' horse?"

Sarge caught the bridle and ran his hand over the animal's roman nose. "Yep. Based on the description the sheriff gave out. It looks like John Coates could be afoot."

15

It was better light now as the sun came sliding over the eastern horizon. John Coates covered a short distance and searched the tree line on both sides of the road as he walked. There was a chance his horse had stopped to graze, and he could run it down. But, of course, John didn't have a saddle now. Carrying a saddle had not been very appealing when he was skeptical of finding his horse. John assured himself that the next horse he stole would have its own saddle.

He pulled his canteen off his shoulder by the strap and realized it was nearly empty. He raised it to his lips and tilted his head back. A series of flashes up the road at the top of a knoll caught his attention. The intermittent reflected sunlight told John instantly that there were several sets of horse's shoes. There it was again! He could barely make out two riders. The men were almost a mile away on the third of five ascending knolls, and the frequency of the flashes before they descended on the other side of the hill told him he'd not be catching them on foot. He willed his eyes to capture the details of their near silhouettes. He gasped. "Son of a...." He breathed. Right in front of him were his two deadliest antagonists. The younger Jones brother, Sarge, was closest. The civilian coat looked familiar even from a distance. The other rider was ahead, leading his missing horse! It had to be the one they called Preacher. He bristled. They were now ahead of him! And they had his horse! He caught the last drops of moisture from the canteen on his tongue. John spotted a lane to his right that seemed to lead back down to the lake. This discovery deserved some thought. In the meantime, he needed to refill his canteen.

At the end of a lane, pulled up on the shore, John found a rough-hewn Jon boat. He had stumbled on someone's access point to the lake. He looked around and up and down the shoreline as far as he could see. There did not seem to be any nearby houses, at least on the lakeside of the road.

Coates walked to the water's edge, and while he stooped and filled his canteen, he considered his options. He could continue walking in hopes of catching Sarge and Preacher, although the frequency of the flashing hoofs told him that their pace made that unlikely until after they camped. What a pleasure it would be to come upon them sitting all cozy by their fire! Or he could try his hand at rowing the boat for a while. He wished he knew the area well enough to know if the road followed the shoreline or not. A shortcut by boat was appealing for his blistered feet. And John was hungry. He remembered his original plan of camping by the water and fishing for his breakfast.

Now that Coates was over his shock, fishing seemed like a pretty good idea again. He was pretty sure that coming across the state line was assurance enough that a Titustown posse would give up before it reached him. Sarge and Preacher were another matter. Their dead friend provided plenty of reason to pursue him forever and plug him at the first opportunity. He stiffened at that thought but replaced it with the memory of his six-gun shooting fire against the back of Bronco's head. *Only two to go.*

One thing was sure; he wanted to come upon them in the dark. He felt his stomach complain again. It made more sense to spend time here by the lake where there was a chance to catch some fish rather than some unknown place up the road that held no such promise. And when he came on them, he'd want them asleep. He pulled some string from the saddlebag. Every boy in Georgia carried a fishhook with him, but the Yankee, whose horse he had stolen, didn't. He swore at the stupidity of Yankees and looked around. Hanging off the back of the boat was a heavy line that might be promising. He clambered to the end and tugged at the line. Sure enough, it was the end of a trotline. He pulled it toward him. Anchored at the other end, John thought he would have to trace it back. But he instantly felt movement. He stretched the line and raised it out of the water. Sure enough, there was a large catfish on the first hook. Coates couldn't believe his luck. He pulled out the hook, tossed the fish on the bank, and set about making a fire. John cleaned the fish and washed it. He searched the saddlebag and found some salt and pepper. So, the Yankee wasn't completely ignorant!

16

Cal Jordon was as done-in when he awoke as he had been when he lay down on the rocky earth. He was glad he sent the search party back to town. Cal was glad his friends and the deputy were not around anymore to hinder him. But he was tired. After a rough night's sleep, the man could tell he wasn't twenty anymore. He shared back problems with his uncle, Pappy Jordon. This journey was going to be tough, but he was determined. At first light, he mounted his horse and rode west. He didn't ask himself where his give-up point was. He didn't want to think about it. In the back of his mind, he knew there was one, but it sure wasn't after four hours of beating the bushes with a scatterbrained deputy and three men who claimed to be his friends. Yeah, he was mad. He didn't want to admit it, but he was. He didn't like being angry, but thinking on it now, he realized he had been upset the whole time Jimmy was gone to war. He had been angry without even recognizing it. He realized it now because when Jimmy got back, the angry went away. For the space of just a few hours, a peace had enfolded him, rejuvenated him. Yes, the farm had deteriorated some. Yes, he was only able to get a small crop planted. But with his son's safe return, the bright sunshine of hope reignited his life. Now Cal was angry again. Angrier than he had ever been. He put his hand on his holster. He realized with a bit of shock that he was killing mad.

He rode for about forty-five minutes before he came upon the gypsy wagon. He followed it a bit before he rode up beside it. He wasn't quite sure how to proceed. What if Coates was in the wagon? He convinced himself that it was unlikely. Cal could see as he got closer that the man, a good bit younger than himself, was accompanied by a young boy and an old woman. He inquired about Coates and was startled when they started to answer his questions before he asked them. Yes, they had encountered the man he described. Yes, he was traveling west down this road. And there were three men on his trail!

Cal felt his heart leap. He glanced back, longingly over his shoulder. If his friends had just stuck with him, they'd all be right here, right now, with this information. They were Southern men who he knew would do the right thing when they caught the damned killer. The Union men were in that respect an unknown quantity.

"This man Coates is evil," The old woman said.

"Be careful," said the man. His dark eyes moved to his son, and he squeezed the boy's shoulder. "He has no soul."

As Cal thanked the family for the information and rode on ahead, he realized something he had hidden even from himself. He wasn't looking for justice. Cal wanted vengeance. He wanted to personally put a rope around John Coates' neck and startle a horse from under him. That singular desire was ugly, but as the distance grew between himself and the gypsy wagon, his appetite for it grew.

An hour later, Cal did not recognize Preacher when he spied him on the road ahead. He was just a rider going in the right direction to make him a suspect. From a distance, Preacher was just a lump on a horse. But as he drew closer, Cal could see that the man wore part of a Yankee uniform and a Yankee cap. Cal remembered seeing Coates no more than a couple of times over a several-year period. So he knew he was unlikely to be wearing a Yankee cap except as a disguise. The man ahead also seemed thicker in the waist than the man Cal remembered. He increased his pace and realized that the rider was one of the Yankees who had initially volunteered to hunt down Coates.

Preacher's attention was directed to his front and either side. He had allowed himself the luxury of a good breakfast while he bided his time before starting, so he was feeling well satisfied. He was pulled out of his pleasant thoughts by a rider just behind him. He turned and recognized Pappy's nephew from the crowd around the jail.

"Well, hello!" Preacher was glad to have company. He smiled. When the man was alongside, he stuck out his hand.

Cal Jordon automatically grabbed it, then relinquished it as though it was a dead mouse.

Preacher laughed. "Kind of takes a minute to sort everything out, doesn't it?" He pulled his hand back. He then relayed the talk with the gypsies and the plan.

Cal nodded. He, too, had talked with the gypsies, but he listened without interruption to Preacher's version of events.

"So, you think we've got Coates somewhere between here and your friends." He pursed his lips and peered down the road.

"Well, that's the way it seems. The two of them could have him in tow by the time we reach them." He looked at Cal expectantly. The man looked skeptical. "Seems almost too easy, doesn't it?" Preacher acknowledged.

Cal made a motion with his hand that was neither pro nor con. "Yeah. Well, it doesn't matter how hard or easy it is. Coates needs catching. I'll take it either way."

17

Pappy Jordan was newly awake. He looked about the room they had helped him into the evening before. There was nothing of particular interest. There was a flower print wallpaper with a short repeat pattern that gave him a headache when he gazed at it too long. It was red, green, and blue on a tan background and grew monotonous very quickly. He wished someone would come in and raise the shade. The light outside was pretty intense around the edges of the window. He felt his beard and estimated the time at about eight on the clock. He ran his left hand lightly over the area of his wound. He had gotten a look at the injury when the doctor changed his bandage. The immediate area around the wound itself was purple from bruising. The holes, front and back, were seeping a bit. Doc said when the seeping lessened and scabbed over some, he could move around more.

There was a knock on the door, followed by a turning of the knob. Pappy saw Sarah framed in the doorway. She came to his bedside and touched his shoulder, then went to the window and raised the shade without his asking. The flood of light hurt his eyes, but he didn't complain. He needed light. He wished he could feel the sun's direct rays soak into him. He raised his hand at the wrist in greeting and let it fall back. He could not overlook the swollen face though she flashed a quick smile and came back to his bedside.

"How are you doing?" Her eyes swept over him and stopped at the approximate area of his wound.

"I think I'll live," he said. "I looked at it last evening. It didn't seem too bad." He motioned to the chair. "Scoot that over there where I can see you."

After she did, Pappy looked into her bereft face and closed his eyes. "I'm sorry." He felt his stomach contract as though punched in the gut. Pain shot through his side as muscles holding his ribs in place pulled at the wound. "I'm sorry!"

Sarah leaned forward. "It's not your fault. I'm the guilty one."

Pappy's eyes widened, and he stared at her. He had not considered anyone else's guilt. Then he told her what had happened with John Coates. He made fists with his hands so tightly that the knuckles turned white. She saw that and covered the near one with both of hers.

"No!" she said. "This began with me." She told him all the reasons why. He told her she was wrong. They each tried to dismiss the other's story. They each longed to shed the guilt they felt, but neither could look into the other's stricken face and feel anything but their own responsibility.

Bronco and Sarge positioned themselves off the road at the top of the highest knoll. "From here, we can see for a good distance and spot him even if he's walking," Sarge said.

"How long do you think it will take him to walk from where the horse caught us?" Bronco asked. He threw his right leg forward over his horse's neck and slid to the ground."

"Probably hour to an hour and a half," Sarge said.

"So, if he keeps coming, we'll be able to spot him over one of those rises. As long as we stay out of sight, we can watch him walk right into our trap." Bronco hunkered down to begin his watch.

Elwood Clemens rode back to his farm, ruminating about his close encounter with Sarah Jordon. She was a pretty little thing. Even with her face puffed up from crying, the tilt of her nose and chin and the ruby lips affected him. Soft as a pillow. He corrected himself. Her shoulders were softer than any pillow he ever felt under his head. He thought he had caught just a whiff of perfume when he briefly pulled her close. Maybe it was in her hair. But then she had detached herself. Had she smiled when she pushed away? He wasn't sure. Perhaps he had imagined that? With women, it was hard to tell sometimes. Elwood had always found women hard to gauge.

There had been a couple of whorehouses on the edge of Titustown before the troops left. He had gone a couple of times, but their offerings were not enough to scratch his itch. They weren't providing any affection. He imagined that "regular women" would be better. He believed that even though his own mother had been colder than a hound's nose. Mrs. Jordon was prettier than any woman he ever knew. And soft! And it was clean, soft. Not sweaty soft like a whore! Elwood knew what he wanted. He just needed a plan and an opportunity. There was some serious planning necessary for sure. Elwood did not usually spend much time contemplating and planning, but the thought of doing that now kind of excited him. Mrs. Jordon excited him for sure. Everything else just followed along.

18

Preacher and Cal settled into silence as they continued along the road. Preacher scrutinized the roadway and nearby clearings, keeping an eye out for Coates. Cal was distracted and retraced the events surrounding the death of his son. First, a group of men heard the report of Coates' weapon and found him fleeing the scene of Pappy's shooting. Since Sarah was so upset, he did not personally talk with her; Emmy told him that Sarah identified John Coates as Jimmy's murderer. Several men watched the man ride off. Several shots were sent his way to no effect. No matter how many times he puzzled through it, he couldn't come up with the answer to the most crucial question that remained, *why?* He was about to run the scenario through again when Preacher abruptly pulled up. A good way up the road, a man was stepping out of the bushes from their right. He was tall with a built described best as lanky, heavily bearded, and even from a distance, unkempt. His eyes were so deeply recessed as to be invisible in the shadow of his heavy brows. His slouch hat tipped up with a jerk when he looked their way, indicating that he had spotted them as well.

Before Preacher or Cal could react, the man brought his rifle to his shoulder and fired. The pellet zipped between the two men. "Down!" Preacher quickly looked left then right and kneed his horse into a rightward course. The big bay shouldered against Cal's horse, forcing that animal to follow his lead. As Preacher cleared from his line of fire, Cal drew his six-gun and fired back in Coates' general direction. The round kicked up dirt about five feet in front of the man as he ducked back into the bushes.

Preacher and Cal hurriedly dismounted and pulled the horses deeper into the foliage. A second bullet passing within two feet of their heads got both men's full attention. Preacher pulled his rifle from his scabbard, and Cal followed suit. "If you catch sight of him, let her rip." Preacher said.

He started to pull both horses further from the edge of the road and under the high canopy. Preacher knew Coates could take advantage of a head start if he could pin them down and ride away before they got organized. "Stay covered and send some lead through the brush from time to time," he called to Cal. "I'm going to go in deeper and see if I can get a clean shot from his flank."

Cal nodded. He fired again and waited for return fire. Nothing happened. He shifted his aim five degrees to the right and fired again. There was no return fire. Was the man running? The thought irked him, and he fired twice more into the bushes clipping off limbs in the bullet's path.

Preacher tied up the horses behind two old-growth pines and moved further to the right so return fire would not hit the animals. He was surprised at the lack of response from Coates. If the man was willing to shoot it out, they could settle things right now. If he tried to escape, it was a good distance to the top of the next knoll. Preacher checked his rifle. His eyes weren't as good as they once had been, but he thought he could still hit a straight-line moving target.

Cal fired again. No response. Preacher was getting antsy. Where was the man? "Cal, you catch sight of him yet?"

"No!" Cal peered out from the roadside bushes. The road was clear. "Dammit! Show yourself!" He shouted into the still air.

"Stay put and guard the road." Preacher edged into the darkness and cautiously worked his way around the fallen timber. He saw no sign of the man. Further to the right, he caught sight of water. They had intermittently seen a body of water for the last half mile. He moved forward step by careful step. Eventually, he came upon the lane. To his left, he could see the entrance from the road. It was clear. The path curved a bit to the right, so he did not have a clear view of the water. He edged ahead until the lake was again in sight. There was no sign of Coates. Moving closer, he came on Coates' dampened campfire. It was still warm. Five feet in from the water, he saw the indentations of a boat in the mud. Preacher hurried to the water's edge and scanned the lake.

Far up the shoreline, just at the end of a point, he spotted a figure in a boat. The man was rowing hard, and while Preacher watched, slipped out of sight behind a stand of trees. "Well, I'll swear!" Preacher slumped. He called out to the other man. "Hey, Cal. He's gone. Would you bring my horse in?" He looked around. "You scoundrel. You finally outsmarted us, didn't you?" As Cal came down the lane with the two horses, Preacher's mind leaped ahead. Maybe they could cut him off? Then his head spun left, right, and around as he surveyed the area. Something was missing.

"He's gone," he said to Cal. "He took off in a boat." Then the rest of the picture clicked, and he added, "But where is his horse?"

19

Beads of sweat dripped off John Coates' nose and eyebrows. He was thankful for his gloves. The oars were rough from weathering, and he could imagine the damage they would do to unprotected hands. He was not an experienced rower, but his predicament was a good incentive to pick up the basics in a hurry. He caught sight of one figure on the shore just before he rounded a point, and the man slid from view. It sure looked like Preacher; stocky, big head, blue cap. Wait a minute! It hit him like a thunderclap. If the man on the shore he saw coming from the east was Preacher, who was the man with him? Who was the man with Sarge who he had seen riding west up the slope earlier? He drifted to catch his breath. The boat rocked with the gentle swells.

Okay, reason this out. The two Yankees were not riding together. Sarge was riding with someone else. The sheriff? For whatever reason, Preacher was well behind him with another stranger. A deputy? Two extra men in total? With Pappy dead, he had expected half the town to turn out for the posse. Bronco's death was probably greeted with a shrug. No, even with Sarge's prodding, Beckett wouldn't be able to raise a posse for a dead Union soldier. Coates started rowing again. For a moment, he wondered if maybe shooting Pappy had not been a good idea. He shook it off. It had felt too good to regret.

But on the other hand, from the very beginning of his flight, he had hoped the state line would finish a posse's pursuit. Seeing just two additional men suggested, maybe he was right. But having only Preacher and Sarge after him, as dangerous as they might be, was a lot more manageable than four. Briefly, he wondered how they knew to take this road. The luck of the draw? It had to be. Chance was never his friend. Then he let his mind dwell on the second shooting. Recalling the slaying of Bronco sent a thrill of satisfaction through him!

Coates dropped the oars and let the boat drift again. His back already ached. He pulled off his bandana to mop his face and neck. What now? He knew he was not going to be able to make much forward progress in the boat. He looked toward the far shore. All he could see was more forest. Damn, he needed a horse!

He froze at another thought. The men pursuing him could ride ahead and come down to the shoreline, and once he came along, it would be like shooting a fish in a barrel. He needed to get back to shore as quickly as he could. At least on foot in the trees, he was less of a target. When he first spotted the two horsemen on the hillock, he planned to lay back and catch them with a night attack. Four men made that a little riskier, but those he didn't kill would get the shit scared out of them! He smiled at that. He picked up the oars and turned the boat toward a narrow beach. He could see the lay of the hills. He could probably make better forward progress walking through the woodland than he could by rowing. If he cleared the hills on foot, he was pretty sure he'd be well to the west side of his pursuers. They would not expect an attack from that direction. He grasped the oars again and put his back into it. The sooner he made it to cover, the better. His brow beaded with sweat once more. Right now, he was a sitting target.

"Riders coming!" Bronco called out. The two men were taking turns watching the road. It was midmorning. A light rain was falling. Sarge had just expressed concern that Preacher had not shown up yet.

"Two riders?" Sarge stepped out toward the center of the road for a better look. "Yep. That's Preacher, all right. Recognize the other man?"

"Nope." Bronco grabbed the bill of his hat and pulled it forward to better shade his eyes. "Preacher, for sure. Dang, I think the other man is Mister Jordon." They waited as the pair of riders traversed the hills and eventually reached their camp.

The men halted and dismounted. "Is that Coates' horse?" Preacher pointed.

"Think so," Bronco said. "He decided he didn't like Coates' company and joined us this morning." Bronco grinned.

Sarge approached the other man and extended his hand. "Mister Jordon, isn't it?"

Cal shook and looked the animal over. "Well, this explains why we caught Coates without a horse a little bit ago."

"You caught up with Coates?" Sarge said.

"We did." Preacher nodded.

Cal looked at the younger man. "Don't they call you Bronco?" He hadn't looked at the young man close enough to recognize the face, but the odd name had stuck with him.

"Yes, sir. I've been real worried about Pappy. Any word?"

"No. I think we left right after you did. Pappy was still unconscious when I looked in on him. He's tough. I'm hoping he makes it."

After unsaddling the horses, the four men sat in a circle at the fire and hashed over the morning's events. Preacher and Cal explained that they had ridden a half-mile ahead and followed a trail down to the shore in hopes of intercepting Coates and his boat, but he never showed up.

"Well, this idea was a bust," Sarge said. "Now Coates knows we're on to him. He either took the boat to the other side of the lake or ditched it and is coming our way on foot. Given his squirrelly nature, just about anything is possible. I'd bet that if he comes for us, it will be at night."

"Or he could slip past us and head on to New Orleans," Bronco said.

"New Orleans?" Cal straightened up.

"Well, we think so." Preacher explained about his earlier run-in with the man.

"Did you give this info to Beckett?" Cal's voice was challenging.

"No. You'll recall that we were disinvited to this party." Preacher said lightly.

"Dammit, Beckett had riders going in every damn direction yesterday!" Cal said. "If he had known about New Orleans, he could have headed this way from the get-go!" His face was beet red.

"In which case, instead of us four, there would be another what, two or three more riders at best?" Sarge asked.

"We figured the posse would thin out by the time it got to the state line. It did, didn't it?" Preacher retorted. "Doesn't the sheriff's authority end at the state line?"

Cal considered it. "Well, yes. Our group was ready to call it quits after four hours of horsing around talking to farmers. But if we knew for sure Coates was headed this way, they might have stuck with it." He did not want to let it go, but the part about losing men at the state line had some validity. He sat back and tucked his chin in, maintaining some silent defiance.

"All right. Enough hashing out what could have been would have been and should have been," Sarge growled. "We've got to expect Coates to come in tonight. Knowing him, he won't be bringing cookies."

20

Sheriff Beckett mopped his forehead. It was an unseasonably warm day, and he was sitting on the porch in front of the jail with young Deputy Shires. The posse had been a disaster. Not only did his group run out of steam after just four hours of making rounds, but both of the other recon groups did too. In the space of thirty minutes, toward the end of the day, the remnants of all three groups arrived back in town with nary a clue as to John Coates' whereabouts. Some of the men had dropped out along the way and gone home without bothering to catch the other groups' reports.

Then when his young deputy explained his theory that since the Yankees had his route covered, everyone should hightail it back down the road toward Birmingham, the older men just shook their heads in disgust and turned their horses homeward.

All of that was bad enough. There was also the situation of Cal pursuing Coates without any backup at all. Beckett understood the man's reluctance to give up, but blast-it! Now they had a man out chasing a killer all by his lonesome! "I'm not so worried about Cal not finding Coates as that he will! You should have ordered him to come back with you!" Beckett sputtered when he heard the story. "He's not a gunman. He's a farmer, for God's sake! He could be dead already."

"I told him he'd best come back with us, sir, but he said when you got the posse together, you were welcome to come to find him." The deputy was also sweating. The posse's total disdain for the logic of his theory shook his confidence. "Besides, the three Union men are between him and Coates anyway. So if anyone finds John, it will be them 'cause they have a head start!"

Beckett chewed that over. Even if the deputy was right, there was still a chance for Cal to end up dead. That was unacceptable. Cal was a friend. And, he reminded himself that in an election year, it was not only unacceptable but suicidal to his election prospects.

"Sheriff Beckett!"

The sheriff turned toward the familiar voice. "Yes, Ma'am?" He felt the iron grip of indigestion in his belly redouble. Mrs. Sarah Jordon looked horrible. She was wearing a newly dyed black dress and her Lucky Star apron, apparently returning to work the day after her husband's death. He had heard that Wanda had put off the funeral indefinitely until Cal got back.

"I just heard that my father-in-law didn't come back with his posse!"

"No, ma'am. He decided to head on over into Alabama on his lonesome, and I'm not happy about it."

Sarah stomped her foot and put her hands on her hips. Her face was ablaze. "Not happy about it? Is that all? Sheriff, John Coates just killed his son and shot his uncle, and now is getting away with it, and you're just not happy?" Her voice rose as she spoke to the level of a high screech by the time she got to the word happy. Sheriff Beckett reflected briefly on how marriage could turn a demure young lady into a raging harpy in the blink of an eye. Then, while she regrouped, he stood up as he felt pretty vulnerable, looking up at the diminutive female standing over him. Out of the corner of his eye, he caught sight of his young deputy getting ready to defend him. The young man had attended school with Mrs. Jordon, so he may have felt qualified to offer friendly advice or another theory about sheriffin'. Beckett held up his hand to the young man to keep quiet and stood as tall and authoritatively as he could.

"Ma'am, given what has happened, I understand you're upset. But Cal Jordon is a grown man. He made the decision his own self. My deputy urged him to return with the posse, and he refused. Would you have him arrest the man?" Sheriff Beckett was beginning to warm to the subject. "We aren't finished with John Coates yet by a long shot. Our goal today was to put everyone in the county on alert. Then, when new information comes in, we're ready to deal with John Coates. So don't worry about that!"

Sarah's eyes were suddenly teary. "In the meantime, Sheriff, Cal is out there alone. If anything happens to him, it will be your responsibility!" Her defiance returned. "Won't it?" She turned and stomped off toward Doctor Jenkins' office.

Sheriff Beckett made up his mind. Even if the chances were slim, he had to go through the motions. "Deputy Shires, get to bed early. Be here at dawn in the morning. You and I are riding out to give Cal some company." The sheriff couldn't help but hope that they'd run into Cal headed back their way. But, without someone spotting Coates in the meantime, he had no choice but to believe that the three Union soldiers had as much chance of coming upon him as anyone. And if they did spot the man, they had as much chance as anyone to run him to the ground.

21

Pappy listened with concern as Sarah related her conversation with the sheriff. He prodded his side. It was still tender. *Of course, it's still sore, you old coot! You was just shot yesterday!* He moved his hand away as his eyes lingered on her troubled face. They shared a sense of guilt over Jimmy. To Pappy, the difference was that she had a long life ahead of her while he could keel over at any minute and be out of his misery. He was willing to do anything he could to alleviate her pain, but his current circumstances curtailed any personal action toward achieving justice. He knew that time could be an enemy, but it could also be her friend. If he supported her now, maybe time would help her achieve acceptance. He went so far as to hope that someday she might even learn to forgive herself.

"Missy, come here," he said. He patted the edge of the bed. He had never called her Missy before, but it felt right. He took her unblemished hand in his old claw and squeezed it. "You're getting overwrought. Beckett is right. Cal is a grown man. He can take care of hisself. He needs to be out there tracking Coates for his own peace of mind, even if there is nothing he can do to bring Jimmy back." At this point, tears welled in Sarah's eyes. Pappy continued. "Nothing can ever change what's happened. But Cal needs to feel like he tried, that he did all he could. We don't know where Coates is. He could have gone anywhere. Chances are Cal won't see hide nor hair of the man. Think of it as Cal just taking a ride. Okay?"

Sarah squeezed his hand and pulled a handkerchief from her apron pocket. She dabbed her eyes. "Okay." She poured some water from a pitcher on a stand and handed Pappy the glass. "Doc said for you to drink a lot of fluids. Take this, and I'll bring back a nice cup of tea in a few minutes. They say it has medicinal benefits."

Pappy accepted the glass and took a sip to please her. Next to the pitcher was a bedpan. He needed it worse than the water. "Make that coffee, instead of tea, if you would. I never had much use for tea."

John Coates motioned the hefty, well-dressed black man away with a wave of his six-gun. John had just relieved the man of his horse. He nestled in the warmth of the saddle and congratulated himself. It felt good. John's eyes were dark and cold. The black man stumbled over his own feet a bit as he backed off for a spell as if hesitant to turn away. A brief shower a little earlier had made the Georgia clay a bit sticky. Coates watched the man hurry east up the hill. He resisted the temptation to use his retreating figure for target practice just for the pleasure of it. The man was overdressed for his station in life. To John, not accustomed to envy toward the negro race, it felt wrong. Unfortunately, the large man's elegant coat would have hung over-large and awkward on his lean frame. Besides, wearing a black man's coat was far too intimate, much more so than using his horse. He almost shivered at the thought of wearing that coat. The man even had some money! It was wrong!

John's reason for not shooting the black man cold was purely practical. He knew that there were at least four men who were serious about finding him. He was pretty confident that they were somewhere up on the nearby hill and probably close enough to hear the report of his weapon. His long, exhausting boat trip around the point and the long trudge along the lake and through the under-growth back up to the road had given him plenty of time to think. His first thought upon finding that they were nearby was revenge. His inner demons spoke forcefully for finishing the job! But he had to conclude that the odds for a successful attack had deteriorated. In addition to Sarge and Preacher, there were now two more men with unknown skills in their arsenals. His close call at Carson's Junction had heightened his sense of vulnerability.

That put him back on track to make his way to New Orleans. The city had a reputation for extravagance and unrestricted com-merce of a nefarious nature that appealed to him at a gut level. Coates had an arrested sex drive and no romantic inclinations at all. Well before full adulthood, John concluded after a few experi-ments that sex paled to its reputation. In the last few years, he had learned that it could not compare with the exquisite experience of putting a bullet between the eyes of someone with the audacity to displease him. John had been a handy target for abuse in his child-hood. Both his father and uncles took their moonshine-generated ire out on him and his cousins almost daily. As a result, other men were usually the object of John's fury. The difference between John and his older Coates relations was that it didn't take liqueur to ignite his wrath. The memory took him full circle in his desire to obtain justice on Sarge and Preacher. He shook it off. No! It was New Or-leans or bust!

Rigid in the saddle, John watched the back of the flapping black coat until the man had stumbled some distance eastward up the in-cline. John reined the horse around. As he approached the junc-tion, he glanced back. He saw the man turn around to check on him. John was somewhat familiar with this road. Two years before, he had been through the area, coming in from the north riding with Captain Owens, the leader of an outlaw gang posing as Confederate partisans. Based on that experience, he was satisfied that the road to his right led to Huntsville, Alabama. The road to the left would take him to Birmingham. The route through Birmingham was the most direct way to get to the Mississippi, where he wanted to catch a riverboat south. Then he remembered his need to confuse those who would pursue him.

On a whim, Coates turned his horse north toward Huntsville. He rode to the top of the hill for the benefit of the figure on the slope. As he gained the apex, he looked again for the retreating black man, but he had disappeared into the forest. John reined his horse around and set back south for Birmingham. He smiled as he spurred the horse toward the next curve. The tracks north might fool the men. John felt good. Still, something was nagging at him. He had been so filled with fear, so busy running, that he had not been able to put his finger on the elusive fragment floating beneath the surface of his consciousness. But now, confident that escape was likely, he was calm enough to retrace recent history, and those thoughts coalesced.

Ironically John's original plan was based on something Bronco Brumley had said while Coates lay bleeding from a pistol blow to his head in northern Alabama. Bronco had mentioned gold. As John mulled those words over, he deduced that Sarge's brother, Tom, had a stash of gold. John had heard about a gold rush in Harlon county twenty years back. He had envisioned a quick raid and a trip to New Orleans for a life of leisure.

However, upon arriving in Titustown, John had found the Union Army garrisoned at Tom Jones' farm and Jones out of his reach in jail. He knew now that those impediments no longer existed. Suddenly that one word again loomed large in his consciousness. Gold! With his successful escape at hand, John suddenly wondered if his original plan still had merit. Suddenly he had a greater mission than mere flight. He had unfinished business! He had a higher goal than mere vengeance. The sleeping coal of greed sparked to life in the deep recesses of his brain. Escape lost its place as his priority. Predictably for John, he changed his mind.

22

"I don't like it," Sarge spoke in low tones and rolled over on his back and surveyed the evening sky through the high forest canopy.

"Oh?" Preacher shifted position as well.

"Waiting around for Coates could be just as fruitless as chasing him in his boat."

The men were hunkered down twenty feet back in the brush from the small campfire they had built, surrounded by four dummied-up figures that appeared to be sleeping by the flames. Looking at the scene from afar as they expected Coates to do, they felt pretty confident about their scheme. They had chosen to lay up on the east side of the fake camp, as far from the road as they could get. They thought their location was the least likely direction for John's approach. They hoped that Coates, in one of his frenzied episodes, would come charging in with guns blazing. That would be their opportunity to take him down.

Cal was asleep. His breathing was steady, almost a purr. Bronco was trying to maintain a good thought for Pappy and Cal. As yet, there had been no discussion about Bronco's part in Pappy and Jimmy's shootings. As far as Cal knew, Coates had suddenly taken with a fit of some kind. For motive, all he could come up with was that some slight, most likely not even intentional, had set the man off. The combination of frustration and long hours in the saddle had worn him down. So now, he slept.

"Well, there are two lures to attract him here," Preacher said. "First, we are still alive, which no doubt bothers him some, and we have horses that he could use to get on his way. Ideally, from his perspective, he kills us all and sells the horses off as he moves on to New Orleans. If he knew about the gold we're carrying, he'd have three reasons to show up."

"Reckon we should have told him?" Preacher's grin reflected the light from the meager fire.

Bronco listened, happy to have something to think about, other than his guilt. He roused himself out of his blanket. "I think I'll check on the horses," he said. He moved back further into the forest. The horses were hobbled since the likelihood of gunfire spooking them was high. He found four of them, in a docile frame of mind, in another clearing twenty yards further east. The fifth horse, the klabruber, ridden earlier by Coates, was the exception. It snorted and nudged against Moon, Cal Jordon's horse. Bronco stepped around a large pine and saw why. The shadowy figure of John Coates appeared to be kneeling in front of the big horse. His back was to Bronco as he worked feverishly to untie the square knot of the hobble cord with his gloved fingers.

Without hesitation, Bronco leaped on the man carrying them both under the horse. The man landed face down in the pine straw. Bronco brought his right fist into the side of the man's jaw just in front of his ear. Suddenly in a fury, Bronco hit him again. Then again. He drew back for another blow but stayed himself. He sat back on his haunches, breathing rapidly. The man appeared to be unconscious. Bronco rolled him over and rested his knees on the man's chest.

"Sarge, Preacher! I've got him!" Bronco called out. Then he heard an exclamation and the thrashing of two men fighting their way through the brush. Then Bronco peered closer in the shifting light cast by the moon. He lit a match. The black man was a stranger to him.

"You got him?" Sarge was incredulous. Preacher was right on Sarge's elbow.

"You got him!"

"Nope. I was wrong. It ain't Coates." Bronco responded. He regained his feet. "This fellow was trying to steal the black. But it's not Coates."

The man tossed his arms about, rolled to his side, and attempted to stand up. He was a large black man, as tall as Coates but more massive. He did wear the same kind of slouch hat. He reached up and rubbed his jaw. "You pack a wallop, young fella!" The voice was deep, with a hint of amusement. His accent seemed eastern but not Boston. Preacher guessed New York.

"You're lucky I didn't shoot you." Bronco's gun hand poised on his holster.

"Well, that would have been unjustified, wouldn't it, seeing as how I'm not armed." His eyes caught on the remnants of Sarge and Preacher's blue uniforms. He grinned. He held the front flaps of his fancy coat away from his sides. "A black man carrying a weapon down here plays a dangerous game."

The three men looked at each other. Just then, Cal crashed through the underbrush. "What's going on?" He was swatting limbs away from his face as he approached behind the stranger. In two more strides, he was standing with his back to the man. He looked around at his startled companions.

The man swiftly pulled Cal's revolver from his holster and wrapped his left arm just under Cal's chin. He placed the barrel against Cal's neck. "I need a horse, gentlemen." His tone was light, almost friendly. "Drop your weapons."

Cal looked around in confusion.

The man cocked the pistol. The men all gingerly pulled their weapons, and they fell invisibly through the darkness and thumped softly on the pine straw. It would have been easy to attempt a shot in the dark, but that cocked gun at zero range discouraged taking a chance. Sarge hooked his thumbs in his belt. "We do have an extra horse, you might say." He glanced at Bronco and Preacher. "Are you headed toward Birmingham or away?"

"What difference does that make?"

"Just curious. We were expecting someone else about now. It seems like a simple question."

The man pulled Cal around, so he was entirely between himself and the questioner. "I ran into a fellow yesterday about dusk. He had a gun but no horse. I had a horse but no gun. So now he has both a horse and a gun. Very unfair trade, I thought." His teeth glinted in the shifting moonglow. "So if one of you gents will fetch me a horse, I'd be very appreciative." He waved toward the hobbled horses with the revolver. "Any of them will do. They all look to be in pretty good shape."

"First, my question," Sarge said.

"Oh! Heading for Atlanta. I ran into the gent I mentioned at the bottom of the hill, a half-mile or so southwest of here. Tall, lean, wore boots a size or two bigger than his feet. Very persuasive. He kind of made my blood run cold. I thought he might kill me. There was something about his eyes, but I complied with his request without argument, so maybe he was impressed with my cooperation. In any event, he took the horse and said I could replace it up here if I could find you."

"He told you that you could get a horse up here?" Bronco repeated.

"Yes, he said you boys were camped up here. Said I had the same chance with you as he would."

"Except for not having a gun," Preacher observed.

"So how did you find us?" Sarge asked the question, although he already knew the answer.

"Not too hard. First, I already knew you were up here. Second, the tracks of five horses are hard to conceal after a rain, and you didn't even try."

"We didn't try it because we wanted to be sure he found us. His name is John Coates, and he's a killer. So you had a good reason for your blood to run cold."

"Okay, questions answered. Kindly fetch me one of the horses. And, throw a saddle on it too."

"Horse, okay, but no saddle," Sarge said.

"Do you want to quibble under the circumstances?" The stranger pushed the barrel of the revolver deeper into Cal's neck.

Cal was now fully alert. The barrel had already worn a forty-four-caliber ring in the side of his neck, and he was tired of it. The big man ducked down, flung his arms up, and threw his considerable weight back into the stranger's body. The man was startled and reacted by throwing his arm up and then bringing it downward in his rush to recover his balance. In the process, he pulled the trigger, and the weapon fired. The slug first passed along Cal's lower leg at an almost vertical angle before it thudded into the ground. Cal spun around with a sworn exclamation and found the man's retreating jaw about where Bronco had softened it up.

The stranger's head jerked. He grimaced and stepped further back. He straightened his arm and pressed the barrel against Cal's forehead. Cal controlled his forward motion just in time.

"Gentlemen, time is a-wasting," the man growled. His attempt to be cordial was no longer evident. His breathing was rapid.

"How bad are you hurt, Cal?" Sarge couldn't see much in the dark.

"It nicked me. Not deep, but it is bleeding like a mother." Cal replied. He the injury with dabbed his finger again, and it came up wet. The three men looked at each other. "I'll get Coates' horse," Bronco said. Sarge and Preacher nodded.

"Thank you. However, before you go and retrieve another weapon, remember how lucky your friend was just now. We don't want any more accidents, do we?"

Bronco brought the horse up, and the stranger took the reins in one hand. "I won't insist on the saddle since, as a rule, I am not a thief. I appreciate the cooperation, such as it is. As we have a mutual aversion for this man Coates, I'll give you one more bit of information. After I got out of his range, I looked back, and he was just reaching a fork that could take him either to Huntsville or Birmingham. He took the road to Huntsville."

"Are you sure?" Sarge eyed him skeptically.

"That's the road I used getting here. I'm traveling from Huntsville, myself." Without further ado, he swung heavily onto the bareback horse, kicked the black's flanks, and headed through the brush back toward the road. The men instantly bent to search through the pine straw for their weapons. As he cleared the near brush, the stranger flung Cal's six-gun back over his shoulder. It landed at Bronco's feet. As the man disappeared into the darkness, Bronco felt it bump his shoe and picked it up.

"I guess he was serious about not carrying a gun," he said as he passed the weapon over to Cal.

23

Sheriff Beckett was pleasantly surprised to find his deputy waiting when he arrived at his office. "On time. That's good."

"Yes, sir. I went to bed early, just like you said. I'm raring to go." Deputy Shires was pleased with himself. He figured the day would work out better if it got off to a good start. "Do you suppose Mister Jordon would check in at the jail or go to his farm if he came in yesterday evening?"

"Damn, good question! Let's go by there before we go tearing off toward Alabama."

The two men made good time getting to the Jordon farm. They found Wanda Jordon on the front porch taking turns with the two girls churning butter. She was a middle-aged woman with wispy hair, and the strain of losing her son had taken a toll on her. Both men tipped their hats, and Beckett inquired as to Cal. She held up her hand to shade her eyes from the rising sun. "We haven't heard a thing, Sheriff. We were hoping Cal would get in last evening, but he didn't. I hope you find him. I can't believe his friends left him out there by himself."

"Well, don't be too hard on your neighbors, Mrs. Jordon. The purpose of our ride yesterday was to alert everyone that Coates was about and what he had done. I guess Cal got impatient and headed toward the border. Don't you worry none. Deputy Shires and I are headed that way, and we will come on him eventually." He detected a teary eye. The girls were more subdued than he had ever seen them. The sheriff reined his horse around and headed for the gate before Mrs. Jordon could bring up the thorny issue that yesterday's posse of neighbors had dwindled to only Beckett and one deputy for today's outing.

Three hours later, they caught sight of a single rider headed their way. Out of habit, Sheriff Beckett put his hand on his revolver while they waited. Unfortunately, he didn't recognize the outline of the man. His hope that it could be Cal diminished as the rider got closer. The slouch hat put his teeth on edge a bit, but as the man grew still nearer, he realized that he was black. That made him pull the weapon. He casually leveled the gun across the front of his saddle. The man pulled up a few feet away.

"Good morning, Sheriff." The black man held his hands up, and he wore no holster. The horse wore an army bridle but no saddle. "I've got news about the four men I met a few miles back."

"Oh?" Beckett holstered his forty-four and leaned forward in his saddle.

"Yes, sir! They were camped out a few miles over the Alabama line when I left them. They're on the trail of a man named Coates."

"They sent you to find me?"

"Well, not exactly." He motioned toward the sheriff's badge. "They said they were after this Coates feller for murder, and you being the sheriff, I thought you'd want to know." His teeth were large and white. His beard was just a day old.

"Was one of the men, Cal Jordon?" Deputy Shires jumped in.

"Well, I believe they did call one of the older men that, yes." The black man squinted and nodded.

"Are they all okay?" Shires liked asking questions.

"Well, I suppose. I didn't see anything seriously wrong with any of them." the man said.

"Well, we'll ride on that way." Beckett nodded down the road. "Are you going with us?"

"Ah, well, no sir. Headed toward Atlanta, myself." His smile broadened. "I have business there."

"Business?" The sheriff could tell the man wasn't from anywhere close to Alabama or Georgia. His accent was pure east coast and north of the Mason-Dixon line. Hearing him say he had 'business' made the hair rise on the back of Beckett's neck. There weren't many blacks in Harlon County, and none of them had ever had 'business' of their own as far as he knew. The only business they ever had was at the behest of a white man.

"Well, alright. Get on with your business," Beckett said. Deputy Shires and I will head on toward the state line."

The man nodded and waved his hand. Then grasping the horse's mane with one hand and the reins with the other, he trotted off before either lawman could think of another question.

"Let's go, Deputy; we have 'business' to take care of ourselves."

24

Sarge and the other three men took time for breakfast. A bandage secured Cal's leg. In the light of day, they could see that it was a scratch that had bled profusely at first, but now, even with the residual soreness, it seemed relatively harmless if he took care of it. Cal rubbed the place on his neck where the pistol had worn it raw. "Damn his hide!" he muttered, thinking of his damage at the hands of the black man.

"Why would Coates head for Huntsville?" Bronco asked. He looked at his two friends.

"I can't think of a reason," Preacher said. "The route to New Orleans is south, not north. I wonder if something changed his mind. If so, we are definitely up a creek."

"I am skeptical too." Sarge threw the blanket on his horse, followed by the saddle. He looked toward the farmer. "Need a hand getting up, Cal?"

Cal put his left foot in the stirrup and swung the injured right leg over the saddle with a grunt. "I'm making it okay." He leaned over as if flexing the leg before he straightened up.

Preacher's saddle creaked as he mounted and settled in. Bronco swung up easily and grinned. "Let's ride!"

Preacher and Sarge glanced at each other. It was good to see Bronco more like himself. Each glanced from the young man to the farmer. There was room for a lot of friction there if Bronco ever spilled his guts about Mrs. Jordon. They took the road down the west side of the hill at a comfortable pace.

"Well, this looks like where our horse thief ran into Coates," Sarge said. "See the prints where the horse danced around while they were jawing?" The brief rain the previous afternoon had only gotten the top half-inch of dirt moist. The bottoms of the shallow horse prints were dry. They could see where their midnight raider had skidded a bit as he headed up the hill on foot. There were no other fresh prints in evidence indicating that the two men were the last to use this section of the road since the shower.

The four men rode to the junction. There were signs of three travelers. On the right, two sets of tracks traveled the Huntsville road toward them, with one turning toward Titustown and the other continuing toward Birmingham. One set of tracks led toward Huntsville.

Sarge studied at the prints as closely as he could from the saddle. "There are the prints headed toward Huntsville, so I guess our midnight guest was telling us the truth."

"Given that Coates stole his horse, it's hard to see why he'd lie to us." Preacher said.

Bronco jumped off his horse. "That's peculiar." He motioned at the prints, both coming and going north toward Huntsville, and the prints headed toward Birmingham. "I'd swear the same horse made all these prints." He looked up at the mounted men and pointed. "See how this shoe is a bit off-kilter? Same here, and here!" He pointed at the two sets of prints coming from Huntsville and the ones headed toward Huntsville.

Preacher couldn't see much at that distance. He rubbed his jaw and kept quiet. Cal strained his eyes, but his vision wasn't too good either. Sarge leaned out of the saddle for a closer look. He reined his horse around. "Maybe! Let's ride on toward Huntsville a bit."

Bronco leaped back into his saddle and followed the other men.

"I'll be dammed!" Cal exclaimed. His horse, Moon, got him to the top of the knoll first. He pointed. "This is where that varmint turned around!" He looked at Bronco with some respect. "You have good eyes, young fella." He swallowed and turned his head toward the others. "My boy, Jimmy, had good eyes, you know."

"Well, we know Coates is a schemer," Sarge said. "I'm thinking he doesn't remember telling you about his New Orleans plans, Preacher. If we had been chasing him cold without that information, we could have headed for Huntsville with nary a thought of paying much further attention to prints."

They descended the hill and stopped again at the fork. Preacher looked at Cal and softly stroked his horse's shoulder. "Cal, this might be a good time for you to head back home. I hate to mention it, but you have a boy to bury and probably a worried family to think about." Preacher said.

"He's right," Sarge said. "Coates is headed to New Orleans. He has almost a full day's head start on us now. We're not going to clear this up today."

Bronco turned toward the older man. His face was suddenly white and rigid with passion. "We will catch John Coates for you, sir. I promise we won't let him get away no matter what."

Cal looked at Bronco, surprised at his intensity. He straightened up and took off his hat. He ran his hand over his balding head while he thought it out. "Everything you say is true. I know my wife is probably beside herself with worry." He looked down at his bandaged leg. By itself, it wasn't a factor in a decision. He knew that the bandage was a reminder of how lucky he had been. He imagined the consequences for his family if the gunshot had killed him. His face flushed red as he considered his dilemma.

On the one hand, he wanted John Coates dead. Not just dead. He wanted a hideous death for him, and he wanted it by his own hand. But he knew he couldn't have that. He had to leave it to these three men. He hated to be in the position of having to rely on three strangers, Yankee strangers at that. But Bronco's intensity won him over. He looked at the young man and nodded. "I believe you." Then, he turned toward Sarge and Preacher. "I do have other responsibilities."

Sarge extended his hand, and they shook. Preacher and Bronco did the same. "One thing is sure." Preacher said. "We are going to New Orleans regardless. So you don't have to worry about us getting tired or disheartened and giving up. We will get this done."

"When this is over, we'll send you the news," Sarge said.

"Thanks." Cal turned his horse toward home. He waved once as he reached the base of the knoll. He stopped there, and they saw his shoulders stiffen for just a moment. Then his horse started up the incline toward Harlon County.

25

John Coates' eureka moment after he left the junction required a new plan. Often, when he had one of his flashes of clarity, he noted that it would have been easier to implement had the idea come just a little sooner. That was the case now as well. He had a good head start on the Yankees should he continue toward New Orleans, but now with his change of plans, that lead had become a time-waster. The tree line fell further away from the road west of the hills in a widening swath of meadow. Eventually, the road crossed a shallow stream. Instead of crossing it, he reined the horse left and followed it a bit until he was back almost in the timber. John rode east and north, shadowing the road from the junction, close to the tree line. Once he was back within sight of the intersection, he concealed the horse and hobbled it to graze in a clearing among the trees. He sat down in the shade to wait. If the Yankees planned an ambush, they'd expect him after dark. If nothing happened overnight, in all likelihood, they would proceed down the west side of the hill the next morning. He had considered trying to sneak past the pursuer's camp at dusk but warned himself that not only were the two Yankees and reinforcements up on the hill, but very likely the black man he had turned loose was lurking somewhere up there as well.

Though it no longer mattered, he was pleased that he would have the opportunity to see first-hand how his trick of misdirection at the fork of the north and south roads would work out. Would they follow his tracks toward Huntsville without noticing his turn-around? Or would there be communication between the black man and his pursuers? Would the five men act on the man's information and head for Huntsville? Now, with his change in plans, they would be wrong regardless of which direction they went. John relished the outcome. But as the day passed, he grew too hungry to maintain his enthusiasm. He impatiently waited. Darkness descended. He fell asleep. A single gunshot awakened him in the early morning hours. It was off in the middle distance, far enough away to limit his panic to a moment of heart thumping. Thinking on it, he grinned. As he pulled the blanket back up over his shoulders, he wondered if the bullet had ended the days of the big black man he had sent to steal a horse or one of the riders trailing him. Then he remembered that the black man was unarmed. He smiled. Either way, it felt good.

Early the following day, John stood among the trees while the junction's drama played itself out. There were the two soldiers he hated so passionately and two civilians that he could not recognize at a distance. The younger one with the wide-brimmed hat seemed to solve the mystery of his actual direction of travel pretty quickly. That was disappointing. He also noted that his escaped army horse did not accompany them. Nor was the black man in tow. He wondered if the man had pulled off the theft. He grunted to himself. Of course, he did! *They are all-natural thieves. It's damn disgusting!*

The fourth man separated from the group and rode back east. John stood in the thick stand of pines and watched the remaining three men ride past in the sure knowledge that he had outwitted the riders who pursued him with his change of plans. He chuckled at that fact. Coates was proud of his efforts toward misdirection, even if they were unsuccessful. He waited another half hour before he rode the horse back out to the road.

Once over the hills, he slowed as he again encountered the tiny hamlet of Turkey Creek. He rode in slowly and once more concluded that there was not much there. A small general store beckoned as a place to spend some of the black man's money. There was no legitimate reason for a black man to have money. Just the concept rubbed John wrong. For a moment, he regretted not plugging the man. It was physically painful to have encountered a man so uppity. John concluded that he had, in truth, rescued the horse he was riding rather than stolen it. He swatted at a fly on the animal's neck, and the horse shivered. This horse was inferior to the one he had lost. This one was older and less agile. But who said he had to stick with it? If he saw something better and the odds were good, he'd trade out!

He wrapped the reins around the hitching post and strode in as if he had been inside a hundred times. It was a typical general store, and the shelves were meagerly stocked. An older man was sweeping behind the counter. He was tall, though not as tall as Coates, and thin with a handsome mustache. He wore wire-rim glasses.

"What can I do you for, stranger?" He leaned the broom against the back wall and rested his knuckles on the counter. The eyes were blue and a little sad. A little red was still visible among the strands of his graying hair.

Coates spied a box with a chewing tobacco sign on the side and pointed. "Give me one of them."

The storekeeper looked over. "Well, mister. I'm all out of the regular chaws. All I've got until more supplies come in is this one Oliver Twist from Denmark, and it's pretty pricey." He picked up the pouch between his thumb and forefinger. "Six bits!" He smiled a little and dropped it back in the box.

Coates frowned. "Denmark, huh? I never heard of it. Is that east or west of here?" The clerk started to respond, but John interrupted him. "Never mind, I'll take it." He felt expansive on the black man's money, though he knew seventy-five cents was more than he should spend regardless of whose money it was.

Coates mentally added his total resources. He would still have plenty for flour, cornmeal, bacon and coffee, and a few more incidentals. He glanced back toward the street as he listed the items one at a time to the clerk who placed them on the counter. No one was in sight. He reflected that he would never stop by here again. Why throw away good money that he could use later? He brushed his wrist against his six-gun for reassurance.

The retailer paused at the coffee. "Sorry, again, stranger. I haven't had coffee of any kind for six months, but they say the embargo is lifted, and it's coming. I do still have some chicory left, though, out of New Orleans." He arched his eyebrows.

"Alright, give me some of the that-there chicory, then." Coates thought he might as well get used to it since he would eventually be adopting New Orleans as his new home. He had heard someplace that folks mixed chicory with real coffee. John knew he could do that if he came on to any of the real thing. He looked around the store and saw nothing more of interest. Satisfied, John was about to draw his six-gun and clean out the till when he heard boots stomping on the steps.

"Howdy, Marshall! I haven't seen you in two weeks. Everything alright over in Barton City?" The man grunted, and the storekeeper gave the new arrival a quick wave. "Be with you in just a moment." He looked back at Coates expectantly.

Without turning around, Coates glanced at the intruder out of the corner of his eye. He was a big man, shorter than Coates, with a strong jaw and an unusually large nose. His tin star was large and well-polished. Coates quickly considered his options. He could probably get the drop on the man and make a get-away. John pondered it for a moment and rejected the notion. It could put another posse after him if he had to shoot the man, whereas a simple robbery might not have. John didn't need that. He turned away from the clerk and exchanged a nod with the marshall.

"Well. I'm on my way." Coates said. He dug in his saddlebag and came up with enough money to pay for his goods.

With Coates' money in his hand, the storekeeper turned conversational. "Where you headed, mister."

"Birmingham," Coates said. "And I need to be getting on." He stuffed the merchandise into his saddlebags and headed for the door. "Have a good day." Coates stopped outside the door and surveyed the street once more.

"Funny," the storekeeper said to the marshal, "I'd swear I saw him come through town heading west just yesterday." He stroked his jaw. "Well, it don't matter. I got rid of that Oliver Twist chew you've been eyeing for the last year." He smiled and watched the lawman's reaction.

The marshal grunted. "Just as well, I'd never been able to afford it on my wages."

26

"Cal's back!" Sarah burst into Pappy's room. Cal Jordon followed her in. "See!" She looked back at the big man. "Pappy's getting better already!" She turned toward Pappy. "Aren't you?"

"Darn right," Pappy muttered. He tried to move, but the pain in his side discouraged it. "I'm fit as a fiddle with a bad string." He looked at his nephew. "Glad you're back. Sarah lit a fire under Beckett to check on you." He frowned. "Well, any news on John Coates?"

Cal shifted his weight off his injured leg. Both Sarah and Pappy noticed. "You okay?" Pappy cocked an eyebrow.

"I'm okay. I found Preacher on my second day out. Preacher and I came on to Coates just across the border, but he got away in a boat." He pointed at his leg. "I got this scratch when a black tried to steal Coates' horse." He threw his hand up to allay further questions. Then he stepped closer and leaned down a bit.

"I need to get home. I know Wanda, and the girls are going to be worried. But when I can get back here, I want to know all about you getting shot. I have to figure out the why of this thing. It's driving me crazy!" He took off his hat and ran his hand over his receding hairline. "I'm really glad you're healing up, Pappy." He glanced at Sarah. He didn't seem to notice that her face was ashen. Instead, he saw her eyes searching Pappy's face.

"I'm sorry, darlin," Cal said. "I'm sick to the core. But like I said, Wanda is bound to be worried. I'll be back in town tomorrow, and we can all talk about this in more detail." He patted her shoulder and clambered down the hall to the front office. They heard him speak briefly with Doctor Jenkins, and then he was gone.

Sarah sat down hard, rocking the bed. Pappy grimaced. She was still white, and she was kneading her hands together.

"What are we going to tell him, Pappy?" She looked at him with wet eyes. "How can I tell him that it's my fault? How can I tell him I got my Jimmy killed?" She leaned forward and dry-heaved. Her stomach was empty. She hadn't eaten since the shooting, and she was half-used to walking around light-headed.

"Tarnation, Girl! You're not going to tell him any such thing!" Pappy gently grabbed her arm and grimaced with the movement. "You let me take care of this. Hear me? Now, pour me some water, will you? All this jawing is making me thirsty."

The Jordon family, though Baptist, invited the Methodist preacher to lead the services for Jimmy Jordon in the Baptist Church. The Baptist minister's position was still unfilled since the church's original minister's death a year before. The church was packed. Jimmy's friends, who had made it back from the war, were among those present. Some wore the remnants of Confederate uniforms, the worn and ripped places now repaired by their mothers' or wives' loving and thankful hands.

Even Brent McGuire came into town with his parents though his injured leg was not yet completely healed. A pretty blond-headed woman sat in front of him, much to his liking. Brent sat with his hand cradled alongside the outside of his leg to protect it from his fidgety younger sister. Mrs. Sarah Jordon sat between Aunt Emmy and Cal Jordon. Miss Maggie Taylor, Preacher's friend from the church, played a piano solo, followed by *Amazing Grace.* Sarah Jordon had such a lump in her throat that she could not carry the tune. There were five verses, and since Sarah knew it by heart, she didn't bother with the hymnal but mouthed the words to each stanza along with the music. Finally, the fifth verse was more than she could bear. *Yea, when this flesh and heart shall fail, and mortal life shall cease, I shall possess within the veil, a life of joy and peace.* She broke down and sobbed into her aunt's shoulder.

Cal Jordon and Wanda, with their two girls, sat in stoic silence. They did not attempt to join in the singing. Instead, they stared at the closed casket. The doctor had explained to them as diplomatically as he could that they, nor anyone else, would want to see the body's condition. Neither shed a tear. Wanda had not recovered from the dual emotional trauma of getting her son back and losing him all in the same day. First, she would find herself going into periods of mumbling, and blackness would come over her, which lasted for five or ten minutes. Then, she would recover and find herself anchored in one spot, with a dish she was drying still grasped in her hand or while stirring soup well past the point when she should have removed it from the stove.

Cal listened to the service and seethed. Doc forbade Pappy from attending the service, but the old man couldn't stand it and prevailed on Howie to help him navigate the two blocks to the church. He limped inside just as the service started. The church was packed, and they stood awkwardly in the doorway, scanning for a place for him to perch. Finally, a friend saw his predicament and got up and gave them his seat in the back pew.

Elmore Clemens sat dark and silent at the far end of the same bench and watched Sarah Jordon through many bobbing heads. Behind his placid exterior, his intense interest was not discernable by the people around him, nor would anyone even remember his presence.

27

After about an hour, Sarge, Bronco, and Preacher stopped to water the horses. "Seems to me that we can pretty much forget catching Coates before he gets to New Orleans. He has too much of a head start," Preacher said.

Sarge nodded and mentally kicked himself. "Yep. We laid around up on that hill for more than half a day. Now, we are only about a day out of Titustown. Unfortunately, I got us fouled up with the ambush plan. Coates is just impossible to predict. He must change his mind a dozen times a day. I already knew that, but I still tried to guess his next move."

Preacher stretched out on a grassy spot and rested on his elbow. "Well, it seemed like the odds were with us. Coates' one goal of late has been to kill us." He looked at Bronco. "You're a walking example of that."

Bronco nodded. "Remember what you told me about not being able to control everything? Well, trying to control or predict what John Coates will do next is impossible. You just have to play the odds." Bronco said. He smiled. "Not that I'm that good at figuring odds."

"Neither am I," Sarge said. "And I thought I wanted to try my hand with poker on a riverboat," he added. "So, are we agreed? We just work our way to New Orleans and hope he stays true to that plan." The other men nodded.

Pappy was back in bed. His excursion to the funeral had stretched places before they were ready to be pulled. He was feeling light-headed by the time they reached the benediction. He gritted his teeth and stuck around long enough to put a consoling hand on Cal's arm and receive brief teary pecks from Sarah, Wanda, and the two girls before returning to Doc's office.

"You know, Doc, what I'd like to do is go lie down at my place." He was watching Doc change his bandage. "I think I'm getting in your way here."

"No. You are not in the way, and no, you aren't ready to move back to your place," Doc said. "Pick your feet up so we can get these boots off. I'm not going to fuss at you for going to the funeral. I'm not going to complain about your hard-headedness. But I'll be damned if I'm going to send you home, so I have to traipse all the way over there when I think I need to check on you. Give this two more days." He held up two fingers. "Two more days, and if your wounds look the way I expect them to, I'll send you home to lay up." Doc laid the flap of Pappy's shirt down over the new bandage. The wound was still seeping a little, but the bruising had gone from purple to an angry ochre. He wadded up the old gauze and turned away. "Lie quiet. Think peaceful thoughts." He left the room. Pappy lay back and contemplated the day. Behind every moment hung the black cloud of memory and guilt. There were no peaceful thoughts.

Sheriff Beckett was holed up in his office when a wagon lumbered down the street and stopped out front. The office door swung open, and he recognized one of old man Coates' boys, though he couldn't recollect the name. He carried the stench of carrion with him.

"Howdy, Sheriff." The man took off his hat and gazed around the room. In his curiosity, there was an alertness to his gaze. "I'm Schooley Coates. Me and my brother, Barney, just got back from Alabama to fetch Willard and Sam's bodies. Some Yankees killed them. Now we can't find nobody out at the farm. The horses are still there. One is even saddled, but there's no sign of Daddy and our brother, Dooley." His eyes came back to the sheriff, and he made a sad gesture with his arms.

Beckett stood up. "I heard about the run-in they had with some Yankees over there. Call your brother in here, and hurry up about it. The stench from that wagon is fouling the air." Or, Beckett wondered, was it the man himself? With both brothers in the office, the sheriff waved toward a couple of chairs and strode over to shut the door.

"Well, boys, I guess there's no easy way to tell you this." He sat down and leaned back in his chair. He started with what he knew and finished with what he suspected. He gave them a moment to absorb the news. "I'm sorry about your daddy and brother. Doc's got their bodies and plans on burying them tomorrow." Beckett was surprised at the lack of emotion on the men's faces. "I guess he can handle two more. I don't suppose you boys got any money, do you?" The two men looked at each other, and Schooley made his hopeless gesture again.

"Well, work that out with Doc. If worse comes to worst, the county has a paupers fund." He stood up. He decided to let Doc fill them in about John's brother Zac. "Just out of curiosity, you boys don't have any idea about what could have set John off, do you? The men looked at each other.

"Well, John has always been wound up tighter than a badger's butt," Schooley said.

"And Pa didn't trust him further than he could toss him," Barney added. He looked at his brother for confirmation. "I guess he was right."

"We have men out looking for John right now. I don't think the chances are good for running him down, though." Beckett walked over to the door and opened it for them. "Now, get that wagon unloaded as quick as you can."

Schooley put his hat back on and pulled the brim down in front. "Thinking on it, Sheriff, we have our graveyard out at the farm. So if it's all the same to you, we'll just pick up our daddy and Dooley and take them back out there."

Beckett brightened up some. "Well, that's fine. Just get that wagon moving!" Since all of the Alabama shoot-out participants of two weeks before were either dead or had left the county, he didn't want to hear any more about it.

28

Sarah lay fully clothed in her black funeral clothes with her face to the wall of her room and repeated the words to the hymn to herself. It was one of the same hymns sung at her parent's funeral ten years earlier. Back then, it had passed through her mind in the haze of loss. At eight years old, only the tune stuck with her. The lyrics had come later as she grew into adulthood. She repeated the last stanza and wondered if Jimmy was indeed possessed "within the veil, a life of joy and peace." She hoped so.

Her mood lifted a fraction at that thought. Hearing a knock at the door, she rose from the bed, went to the front bedroom window, and looked out. She could see the man's head thrust forward as if peering through the glass into the interior. He held something in his hand. Not being able to discern his face, she opened her bedroom door. From that angle, she could see that the man was Mister Elwood Clemens. He was holding a spray of flowers. Sarah stepped back and considered if she wanted to go to the door. The flowers were a friendly gesture, but the man who stood holding them on her front porch was an enigma. Of late, he seemed to materialize in her presence with increasing frequency.

She stepped back into the bedroom and glanced in the mirror. Lying about could play havoc with your clothes. She gave her apparel a passing grade for answering the door and stepped into the living room to do so.

"Howdy, ma'am." Elwood stuck out the flowers. "I was just riding home after the funeral, and you know, out in front of a house on the way, I seen these flowers. I thought they was right purdy, and so with the funeral and all today, I brung you some." He grinned foolishly, and she saw that his eyetooth was missing on the right side. The combination of the flowers, her nervousness, and the missing tooth from a mouth of otherwise well-stained incisors gave her pause.

"Well, thank you, Mister Clemens. I appreciate your kindness." Sarah accepted the flowers and put her hand on the knob.

"Well, I hope you like them." Elmore took a step back. Sarah started to close the door. Then Elmore stepped forward again. "I could get you more if you'd like."

"Thank you, Mister Clemens, but these will be just fine. I'll put them in water right away."

"All right then." Elmore put his hat on and backed up two steps. Sarah closed the door and took the flowers to the sink, where she pulled a vase from the shelf. Sarah poured a bit of water from the well-bucket and put the fistful of flowers in. They were pretty, and she was grateful for a moment's pause from her naked grief. Sarah did not hear the door open. Nor was she conscious of the footsteps approaching her from behind. The flowers were exceptionally beautiful. She was about to arrange them when an arm clamped around her middle just below her bosom and a hand, clasping a damp cloth, clamped forcefully across her mouth and nose.

"I don't mean to hurt you none, ma'am!" The voice growled close to her ear. "So. don't go making any noise."

Sarah's eyes went wide with surprise. She struggled to breathe. The hand across her mouth was unyielding. The cloth reeked of both smoking tobacco and something else. In that instant, before the ether-soaked rag did its work, she discerned that the foulness was sweet and sour at the same time. She had been in the presence of this person before. The vase slipped from her grasp into the sink. It landed bottom-side down on the cast iron and cracked around the base. The water started to dribble away out the sides. She felt the strength leave her legs. The man swore as she went inert and wilted like a leaf of spinach in hot oil. His hand fumbled a bit as he gathered the folds of her black skirt to get his hand beneath her sagging legs. His breath came in quick, flustered gasps. He had imagined that she would be lighter.

Pappy was sleeping in his clothes when awakened by a tap on the door. Miss Emmy cracked it, and seeing his eyes flutter, the old lady pushed it fully open and glanced around the room.

"Have you seen Sarah?" Intently, she leaned over the old man. She was a little too close for comfort, so he waved her back and gingerly scooted to a more upright position. She grasped his intention, grabbed his pillow, and moved it higher against the headboard.

"No?" Pappy rubbed his eyes briefly and tried to focus on her looming presence. "Sit down over there." He said irritably, pointing to the chair. "What are you saying?"

"I'm saying I can't find her!" Emmy exclaimed. She waved her arms about in an agitated manner that was unlike her.

Pappy was about to suggest home, but that was too obvious. "Sarah had a lot of friends at church. Maybe she went home with one of them?" He eyed her expectantly.

"No! I walked home with her and put her to bed. She was too upset. She wouldn't be interested in visiting with any of them." Emmy walked to the window and peered out at the street. There was a wagon with two men tying up outside the doctor's office. "Coates, cousins," she said out loud without realizing she had spoken.

"Huh?" Pappy was getting frustrated with the conversation.

"John Coates' cousin's just tied up outside."

Pappy started to rise but decided against it. No member of the Coates clan was worth a moment's pain, as far as he was concerned. "Well, as far as I know, the oldest one's name is.... Schooley! Probably the smartest of the bunch, including the old man. I don't recollect the others." He shook his head to clear it.

"Getting back to Sarah," he said." Maybe Cal and Wanda picked her up?"

Emmy considered. "I guess that could have happened."

"That's got to be it." Pappy closed his eyes in dismissal.

Emmy fanned her face with her hand. "Oh, my. I had myself going, didn't I?" She chuckled a little with some embarrassment. "Well, I need to get back to the Star."

Pappy nodded and gingerly edged back down on the bed, pulling the pillow with him. "She's fine," he declared and closed his eyes again.

29

Sheriff Beckett was half dozing in his chair. The under-edge of his white mustache was tinted caramel from his recent cup of coffee. The previous day had started about three hours earlier than usual. He and his young deputy had encountered Cal about two hours out of town, and they had all ridden back together. Today he had been forced by circumstances to arise early again. He was still feeling the effects of lunch while sitting through Jimmy Jordon's afternoon funeral. With the funeral over, and John Coates, now known to be far out of his jurisdiction, about all he could do on that score, was send out another wave of telegraph messages to law enforcement officers in Alabama, along the route to New Orleans. At least Cal's time with the Yankees had provided that helpful information. He thought that maybe things could get back to normal now.

His eyes were just starting to close when Cal Jordon pushed the door open and stood back so Miss Emmy Lawson could bustle into his office. She was stewing about something. He found himself thinking about how her manner reminded him of her niece, Sarah, when she was having a hissy.

"Sheriff, Sarah is missing," Emmy said without preamble.

"Oh?" Beckett opened one eye and placed both hands palms down on the desk before sliding them into his lap while leaning back in his chair. "I saw her at the funeral. She looked about as well as you could expect." He crossed his arms, leaned further back, and looked at Cal for verification.

Cal took three limping steps to one of the chairs opposite the desk and plopped down. He looked concerned but not nearly as upset as Emmy.

Emmy came up to the desk and loomed over the half-reclining sheriff. "Did you hear what I said? She's missing! I took her home and left her there. When I checked on her later, she was gone. I naturally checked with Pappy, thinking she went to visit him. He hadn't seen her since the service. He and I thought maybe Cal picked her up to go out to the farm to be with the family. That was two hours ago. Now, Cal is back in town, and he hasn't seen her either!" She ran out of breath and looked at Cal for verification.

Cal took off his hat and wiped his balding head. "Sheriff, as best as we can tell, Sarah has just disappeared. Neither of us can think of any more possibilities."

"Sarah's best friend is Nellie Black, north of town," Emmy said. Her breathing was back to normal. "As a last resort, Cal rode out there. She's not there. I'm beside myself!" She reached out and pulled the spare chair close to the desk, sat down, and looked back and forth between the two men. "Well, what are we going to do?"

"Well, what do you want to do?" Beckett was at a loss and wanted to gain some sense of direction.

Miss Emmy jumped to her feet. "We want to find her, you oaf!"

Cal grabbed her wrist, but she shook him off. "That girl could be anywhere. She could be lying in a ditch somewhere. She's terribly upset about losing Jimmy. Maybe she had some kind of a stroke and wandered off. I don't know." Her knees weakened from the exertion, and she sank back down in the chair.

Beckett mentally put on his sheriffin' hat and looked down for a minute. "All right. The first thing to do is round up my deputies to search the town and nearby farms as quickly as possible. If she's gone visiting or wandered off, we'll probably find her inside an hour. If not, we'll think of something else." He rose to his feet. "Cal, are you going to be in town for a while?"

Cal got up. "I'll be at the Lucky Star with Emmy, Ben. I sure hope you find her. Come on, Emmy, I'll walk you over there."

Miss Emmy didn't move for a moment. She seemed distracted as she spoke. "She didn't have a horse or wagon to go anywhere. Surely, if she's walking, she won't be hard to find." She rose and allowed Cal to escort her out the door and toward the Star.

Beckett put on his hat and headed four doors down the block to the pool hall. His two deputies hung out there when there were no chores to take care of at the jail. He had Deputy Shires saddled up and heading out north in ten minutes, and Deputy Boggs headed south. They had instructions to go no further than the nearest farms. For his part, he started legging it from store to store to make sure the girl had not decided to go on a shopping spree to assuage the pain of losing her husband. He knew that people acted in peculiar ways at a time of traumatic loss. He was not feeling right about this. The Yankee troops were long gone, but there were a few low-life Confederate boys without jobs or prospects that came too readily to mind. A good number of them had been at Jimmy's funeral, and he'd overheard some of them grousing after the service about how tough things were. A man feeling sorry for himself tended to do stupid things.

Sarah had been a popular girl among the young men up until she married Jimmy. Well, even afterward, if you counted Bronco Brumley. Sheriff Beckett had been in his position since well before the war, and nothing had changed when it came to the combination of discontented men and liquor. He stuck his head into the hardware store and had a quick look-see. Then, just to be thorough, he stopped at the livery stable to see if Sarah might have rented a horse or wagon. No luck there. Every dead end raised the rawness level in his gut another peg. A missing girl was not good. The town business section searched, the sheriff made his last stop at Doc's office to check with Pappy.

The old man startled awake. Emmy and Cal had headed straight to the Star after Beckett's visit but backtracked, remembering that Pappy was in the dark regarding recent developments.

"So, you've searched the town?" Pappy ran his forefinger over his mustache.

"Every store and shop, including the livery stable. I looked into the Baptist and Methodist churches. Brother Thomas was back in his office. She hasn't been there."

"What about Maggie Taylor?"

The sheriff considered. "I should check with her! She is something of an unofficial soft shoulder for the younger women. I'll be right back." While he was gone, Pappy ran through a negligible catalog of possibilities. Beckett returned fifteen minutes later.

"Nope. Miss Maggie hasn't seen her either." He sat down in the chair and ran his hand from his brow, over his nose, to his chin. "She came up with a funny idea. She said we should get those Yankees back here."

At that moment, Cal limped through the door. He looked at the two men. "If I stayed over at the Star much longer, I'd start drinking from the aggravation, and I need my wits about me. Anything?"

"Nope." The sheriff sat in one of the chairs.

"The sheriff did pick up a good idea, though," Pappy said.

"I did?" Beckett said in surprise.

"Yep. Maggie Taylor suggested we get Sarge, Preacher, and Bronco back here."

"That's foolish," the sheriff said.

"Madison figured out the last little mystery we had going on here," Pappy said.

"Yes, but still...." The sheriff looked dubious.

Cal looked at the sheriff. "Pappy's right. If your deputies come up dry, we're stuck. Don't forget; I spent some time with them. I know they're Yankees, except for Madison, of course, but from what I've seen, they are smart." He looked at the other two men. "More important, they never give up." His tone was razor sharp with meaning.

"Well, I can send out some more telegrams to law enforcement along their trail toward Birmingham." Beckett allowed. He was dead set against bringing the Yankees back, but Cal was a friend. He also had influence. At the moment, there did not appear to be any real upside.

"That's too hit and miss," Cal said. "I think you should send your young deputy, Shires, out to try and catch them." His tone made the idea seem more than just a suggestion.

Beckett looked at Pappy, and the old man was nodding his head in agreement. The sheriff shrugged and put his hand on the doorknob. He was not a man to procrastinate once he made a decision. "All right. If my deputies come back empty-handed, I'll head over to the telegraph office."

30

John Coates mounted his horse outside the general store in Turkey Creek and stuffed a new Danish tobacco chaw into his cheek. The evening shadows were lengthening. This chaw was sweeter than the tobacco he was used to. He licked his lips. It was almost like candy. The first juices built up strong, and he needed to spit a few times, but he was swallowing a trickle in a couple of minutes. His empty stomach appreciated the sweetness.

Coates was intent on making the ride to Titustown in one straight shot. That required that he keep a slower pace and not wear out his horse. Every hour or so, John dismounted and walked the horse for a bit despite his sore feet. He took every opportunity to stop for water. It was well before sunrise when he rode in past the sagging, open gate of the Elwood Clemens farm at the end of a lonesome country road. As it was early morning, the house was dark. Coates walked the horse to the barn and threw the saddle onto a rack. Returning to the porch, he tried the door. As expected, it was unlocked. A look in the bedroom found his cousin, Elwood Clemens, asleep. Coates moved to the second bedroom and found the bed covered with debris. Two minutes later, he had unloaded it down to the tick. Coates kicked off his fancy boots, settled in on the bare mattress, and was instantly asleep.

Bronco Brumley rode between Sarge and Preacher. From time to time, he'd trot ahead a bit and then drop back. It was a harmless way to entertain himself on long rides. His companions ignored him and kept a steady pace. The sun had set on the western hills as they continued south through the wide valley floor. The day faded, and given that they had let go of the idea of catching John Coates en route to New Orleans, Bronco cast his eyes to the left and right of the road, looking for a potential camping spot. When he saw a likely place close to a small stream, he thrust his arm out, pointing. Sarge and Preacher signaled their agreement by changing their heading and halting at the water's edge.

"You know, Barton City is just a mile or two ahead," Preacher mentioned after they dismounted and the horses lined up at the water's edge.

"You thinking there might be a place to stay the night?" Sarge asked as he walked over to a large rock to relieve himself.

Bronco didn't respond. It was hard for him to overcome his miserly ways. There hadn't been much beyond necessities when he was growing up in Ohio. As an army private, he was always on the low end of the pay scale. He had gotten along by doling out his meager funds carefully. He still viewed hotels as a luxury despite his newly acquired wealth. He lay his hand on his saddlebag to verify the reality of the lump.

"Might be. If not, we could camp on the other side. You okay with that?" Sarge said, looking toward Bronco.

"I guess so." Bronco took off his new hat and admired it again.

"If not a hotel, they probably have a livery stable." Preacher said with a poker face. His eyes lit up a bit with amusement. In the past, Bronco had shown a liking to sleeping with the horses.

Sarge's head swiveled in his direction. Preacher slapped his leg and laughed, and Bronco grinned. "Well, horses don't snore like you two, and straw makes a good mattress." Then, he paused, "and it is a darn sight cheaper!"

"Okay then, let's press on and see if we can improve on sleeping in the wild. I'm spoiled of late. My old bed on the farm was a good one." Sarge put his foot in the stirrup and swung his leg over. His horse snorted. It, too, had probably been thinking they had reached the end of the day's ride.

It was late dusk by the time they covered the remaining mile and a half to Barton City. They rode in slowly, scanning the storefronts for a sign that would provide them with a place to spend the night.

"You gents looking for something?" A large man approached from the boardwalk and tipped his hat back. There was a shotgun in his hand and a big star on his chest. Even in the semi-darkness, his face looked large and commanding.

Sarge halted his horse. "Matter of fact, we are, Sheriff. Is there a hotel in Barton City?"

"Marshall, it's Marshall Holifield. Where are you folks from?" He switched hands on the shotgun.

"Most recently, Titustown," Sarge said. He made sure his voice reflected his southern upbringing.

"Any chance you go by the name of Madison Jones?"

Sarge's head whipped around to look at Preacher and Bronco. Then, his eyes returned to the lawman. "Well, as a matter of fact, it is, Marshall. Why do you ask?"

Marshall Holifield thumbed his big nose. He reached in his pocket and pulled out a sheet of paper. "Says here, you boys are wanted in Titustown."

"Wanted?" Preacher was astonished. Bronco's horse danced a few steps as if the word had spooked it. Sarge eyed the badge suspiciously.

The lawman laughed. "Maybe that was not the right word. This telegram says you are 'needed' in Titustown." He handed the paper up to Sarge. Sarge squinted but couldn't read it in the darkness.

"Come on over to the jail where the light is better," Holifield said. He parked the shotgun on his shoulder and strode back to the boardwalk. The three men clicked their tongues for their horses to follow along. Despite the darkness, Sarge kept moving the paper close to his eyes, trying to read it. He could feel a twinge of anxiety. Two blocks down the street, they caught the tinny sound of a piano. It appeared Barton City did have some life, so maybe there was a hotel as well.

The marshall opened the jail's front door and put the shotgun in the rack on his way to his desk. Sarge followed him in and read the message while walking to the desk where Holifield had taken a chair.

Sarge looked at the other men. "This telegram is from our friend, Sheriff Beckett. It says Sarah Jordon is missing. He says she may have been kidnapped!"

"Kidnapped?" Bronco's eyes went wide. He could feel his gut tighten.

"I'll be!" Preacher pulled out a chair and dropped down.

Sarge looked at the marshall, who shrugged. "All I know is what's written on the paper you have in your hand."

Sarge took the other side chair and ran his open hand along his jawline. He handed the telegram up to Bronco, who scanned it twice, absorbing the message and trying to find something more between the lines. Then, finally, he flapped the paper against Preacher's shoulder. Preacher reached up and accepted it. His big head moved up and down a bit as he focused his eyes.

The marshal eyed Sarge and Preacher's blue caps in turn. He had not picked up on them in the dark street. Sarge's accent was not from Yankee land. These men wearing Union uniforms raised his hackles some, but he knew Sheriff Beckett a little. That the telegram came from him was a point in their favor. Sarge's accent, and the word 'needed' on the telegram, were just enough to make him co-operative.

"Back to your question, Jones. We don't have a hotel in Barton City. We have a boarding house, but it's been full up for the last year and a half. They found a new low-grade gold vein in the hills, and Jefferson Davis needed all the gold he could get. So they're still at it, but now that the war is over, they probably won't be able to hang on much longer."

"Well, I guess we can ride back out to the spot Bronco picked out before we decided to come to town," Preacher said.

Marshal Holifield tapped his fingers on his desk for a moment. "Well, there is another option." He motioned toward the back. "I could put you up here for one night." He scratched the back of his neck. "' Course, I'd have to charge you something. Say four bits, apiece?" He leaned forward. "Just a suggestion. Some folks get spooked at the idea of sleeping in jail."

"Well, we've...." Bronco started to speak.

Sarge cut him off with a 'stay still' motion of his hand. "Well, Marshall, given the lateness of the hour, I'm for accepting your hospitality." He looked over at Preacher, who nodded. He glanced at Bronco, who accepted his mild interruption without comment, and sheepishly nodded as well.

31

Cal was sitting in Pappy's room watching him drink his morning coffee when a sharp knock on the door brought in Sheriff Beckett. He had a paper in his hand. "Well, they're coming!" He had developed some enthusiasm regarding the return of the Yankee soldiers. Besides his personal feelings on the matter of the missing girl, he had learned to weigh events, at least in part, by their impact on his reelection prospects. So he now calculated that having the three men return was probably a good thing, as it removed some of the responsibility for finding Cal's daughter-in-law from his shoulders.

He handed the telegram to Cal. The man carried it to the window to catch the sun. "Three Yankees headed your way." He skipped the stops between sentences. "Headed out this morning. It is signed Holifield."

"Well, that is fine," Cal said. He handed the message to Pappy, who gave it a quick look before returning it to the sheriff. His eyes would have had trouble with it, even in the light of the window.

"Yes, sir. Now we're going places," Pappy said. "But it's going to take them at least a full day to get here from Barton City."

"Meanwhile, are we just going to sit around and wait?" Cal looked at Beckett.

The sheriff scratched the back of his head. "Have you got any ideas, Cal?" His eyes shifted to Pappy, who picked that moment to fluff his pillows.

John Coates was lying deep in the lumpy mattress, with his coat draped over his chest. He slowly became aware of a change in the atmosphere of the room. Groggy, he let the feeling drift for a moment. Yes, there was, without doubt, a looming presence. His hand automatically reached for his forty-four even before he opened his eyes. He felt an immense paw stay his gun hand. He was no longer alone. Thick fingers grasped the gun, and the revolver slid smoothly from the holster. It took him a moment to orient himself. The only light was sneaking in from around the window coverings.

A dark bushy curtain of lank beard descended swiftly to within inches of his face. He could smell the unwashed body odor only because it was slightly more acidic than his own. His mouth was half-open, and the remains of a chaw pushed out one cheek. His tongue felt as dry and rough as a corn cob.

A familiar voice challenged him. "What the hell are you doing here!" Elwood Clemens poked Coates in the chest with his gun. The inquiry was a growl. "What the hell are you doing here!" He poked the place again. Then he pulled back the hammer and stuck the barrel in Coates' half-open mouth. "Start talking." With that demand, he pushed the barrel deep in John's throat.

John didn't think he could remember seeing his cousin so wrought up. He waved both hands in a motion for the man to back away. John put one finger on the trigger guard and pushed it away very gently. When the barrel was out of his mouth, he took a gasping breath and finally was able to speak.

"Now, Elwood, be careful with that gun. It has a hair-trigger. If you ain't careful, you're gonna shoot me accidentally, and I'll bleed all over this here bed." His voice was an octave higher than usual.

Elwood knew his cousin well enough to know that what was to follow would be pure bullshit. They had grown up together over in Washington County. However, the anxiety in John's voice was genuine, so Elwood backed the hammer off and pulled the pistol back a tad. He felt around behind himself and turned a ladder-backed chair half over, so the accumulated odds and ends piled there slid to the floor.

"Answer my question, John." Elwood kept the gun on John while he sat down. Coates half sat up and swung his double-stockinged feet out as he leaned against the wall.

"Well, the law is after me, El." He put a pathetic look on his face. "They say I killed Bronco Brumley and Pappy Jordon. But I swear I didn't."

Elwood shook his head from side to side. "You know, John, as much as you lie, you'd think you'd get good at it. It's kind of funny that this lie is half true, and I'd bet my momma's tombstone you don't know it?"

John opened his mouth to reply, but nothing came out for a second. "Huh?"

"To begin with, you didn't kill Pappy. You wounded him, and he is getting healed up in town at the doctor's office. Secondly, you didn't kill no Union soldier. You shot Jimmy Jordon dead as a doornail."

"I didn't? I did?" John worked his mouth while the information swirled around in his brain. "Well, good for Pappy!" He forced a smile. That was disappointing. Then, his mind swirled on and caught up with the news about Jimmy Jordon. "I don't know anything about killing Jimmy!" He was preparing a defense when Elwood dropped the last of the bombs.

"Don't start to tell me you didn't kill Jimmy. Don't go into a long rigmarole about that 'cause I saw it happen. After thinking on it,

I figure you thought you was shooting that worthless Yankee they call Bronco, but you plugged Jimmy."

John opened his mouth. "But."

"No buts about it. I saw it happen."

John let himself slide sideways back flat on the bed. He closed his eyes and ran through recent events. Now, John's brain lit up as he realized that the older man he had seen with Preacher out on the road was probably Jimmy's father, Cal Jordon. He went a little cold, thinking what would have happened if the man had gotten the drop on him. Then, he thought about the other three riders out at the junction the following day. He knew two of them were Preacher and Madison Jones. And the third one had to be Bronco Brumley! That last realization hit him hard and started everything whirling again.

"That damned Jimmy Jordon switched places with the Yankee?"

"Yep. You killed Jimmy, and Bronco Brumley and his two friends have left town." Elwood leaned forward. The forty-four again pointed at Coates' forehead. "Now, tell me why I shouldn't march you over to the jail and turn in your sorry ass!"

32

The room was dark. The figure of a small woman, reclining on the narrow bed, stirred. The bed was constructed with rough-cut four-by-fours, and several one-by-four sized lumber boards with a lumpy mattress, supported by a rope weaved between the horizontal sideboards. Mrs. Sarah Jordon pushed away from the wall. Though she was blindfolded, an assortment of smells and sounds filtered through to her. They hinted that she was in a strange house. She shivered in the coolness of the evening. By tilting her head just so, she could see a tiny sliver of light through a gap by the bridge of her nose. Since she had regained consciousness, her only means of gauging time was the shifting light pattern around the heavy fabric covering a window. Sarah tested the bindings on her hands. Eventually, as the day waned, the light faded into darkness. A man came into the room. He brought a chamber pot for her to use to relieve herself. He reeked with a familiar body odor. She found his presence terrifying, and the humiliation of such intimacy with this stranger was devastating. Sarah weighed the options and found none. He untied her wrists and made out like he was turning away. She enhanced her sense of privacy by draping the voluminous black dress around the chamber pot before squatting. She felt her face flush scarlet, from the first tinny sound of the tinkle of urine on metal to the last when she stood and gathered her dress up and away from the container. She stumbled on her undergarment and feared she would upset the pot, but it remained in place.

Until he delivered directions on using the chamber pot, neither of them had spoken since the man's warning in her ear about screaming. The last sound she remembered was her own muffled gasp as the ether-saturated cloth pressed over her nose.

"Okay, I'm leaving out now," he said. The man did not retie her wrists. She heard the rattle of the handle on the pot, the door opening and closing, and the key in the lock, followed by feet thumping down the hall. Her aloneness was the only comfort she had. She longed for it to last forever. The moment the door closed, she tore off the eye covering, but doing so revealed nothing useful in her strange surroundings. The room was stark in the gloom. It appeared to have been used only for storage until her arrival. Exhausted and dizzy, she returned to the bed and fell asleep, dreading the man's next visit.

The man returned early the following day. The lack of eye cover allowed her to verify that her captor was Elwood Clemens. With minimal oral communication, they replayed the scene from the previous evening. The identity of her abductor only heightened her distress. Mister Clemens provided unnecessary assistance, helping her up from the bed. She sensed his helpfulness had everything to do with achieving familial closeness. He watched her locate the pot with the toe of her foot under the shelter of her skirt. Her business completed; he gave her a bowl of oatmeal. The portion was generous. Her fear was alleviated a bit by the realization that he didn't mean to starve her. All of her life, Sarah had lived within the rules. She was now on high alert to know the rules in this strange place without realizing it. She had questions, but she remained mute out of fear of encouraging more familiarity and the dreaded finality of the answers.

The man helped her sit back on the bed. His instructions were low murmurs as if to soothe her. Then, he leaned close and said the first words requiring a response.

"I could bring you some tea, ma'am. Would you like that?"

She nodded. Any action by the man that she could construe as kindness was a balm to her inner panic. He picked up the pot and carried it out. She heard the lock click as the bolt slid into place. With a jolt, she realized instinctively that every sight, sound, touch, or smell, could be crucial to her survival. She resolved to let no clue pass unnoted.

Elwood carefully carried the chamber pot through the back door, across the insubstantial porch, down two steps, and several more paces toward a rough drainage ditch, and dumped the contents in the weeds. A small smile passed across his face as he walked back and joined John Coates.

"How'd it go?" Coates tilted his chair back against the wall and caught the man's smile. His cousin's exaggerated reaction to his camping out in the spare room had been way out of proportion to any apparent offense. John's suspicion was justified. It had taken some conniving for him to draw out the story regarding the presence of the girl.

Once his suspicions dawned, he had played a version of the old twenty questions game to elicit the truth. He was bemused by the whole situation. His cousin had some wily attributes that he had never discerned before. He was almost glad Pappy's revolver had run out of bullets when he put the muzzle against the young lady's forehead. This little drama could prove to be entertaining. He and Elwood had negotiated a bit of a truce earlier. He agreed that he was to stay away from Sarah Jordon, and he was not to mix Elwood up in any of his schemes. In trade, Elwood would fetch any provisions needed so he wouldn't be required to travel in daylight. It was good enough at the moment.

"Okay, I guess. The girl hasn't said much of anything yet. Course, I had her gagged at first." He sat down in the other chair and looked off into the woods. "I told you, I'm going to court her. I've heard courtin' takes time if it is done proper." He snapped his fingers. "I forgot. I promised her a cup of tea." He lumbered to his feet and hurried back through the door.

John could hear a pot landing noisily on the stove. Water splashed briefly. John smiled. Elwood was humming some rabid ditty a slut would sing in a saloon. This courting was going to be courtin' like he had never seen before. John took a deep breath and thought he detected the slightly yeasty smell of fresh urine. He wrinkled his nose and leaped to his feet to slide his chair six feet closer to the corner of the porch, where a breeze was moving the leaves of an overgrown lilac bush a bit. John Coates prided himself on his keen sense of smell. Sometimes, it was a burden, though. Now that he was more up-wind from the scent, he could concentrate on figuring out the details of his latest scheme.

Through the kitchen window, Elwood could see his cousin move his chair. There was no apparent reason for him to do that as far as he knew. For as many years as he cared to remember, the chair had been sitting within six inches of the same spot. Now, all of a sudden, it had a new resting place. That was just like John. He was always doing the unexpected. When they'd been kids, they'd be playing a game, and suddenly John would come up with a new rule or suspend an old one right out of the blue. It was disconcerting to the other kids. It was disturbing to Elwood, and he was big enough to overrule the younger child's changes when he chose. Sometimes he did, but he remembered occasionally going along just to see what the outcome would be. John's new scheme intrigued him some. As an adult, John's plans and back-assed ways of doing things were almost always associated with making a lot of money in a hurry. Of course, "coming on to things" that weren't nailed down had been part of both boys' upbringing. Making a lot of money in a hurry was nearly always illegal. The unlawful part did not bother Elwood. The only reason he had decided to let John hang around, instead of hauling his ass to the sheriff as he had threatened, was the unlikely prospect of his getting some of the loot for himself, and of course, Sarah.

Once Elwood admitted to his cousin that he had taken Sarah against her will, the two men were in a stalemate regarding John's hanging around. Elwood had to hand it to John. The man knew how to pull information out of a body. Anyway, he figured he had nothing to lose and maybe a chance of some gain. Elwood smiled at the prospect as he poured the hot water into a cup with the tea leaves and let them settle. He liked the idea of hosting the pretty gal and taking her tea. Elwood could foresee a real relationship growing from these little niceties. He picked up the cup. He put it on a plate for lack of saucers. She was so soft. Even in the ugly black dress, she was beautiful. Smooth and pink and a lot cleaner than a whore.

33

Sarge, Bronco, and Preacher were riding east down the main street of Turkey Creek when they spotted Deputy Shires coming out of the general store. He caught sight of them at the exact moment and grinned. Shires held an apple in his hand. He took a bite out of it while he waited for them to join him.

"Been riding since before light, hoping to catch you boys," he said. He savored the apple juice for a moment before he swallowed.

"Well, we started early, too," Bronco said. "We got the telegram from Sheriff Beckett yesterday evening. We could have started last night, but the horses were already worn out." Bronco eyed the apple and awaited any news.

"Anything happen since Beckett sent the wire?" Preacher asked.

"Well, no. I mean, the whole town is stirred up. Miss Emmy is buzzing like a yeller-jacket. She has all the womenfolk in town buzzing along with her. Nothing figured out yet." Shires took another bite of the apple, chewed, and swallowed it before he continued. "Pappy and Cal were the ones that pushed to have you boys come back, but I don't see what you can do. There just ain't no clues." He stopped. "Well, none that we have been able to come up with yet."

"So, Pappy is alright?" Bronco leaned forward.

"Yep. I haven't seen him myself except at Jimmy's funeral. Laid up at Doc's, but they say he's coming along.

Sarge took all of it in and dismounted. "That apple looks awful appealing. Think I'll get one."

Bronco was off his horse in an instant. "You want one, Preacher?"

"You bet!" Preacher climbed down and followed everyone else inside the store.

"Welcome, gentlemen. What can I do you for?" The gray-haired clerk looked over the top of his wire-rimmed glasses and leaned on the counter with his knuckles. "I was just telling the deputy that I'm kind of low on stock right now. I expect to have more in a couple of weeks. Don't even have chewing tobacco. Sold the last one I had yesterday."

Sarge looked around the store. Many of the shelves were bare. "Hard to be in business without merchandise, isn't it?" He walked over to the apple barrel, leaned in, and picked out a likely fruit. He tossed it to Bronco. Another went to Preacher before he clutched another and rubbed it against his ribs. "Apples look pretty good."

"Yes, sir! They've been sitting in that-there barrel since last October, just waiting for you boys to come along and eat-um-up. Sure, you don't want to take some for the road?"

Sarge considered. He nodded and reached down for four more. "Say, just out of curiosity, did a tall skinny fella come through here going west a couple of days ago?" He glanced at Preacher and Bronco and shrugged. "Just curious," he said.

"Well, yes, sir. I first saw him ride through two days ago. He didn't stop." He pulled out a sack and offered it to Sarge, who shook his head, turning it down. He put his extra apple in his coat pocket and handed out the other three.

"Sounds about right," Preacher said.

"Then he was by here yesterday. Said he was going west again."
The clerk put the sack back.

"Huh?" Bronco squinted and tilted his head sidewise.

Preacher slipped the second apple into his coat. "Don't see how
that could have happened."

"Does seem odd," the clerk allowed. "He was in here yesterday
buying provisions and said he was going west. Again." He considered for a minute. "But I would have sworn he rode in from the west
like you boys." He brightened. "I think I've got it! Maybe he camped
to the west of town and then came back in for provisions before
heading back west." He snapped his fingers. "That's got to be it. It's
the only thing that makes sense." He straightened up and grinned
with satisfaction at solving the mystery. "Yep."

Sarge dropped a half dollar on the counter and headed out the
door. The other men nodded at the puzzled storekeeper and swept
out behind him. Sarge and the others mounted their horses. Sarge
stood in stirrups for a moment, turned back, and faced them. "Well,
obviously, John Coates somehow got behind us and is now going
east. Gentlemen, for whatever reason, he has changed his plans and
has returned to Harlon County!" He shook his head in wonderment.
He reined his horse away from the hitching post.

"We need to get moving. Where Coates goes, trouble follows,"
Preacher said. The other three men took bites out of their apples
and clucked to their horses. It was still a good way to Titustown.
Deputy Shires reached forward and fed the leftover apple core to
his horse and hurried to follow. Though tempted to start the second
apple, he resolved to save it for a while.

34

John Coates sat on the back porch and contemplated his next move. The fact that all of the farmers, merchants, and lawmen in the area were looking to either put a bullet in his hide or string him up hindered his plans. "Damn!" The bad luck switch of Jimmy Jordon for Bronco Brumley on the front porch swing was uncanny. Shooting Bronco wouldn't have raised an eyebrow among the good citizens of Harlon County. 'The only good Yankee is a dead Yankee,' was a common opinion in the south, from the lowest cracker on an isolated farm to the highest public officials. His mind slid neatly over the fact that killing Pappy would have had a similarly negative effect. Somehow, Pappy still being alive was a good thing, at least at the moment.

John ran his fingers through his thick black beard. He found the itchy spot and scratched it while he worked out a plan. All of his movements would have to be at night. One sighting and the game would be over. The man he had seen turn back toward home, on the other side of the mountains, would spread the word that he was well over the border. That was to his advantage. He needed to change his appearance on the chance he somehow ran into someone who could recognize him. He grabbed a tuff of his ten-inch-long beard. Getting rid of that could be the start of a disguise. He got up and walked into the house.

Elwood came out of the Jordon gal's room. He carried the empty cup and plate. He was all smiles. "That's one purdy gal in there, John." He sat the dishes in the sink and smiled. "I'm thinking she is going to come around!"

John shook his head. *Hopeless!* "Do you have a straight razor, Elwood?"

Clemens' eyes came back into focus. "I do. I used it just a couple of years ago." He opened the kitchen cabinet, pulled out a brush, a cup with a lump of cracked soap stuck to the bottom, and an old straight razor. He glanced at it briefly and handed the works to his cousin.

John set a deep pan in the sink and added the remaining hot water left from the tea. He filled the container again and placed it on the stove to heat up while Elwood wandered out to the back porch. By the time it was starting to steam, John had done what he could with a whetstone to sharpen the rusty razor. He puzzled for a moment on how to start. John looked into the cabinet again and saw a pair of scissors. He finally settled on attacking the thick growth with the shears first. It took him five minutes of whittling to get it down to what he considered shaving length. In another fifteen minutes, three nicks, and several abrasions later, John was dabbing fresh blood from the corner of his mouth. He looked in the little mirror and approved the results. John noted how strong the family resemblance was between himself and Elwood. Even with the beard, he had favored his cousin enough to pass for a younger brother. John remembered how much they favored each other as kids. Though similar in height, he was several pounds lighter and thus a gaunter version of the big man.

Shaving was a pain in the ass, but John did look different now. He used the scissors to even up the bottom of his longish hair. He carried the pan out and dumped it in the same place Elwood had emptied the bedpan. John tramped back inside and looked at the pegs lined up on the wall next to the front door. He had noticed several shirts hung one on the other. John tried on a broad-brimmed black hat to replace his slough hat. Then, after comparing one smelly garment to another, he settled on a red shirt. Coates stripped off his shirt and draped on the new one. It was too large on him, but he couldn't be choosey.

He walked back out to the back porch, where Elwood was still basking in his imaginary romance. "What do you think?"

Elwood eyed him. "That's one of my best shirts." He looked down at his own. "It's almost just like this one but newer. Take care of it." Then he studied Coates' face. "You do look some different. In the dark, you can probably fool anyone who don't know you too well."

The road out toward the Jones farm was uninhabited after dark. John rode out on his stolen horse and congratulated himself on switching animals while on his curtailed trip south. Anyone who had seen him ride away from the murder scene at Emmy's house would have no clue as to his new mount. He chose to ignore the fact that the switch-out had not been voluntary. Nor did he dwell on the fact that in quality, the new horse was a severe downgrade.

Every once in a while, he ran his hand over his newly shaved face and marveled at the planes and creases he encountered there. It was at least five years since he had shaved his heavy beard down to the bare skin. He absently tried to remember what the occasion was the last time he had done that. He couldn't recollect. He wondered if the dent in the back of his head had anything to do with his loss of memory. Damn Sarge! He was about to dredge up all of his old hatreds. He had to force himself to pull his thinking back to the present. Gold!

Early in his family's settling in Harlon County, the year before the war started, he observed that Tom Jones was a prosperous farmer from afar. He operated a sawmill, had a few slaves that he used for his business and farming. Tom switched them over to farm work when cotton needed planting, hoeing, and picking. Once the war began, Jones headed for the battlefield, as a captain no less, and his slaves had run off. That was the end of planting, hoeing, and picking for the next four long years.

Since his revelation on the road to New Orleans, the outlaw had been straining over the question of precisely what he had overheard Bronco say while he was playing possum. He had barely been clinging to consciousness through a stunned fog at the time. Only the word gold had stuck out clearly from the general mumble of conversation between the men that penetrated his consciousness. Gold! Once he slipped into that promising groove, he couldn't get the word out of his head. Bronco Brumley brought up gold out on the trail. Tom Jones was a wealthy man. It was a well-known fact that a man could pan gold in Harlon County on or near Tom's farm in years past. The factors added up to only one conclusion. It was obvious. That damn Tom Jones was a stinking-rich farmer who probably staked his brother and friends for their ride west. It all made perfect sense now that the light had dawned. With that thought in mind, he saddled up for a nighttime visit to the Jones' farm.

Riding along, he readily forgave himself for getting side-tracked. Looking back, it made sense. When John first returned to Harlon County, Tom was in jail and out of the picture. Tom's farm was in the hands of a troop of newly victorious Yankees. Coates, forced to come up with an alternate money-making scheme, had formulated the perfect plan. But somehow, through no fault of his own, things went sideways. John's attention had fervently turned to escape. Just the memory of the fear that screamed through him as he rode out of town after the disaster made him shiver. Well, now he was going to collect. It seemed pretty straightforward. He'd ride out to the Jones farm. He'd bust in, force Tom to hand over a big sack of gold and skedaddle. Given that his chief adversaries were more than a full day's ride away chasing his ghost, it seemed like a piece of cake.

John's train of thought was interrupted by his arrival at the Jones' farm. Thankful for the dark, he tied his horse to a bush behind a shed. He moved from shadow to shadow and up on the porch until he had a view of the interior. It was a large high-beamed parlor with a fireplace, with four men standing around talking. Damn! That was a disappointing discovery, given his plans. For some reason, he had anticipated that Tom would be alone. Well, maybe they were just visiting. Coates chided himself for his momentary alarm. But, of course, it was plausible that Jones might have visitors. The men were all younger than Tom, and two were still wearing partial Confederate uniforms. All three of the visitors were packing six-shooters. Tom stood in the middle of the group with his half-wing tucked close to his side. His left hand was gesturing. The men nodded assent, rose, and without further ado, everyone headed toward the back of the house. Damn. His initial conclusion had been accurate. It appeared that Tom Jones was not living alone and defenseless. Everything became more complicated. This development required some planning. If he went in guns blazing, he could accidentally kill Tom before the man could reveal the location of his gold stash. One of the men might get a shot off at him. The gold had to be well concealed. If not, the Yankees would have found it looking for the stolen payroll. John Coates spit out his Danish chaw. The sweetness distracted him. How was he going to go up against Tom and three gunslingers and come out ahead? He walked back to the shed and mounted his horse. It seemed that more thinking was required. Coates was satisfied that he would come up with a plan. He always did.

35

Sarah Jordon sat in the room's only chair while being ogled by Elwood. Her muscles ached from tension. She placed the chair as far from the bed as possible to avoid accidentally suggesting any unintended intimacy. She pulled herself together as her second night in captivity approached.

Elwood left the room with a grin on his face. When he returned, she accepted the bowl of soup with an assurance and quiet composure that baffled him a bit. But since she didn't go screeching for the open door, it confirmed his hope that maybe she had accepted her confinement. He was more confident than ever that she would eventually come around to his way of thinking. He was sure that this courting was not going to be as hard as John had let on.

Cal and Miss Emmy were keeping Sheriff Beckett company at the jail. They arrived at mid-afternoon with a pot of Lucky Star coffee, and things settled into silence after the initial greetings. Miss Emmy was ecstatic at the news of the Yankees' return. That amused the sheriff some since he remembered that only a week before, just the sight of Bronco Brumley had brought a tossed head and a disparaging mumble from Miss Emmy. After a while, the lady left, saying she'd check on Pappy and the girl she had left in charge of the Star.

Cal dozed off. While he purred, Sheriff Beckett quietly slipped out the front door to the porch, sat down on the bench, and surveyed the street. The sheriff liked a peaceful town and tended to give himself credit for keeping his pretty quiet. He was glad the minor upheaval created first by the Confederates, and then the troop of Union soldiers was over. The abandonment of Tom's farm by both armies cost the town a few scandalous businesses operating out of tents in various vacant lots at the town's city limit, but Beckett said, 'good riddance!' If that damn John Coates had not come home in April, everything would have been a whole lot better. Having a killer running loose was not good for his reelection prospects. John was gone now, but the missing Mrs. Jordon and returning Yankees were a serious cloud over his office. The next couple of days could go either way. He kept running the events through his mind. What could have happened to the young woman? How was it possible for a person to just disappear without a trace? It seemed especially unlikely in the small town of Titustown, Georgia. Honestly, it gave him a headache trying to reason it out.

Then, silhouetted, with the sun to their backs, four riders were visible coming down the street. Two of the men wore wide-brimmed hats, while the two others wore blue Union caps. The torso of one of the wide-brimmed hats had a shiny object flashing on its chest in the last light of the afternoon. Beckett stood and opened the office door.

"Cal, the cavalry has arrived," Sheriff Beckett called out a bit sarcastically. A chair scraped noisily, and the big man's heavy footsteps thumped across the floor toward the door.

Cal joined the sheriff and put his hand over his eyes to make out the riders. With their backs to the now setting sun, they were barely more than silhouettes. As they drew closer, he stepped down from the porch, and he gave them a wave. "Good to see you, boys."

The deputy was the only one to dismount. "I found them, Sheriff!" He paused. "Or they found me." He grinned. He looked expectantly at the older man.

Beckett nodded. Shire's reward was brief. "Good job." The sheriff cleared his throat. "I'm sorry if we interfered with your hunt for Coates, Madison. Pappy, Cal, and Miss Emmy are so worried about Mrs. Jordon that it just seemed the right thing to do to call you back here." Beyond that simple statement, Beckett found himself at a loss of words. They knew so little that there was simply nothing left to be said.

Sarge nodded. "Well, as much as we'd like to, we don't know that we can add anything. You know the people around here a lot better than we do. Do you have any ideas at all?"

Cal and the sheriff looked at each other and did a mutual side-to-side head shake. "Why don't you boys come in, and we can talk things over. Well, better yet, you are probably hungry. Why don't we all go over to the Lucky Star so Miss Emmy can put in her two cents." He looked at Cal, "Well, maybe more than two cents." He turned to his deputy. "Shires, go down to the pool hall and rustle up Deputy Boggs to cover the jail and then go over to Doc's and see if Pappy is strong enough to join us."

"Yes, sir!" The deputy was eager to be part of some real sheriffin. He jumped back on his horse to make the short trip to the pool hall and then the doctor's office to wake up Pappy from an afternoon snooze. The remaining three men rode along, keeping a walking pace with the sheriff and Cal Jordon.

Bronco loosened the drawcord of his new hat. He had a knot in his gut that seemed to get bigger with every development. A dozen questions haunted him, but the presence of Cal, who knew nothing, and the sheriff, who knew a lot about his past relationship with Sarah, was a stumbling block. At the war's end, it had seemed like a simple decision to travel from northern Alabama to northwest

Georgia to help Sarge retrieve his inheritance. But, as it turned out, there just seemed to be a constant string of events in opposition to every plan they put together.

For Bronco, the idea that Miss Sarah could be lost forever was the most stunning aspect of their dilemma. The fact that the beautiful young woman had rejected him in favor of her returning husband held a sting he was unable to shake. He wanted to forgive that decision for his peace of mind but had not managed it yet. That decision blocked any prospect of reconciliation from his mind. Even setting his personal interest in the girl aside, he was anxious at her disappearance. It was not hard for him to conjure up several horrible ways for this mystery to end. In a way, it was like two roosters in a cockfight. First, one thought would set him back, and then another would counter it. Behind everything else, in a black and insurgent backdrop, he feared that somehow, he was responsible for this latest disaster as well.

36

The men huddled at two tables pushed together in the back of the diner. Miss Emmy ordered a big plate of sandwiches to come out with the coffee. She clucked over everyone as she was pleased to be cast as the hostess of the meeting. Her recent cranky demeanor dissolved into stoic resolve. Miss Emmy noted that Bronco barely noticed the pretty girl she had hired to cover for Sarah. She took their orders, brought out the food and coffee, and retired to the kitchen without comment or special attention from the men.

Preacher asked the first question. "When did Mrs. Jordon disappear?" Miss Emmy explained the funeral's timeline at the church and cemetery, the walk home to rest, and her return to run the Star. She was interrupted by the arrival of Pappy and Deputy Shires. It took a couple of minutes to get the old man settled before she continued.

"She was so upset during the funeral. Once I got her settled at home, it didn't feel right to leave her there by herself for too long. After about an hour, I went to check on her, and she was gone. I checked with Pappy, and he hadn't seen her. So we finally decided that Cal must have picked her up to take her out to the farm. After another hour or so, I saw Cal, and he hadn't seen her since the funeral." By now, Emmy's eyes were brimming. "Sheriff Beckett, his deputies, Cal, and I have searched high and low all over town and round-about. No one has seen her since I left her at home. It's just like she vanished into thin air. I don't know what to do." She looked pleadingly at the three Yankees. "I would be so grateful if you could figure this out." She brought the hem of her apron to her eyes to blot her tears. "What if she is hurt somewhere?"

Sarge looked at his two friends, but their faces revealed bafflement that matched his own. He turned to Pappy. "Is there anything else. Anything at all?"

Pappy was looking intently at Miss Emmy while she finished her story. He turned toward Sarge, holding his side, trying to keep the pain at a minimum. He ran his forefinger across his mustache. All he could come up with was a shorter synopsis of events. "We had the funeral. I went back to Doc's office. A while later, Emmy came by looking for Sarah. Cal came back to town, and he hadn't seen her either. End of story."

Finally, Bronco spoke up. "Ma'am, this whole thing happened at your house, and that was the last place anyone saw her. Maybe we should take a look there first?" He looked around.

Preacher nodded. "We have to start somewhere. Ma'am, would it be all right for us to go over there to have a look around? The lack of evidence or a sighting seems to indicate that someone took her. Maybe we can find out something there to give us a clue."

Miss Emmy nodded and pushed her chair back. Once on her feet, she called to the young lady and kitchen workers. "I'll be back soon."

Sarge rose. "One more thing. What little I've read on this kind of thing suggests that we need to keep our number of investigators small. Sheriff, would it be all right if we do our snooping around quietly and report what we find to you? Hopefully, at some point, we may need your authority to deal with whoever is responsible."

Beckett ran his hand over the back of his neck. The idea of excluding him from the actual investigating raised his hackles slightly, but he didn't want to throw a log in the road.

"Alright, that's fine, but I expect regular reports." He stood as well and put his hand on Deputy Shires' shoulder. "If you come on to anything, we will be ready to step in and help out." The deputy nodded though he looked a bit disappointed that he wasn't going to the possible scene of the crime. Cal Jordon frowned, but lacking a plan of his own, he nodded. The farmer and two lawmen headed out the door toward the jail where Cal had left his horse.

Miss Emmy led the three Yankees down the street and around the corner to the left toward her house.

Sarge said, "Let's do this, Miss Emmy. You take us in and point out anything you think is important. Then we'll have a look around. Is that all right?"

Miss Emmy nodded eagerly and opened the door. The three men shuffled in after her. The still air inside was heavy and stale, as the windows were closed following the recent rain. "Sarah and I spend so much time at the Star that we don't do much to keep the place picked up." Miss Emmy said. She scooted a chair up closer against the dining table. Then she pointed out Sarah's and her rooms. "The last time I saw her, she was lying in that bed." She pointed. She stood in the doorway and looked back into the living room. "You can see everything from right here. The kitchen hardly ever gets used because Sarah and I eat almost all of our meals at the Star." With four people bunched up together, the room was feeling over-crowded. She shrugged. She seemed to realize that she was feeling a little claustrophobic, and the repeated mentions of Sarah and herself together in this house were very upsetting. "I don't see how you could learn much here. So, is it alright for me to wait outside?"

"Just one question, ma'am," Preacher swept his arm around. "Was anything upset when you came to see Mrs. Jordon? Was a chair out of place, a table overturned?" He glanced down at the door. "Was the door forced?"

"No," Miss Emmy said. "We never lock the doors. Everything looked normal when I came in." She turned the knob and stepped out on the porch, and sat down on the swing. Through the window, Sarge could see her sit, look around, and then jump up and move over to sit on the step. Sarge surmised that she had probably remembered that the swing was the murder scene.

Bronco stood with his back to the kitchen table. The room crowded with just the three of them seemed oppressive. He pointed around the room. "Things got messed up some when Miss Sarah and Pappy corralled Coates. That chair got overturned. Some books got knocked out of that bookcase." He turned in a slow circle. "I imagine Miss Sarah must have straightened everything up after all of us left." He frowned, remembering his hasty departure. "Of course, Miss Sarah disappeared several days later."

Sarge squeezed around Bronco and stepped into the kitchen. He nodded toward the back door. "So this is where Pappy left with Coates. Is that right?"

Bronco nodded. "Once Pappy had Coates tied up with the cords off the apron draped on that chair, they headed out the back, and Miss Sarah came out on the front porch to sit in the swing with me." His eyes dropped to the floor. "If I had gone with him instead of with her, none of this would have happened."

"Life is pretty iffy. Let's not get off the track," Sarge grunted. He walked to the kitchen sink and looked out the window into the back alley. It was shaded by large bushes and a row of buildings. Miss Emmy's house, fronting on Pepper Street, ran north and south. The row of retail establishments that fronted on Main Street created a tee-shaped alley. His eyes fell, and he noticed a small vase of flowers sitting in the sink. It had a crack about a quarter-inch high, encircling the bottom. The flowers were beginning to wilt as the water remaining after the break in the base had evaporated. However, the blooms still maintained their assorted though faded colors. The stems and flowers were held erect by the remaining eight-inch tall circle of detached but intact glass.

"Bronco, have you seen these before?" Sarge stood aside so Bronco could approach. Bronco approached and looked at the contents of the sink.

"No."

"They weren't perhaps on the table?"

"I don't know. I only came inside for a second. If they were, I didn't notice them."

"Preacher, call in Miss Emmy," Sarge said. He and Bronco stood aside while the woman joined them at the sink.

"My lands! That's my favorite vase. How did it get broken?" Emmy pulled one of the stems from the grouping and held it to her nose. "This is lavender. It's just a green stalk this early in the year, but just the stems put off a nice fragrance. This one is a cornflower." She picked up a blue flower. She pulled the third bloom from the bunch, and this one is called cosmos. I wonder how they got here."

"So, it's not something you or Sarah would have put in the vase?"

"Not unless someone gave them to us. I don't know of any of these particular flowers growing nearby. The lavender is a perennial with nice purple-blue flowers once it blooms."

Sarge looked around and smiled a little for the first time. "Folks, I think we have our first clue."

37

The three men rode to the sheriff's office to report. The sheriff and Deputy Shires were busy. The sheriff was going through an old batch of wanted posters. The deputy was sweeping out the cells. He put his broom aside when he heard the voices in the front office. After their report, Sheriff Beckett leaned back from his desk and put his hands behind his head.

"So, you think whoever showed up with the flowers is the person who took off with Mrs. Jordon. It makes sense, I guess. Bringing flowers to a widow after a funeral seems a pretty innocent thing to do. I wonder why no one saw anything."

"Well, this supposedly happened right after the funeral and cemetery service. I suspect there was a lot of traffic in the street, what with everyone coming and going to the cemetery or back home." Preacher said. "People kind of shut down at funerals, especially when the circumstances are as grim as they were for this one."

The sheriff nodded. "I remember." He stood up. "I guess this is one thing we can't lay at the feet of John Coates. He hightailed it away from town with you on his trail."

Deputy Shires straightened. He looked like a man whose light had just come on. "That is true, Sheriff. He was gone then. But one thing we forgot to tell you. John Coates is probably back in Harlon

County now. He gave them the slip!" He glanced at the three men sheepishly as though embarrassed at using the words *they* and *slip.*

"No!" The sheriff was incredulous as he stiffened in his chair. His eyes moved from the deputy to Bronco to Preacher and then to Sarge. All four men were nodding their heads in the affirmative.

"Afraid so, Sheriff. Coates took a notion to come back east," Sarge said. "On our way back, we came across a storekeeper who recognized him from our description."

The sheriff walked to the front door and out on the porch. The other men followed and watched as he took a deep breath. He looked far down the peaceful street of his town and took another deep breath.

"Mrs. Sarah Jordon is missing, and John Coates is probably back in the area, but with him in Alabama when it happened, there is no way that the two can be connected! Good Lord, what next?"

Elwood checked on Sarah. She appeared to be asleep. He was confident she would not escape in his absence. According to Elwood's father, his mother had insisted on installing heavy locks on the door and bars on the windows. The farm was at the end of a lane well back from the road. The neglected field behind the house backed up to the west side of Homestead Mountain, a forested area that had been breached only by loggers since the Creeks went west years before. Around the other side of the mountain, a lumbering operation shut down after the war started. Elwood was not a sociable man and never had visitors. He realized that John was late to return from his scouting mission at the Jones' farm.

Elwood locked up both the spare room and the house. If John returned while he was gone, he would just have to sit out on the back porch until Elwood got back. Elwood drove his wagon into town. He was concerned. If someone had spotted him hauling a large bundle from the house and depositing it in his wagon, he could be in trouble. Elwood relaxed a bit when his arrival elicited no reaction that he could see. One problem faced him with both Sarah and John under his roof. He did not have much money and was suddenly feeding three people. It was still early for garden produce. The tomatoes were still mostly green. His two hens produced enough eggs for him but could leave him short with two guests. He could fry up some of the green tomatoes, but it was lean pickings. He put it on his mental list to hunt up some squirrels or rabbits for meat because he wanted to do right by the purdy gal in the backroom. He wanted to give her every chance to come around. His eyes hardened for just a moment. If she didn't, he'd have to adopt another strategy. He had hit John up for a couple of bills to shop for more oats and some bacon.

Since John had picked up some supplies of his own on his way back to Titustown, they would be good for a week or so. Elwood reflected on his questioning of John., The big man had insisted that in a few days, he'd be gone. More importantly, he promised that Elwood and Mrs. Jordon would get some of the gold he would take away from Tom Jones. Elwood wanted John well on his way before he brought Mrs. Jordon out of her room. It did not require much imagination to foresee her potential reaction. Elwood did not want Sarah to learn that John was even in the house. That knowledge could set back all of the progress he had made with her. Elwood knew the man well enough to be skeptical of any promise from John. Yet, he found his enthusiasm building for his cousin's scheme. According to John, Elwood would not have to participate beyond providing him a temporary hideout. So, after all, anything he got from the man was gravy.

He walked into the store and told the clerk what he needed. The subject of Mrs. Jordon's disappearance was the talk of the town. A couple of ladies were whispering about it when he entered the store.

One was saying how awful it was, while the other nodded enthusiastically. Elwood sensed from their tone that the disappearance had become a scandal. They assumed the abductor to be a man. Elwood allowed a little secret smile to himself. He spotted a display of ribbons. Elwood picked a pretty red one and lay it on the counter with his other supplies. He thought it would look good in the young woman's hair. Clemens handed over one of the dollars and jammed the remaining dollar and the change back into his pocket. He didn't think the girl wanted to escape very badly. After just two days, she had smiled at him shyly the day before when she handed him the pot at the door. Of course, now that he could trust her some, he gallantly left the room while she dealt with the matter by herself.

38

Sarah opened one eye as the door closed behind Elwood. The key turned in the lock. She heard his heavy footfalls before a pause, and then a distant door slammed shut. He was gone. She had learned that she could limit her encounters with the man by pretending to be asleep. In the time since Elwood had consented to her freed hands and unblindfolded eyes on the unspoken promise that she would not try to escape, she had had enough time to inspect her surroundings. The worst times were when she would awake from an exhausted sleep and find him sitting in the nearby chair admiring her. The look in his eyes felt like a violation all by itself.

With the slamming door, Sarah felt a release of tension run through her entire body. She let the feeling ebb away and again turned her attention to her prison. The room was small. It was a lean-to add-on that jutted out from the original house structure. She had heard muffled voices, both male, earlier in the day. Since the thick outside wall between the room and the rest of the house remained, the sound did not carry very well. She wondered if the other man knew she was there and would he ever open the door to converse with her. How should she respond if he did? Her sudden abduction, unconsciousness, and brief interactions with Elwood had been both confusing and frightening. The fact that there were two men rather than one sent a new stab of desperation through her. The fact that Elwood, aside from knocking her out, abducting her, and holding her prisoner, seemed relatively benign up to now did not mean the other man would be the same. She had heard horror stories of women at the mercy of lustful monsters.

Just for verification, she checked the door and found it locked. Elwoods' departure provided her first opportunity to examine the window without fear of being caught. She pulled the filthy curtain aside and saw the view obscured by a thick film of dirt deposited by rainwater off the roof over at least a decade. She held some hope for escape through that window. But as she peered through the dirt, she realized that the window was barred! The realization was like a physical blow. With no buildings other than the barn far to the left in her line of sight, the house appeared to be well out in the countryside. She moved from the window to the small mounds of belongings that seemed to have accumulated in the room in random piles over time. She looked under the bed for something useful. Nothing! She wondered how long she would have alone before Elwood returned.

At that moment, her thoughts were interrupted by a pounding noise from the other side of the house. It sounded like a fist was mistreating the outside door. Sarah's heart raced. Perhaps she was being rescued! Her heart started to thud in her chest. She listened carefully. The extent of the muffling told her that there was no use in her responding as yet. She ran to the window and waited. Surely her rescuers wouldn't just knock on the front door and go away! Presently she saw a figure come into her line of sight from the front of the house. He was a lean man leading a horse. It could be either Sarge or Bronco! She cursed the dirt and poised her hand, ready to draw his attention. Closer! Closer! She watched the man come almost even with her window. But something about his gait was wrong. Something about the silhouette was off. Then, finally, she made out the thin-lipped mouth that carried a perpetual sneer. She drew back in horror! John Coates was passing ten feet away from her! He was recently shaven but recognizable even through the hazy glass. That nose, those eyes, and that sneer were indelibly etched in her mind.

Suddenly in that realization, the locked doors and window that held her prisoner were transformed in her mind into the barriers that must keep John Coates out! She scrambled away from the window, dropped down on the side of the bed, shaking. She put her hands to each side of her face and recalled every terrifying moment of the murder of her young husband. John Coates was here! Sarah closed her eyes and saw the revolver thrust against her forehead with such force that her flesh still held a memory. Eyes closed, she listened for the explosion that would end in blackness. Sarah's fingers reached up and found the spot on her forehead. She rubbed it gently. After a moment, her eyes opened, and she roamed about the room searching for something she had missed. Then she saw a possibility.

39

John Coates' night ride to the Jones farm had produced little to encourage him. He had anticipated that Jones would be alone, but apparently, he had hired help now. That was good and bad. Hired help did not come free. It supported his belief that Jones had money and, at the same time, added to the obstacles standing in the way of his getting some of it away from him. After watching the house for a while to make sure the hired hands stayed put, Coates rode on into town.

The danger of riding down the mostly deserted Main Street past the jail and Lucky Star was reduced immensely by the darkness. And he was unlikely to run into anyone who had seen his face clean-shaven. Coates wanted a drink more than anything else. However, the safety of darkness would not follow him inside the watering holes he rode past. He had finished off Elwood's limited supply of whiskey in just a day lounging around on the back porch. His mission right now was to take care of his immediate needs and, at the same time, replenish the supply at Elwood's farm. He studied on that while his eyes moved from one storefront to the next until he located the store that interested him. He was not accustomed to buying his liquor. His usual source had always been his Uncle Rufus. But, of course, Uncle Rufus and his cousin Dooley were both dead now. John still considered that tradeoff acceptable. John kept the location in mind as he turned into the alley and rode along the buildings' backside parallel to his route down the street.

As John rode through the alley looking for the liquor store, he depended on the discarded boxes and such to keep him oriented. He stopped outside a door. The sign said *deliveries.* Based on the empty wooden crates piled next to the outhouse, he guessed he was looking at the backdoor of the store he had targeted. Coates licked his lips. He scanned the wall. There were no windows, and the door looked formidable. There was only one way to handle the situation. Coates tied his horse securely to a post, pulled his revolver, and sent a bullet into the lock. The round destroyed the mechanism as if a bolt of lightning had hit it. The noise level was equivalent. John kicked the door to one side, rushed in, grabbed one of the handy crates of liquor bottles, and headed back outside. He hoisted the container up in front of the saddle while he inserted his foot in the stirrup. John stood briefly in the stirrup on his left leg while sliding the crate to the side and dangled it off the horse's right shoulder. He gained the saddle, positioned the rattling bottles against his leg, and listened. After a brief interruption, following the gunshot, the crickets were the only sound as they resumed their chirping in the patches of grass and weeds.

Coates spurred his horse down the alley past the place where he shot Pappy Jordon. He formed a wad of phlegm and Danish tobacco on his tongue and sent a stream toward the place Pappy landed. Then, continuing to retrace his route, John turned the horse through the space between Miss Emmy's house and her-next door neighbor. As he passed the murder scene where he shot Jimmy Jordon and onto Pepper Street, John's only regret was that he hadn't saved his chew to memorialize the spot where Jimmy Jordon had met his fate.

Given the town's lack of visible response to his first shot, he fired his pistol into the still night air a second time as he cleared the last house on his way out of town. A mile further along, a familiar barn was off to his right, standing alone in a field. Coates held up, then wheeled about and rode to the far side. He laughed to himself as he pulled up, sat the crate of liquor up in front of him, and dismounted. He hauled his treasure toward the barn. Recollecting his experience in Alabama, Coates secured the horse just inside. He sat down and leaned against the wall. Without even looking at the label, he muscled the top off and took a deep drink. The liquid burned all the way down. He smiled. This night with a bottle was the life he liked. He could take what he wanted. He took another swig and looked up at the stars. In the middle of the second bottle, Coates dozed off.

It was well into the morning when John returned to Elwood's farm. He had ridden the miles with some anxiety in broad daylight. At the door, John found that his stupid cousin had locked him out of the house while he was in town! He could use some coffee and eggs. John stomped around the front porch for a minute. He considered kicking the door in, but raising his cousin's ire was not a path to get the cooperation he needed from Elwood. So instead, Coates walked the horse around the house to the back porch. He set the wooden crate on the corner and continued to the barn, where he unsaddled the animal and turned it out to pasture. He climbed up on the back porch to be with his crate of whiskey and settled in to wait. There was gold to be had. Though sidetracked a bit, he was ready to zero in on the goal now. It felt good!

40

Bronco opened the paper tube he had fashioned containing a sample of the flowers they had found in Miss Emmy's kitchen to remind himself once again what he was seeking. Houses were few and far between out in the direction he was searching. His chances of finding a match were looking pretty slim. He was on a dirt road east of town when he spotted a hint of color ahead. When he approached, he found a poorly kept up house sitting close to the road. There was a white picket fence across the front, peeling badly. In dramatic contrast, the flowers grew in abundance, with quite a number sticking out between the pickets. They could easily invite picking by someone so inclined. Bronco reined in and contemplated the scene for a moment. He told himself that this could be the place and anticipation replaced the anxiety he had carried all morning. He couldn't shake the notion that he was responsible in some way for Sarah's disappearance though he couldn't put his finger on how.

There was no one in sight. Bronco dismounted and opened the gate, intending to knock on the door. The flower garden continued up both sides of the walk and wrapped around the front corners of the house.

Suddenly, there was a clawing sound behind the front door. The door opened. An attractive, middle-aged woman appeared with a large mixed breed brindle-coated dog at her side. Before she could speak, the dog lunged toward Bronco with a low growl. Bronco hastily backpedaled and got the gate shut before the dog could reach him.

"Howdy, ma'am." Bronco doffed his new hat.

The woman was pleasant-looking with light brown hair. Her blue eyes were magnified by a pair of glasses that partially hit shapely eyebrows. She wore a full-skirted dress with a contrasting sash.

"Hello!" she said. She seemed undecided at the moment as to what expression to assume. Her mouth pursed between a smile and a frown.

"Ma'am, my name is Bill Brumley. People call me Bronco on account I used to break horses back home. I don't mean to bother you none, but I must find a match up with these flowers." He held up his tube of wilted plants.

The woman hushed the dog and advanced to stand on the other side of the sagging gate. She could see that the young man was clean-shaven and wore a new shirt and hat making him look a good deal more respectable in her eyes than most of the men and boys she saw out and about.

"Really?" She put her hand out and touched the flowers as Bronco unwound the tube. "Well, Mister Brumley, my name is Mrs. Wood." She picked out a slim stem and brought it to her nose. "I'd have to say that the lavender matches mine over there at the corner. Cornflowers also match. Of course, you can see all the cosmos that I have." She looked up. "So yes, I'd say you have found a match." Her eyes squinted. "So why are you looking for flowers, young man?"

Bronco smiled. "Well, ma'am. You may have heard about Mrs. Sarah Jordon's kidnapping?"

The woman nodded, frowned, and looked closer at his face. "You're not wearing your uniform anymore, but you're one of those

Yankees, aren't you?" Her pleasant tone curdled. "I don't see what my flowers have to do with that."

"Well, ma'am. You see..."

"I'd thank you to get back on your horse, sir."

Bronco stepped back. Her hand was on the gate latch as if preparing to open it for the brindle dog. The animal appeared to be sensitive to her change of tone and had resumed its growling. "Ma'am, I don't mean to bother you. I'm just asking if you saw anyone pick a few of your flowers in the last couple of days?"

"No, sir. I did not!" She waved her hand toward the road. "Now, be off!" She grabbed the dog's collar and made an effort to motivate it back toward the porch.

"Ma'am, if your husband is home, I'd be much obliged if you'd mention this to him? If he has seen anything, it would be right helpful if he'd contact Sheriff Beckett!"

"No, sir. My husband is not home! He currently resides in the Baptist Cemetery about a hundred yards from where we buried Mister Jimmy Jordon the day before yesterday! He was likely sent there by some idiot boy like you from up north!" She turned just as she reached the entrance, kneed the dog inside, and slammed the door behind her.

41

Preacher made his rounds looking for a match for the flowers peeking out of his shirt pocket. His goal had been to check among the farms and houses in the northern area of town. He had done so without success. There was a great deal of clover, sometimes stretching for long stretches of the road and fields. He spotted some daisies at two houses. He had a sense of foreboding that he and his friends were failing the young widow. Perhaps Pappy and the family had been too optimistic, trusting in their chances of success. When his travels were complete, Preacher returned to town. On his way to report at the sheriff's office, he decided to stop in briefly at the general store to shop for a hat. Every day, his Union cap seemed to attract more unwanted attention. He was tired of the looks he was getting from people he encountered on his ride. He suspected the reason was the daily reports about northerners flooding into the south to pursue money-making schemes to the detriment of the natives. The local weekly newspaper was carrying a negative story about such doings. The paper's approach suggested that it would be a regular feature. He was just about to duck in when he met Miss Maggie Taylor on her way out.

"Well, Mister Gracey, what a pleasant surprise!" Miss Taylor was an attractive middle-aged lady he had met at the Baptist Church before leaving town in pursuit of John Coates. She was the pianist at the local baptist church. In a bit, Maggie would cross the invisible bridge of years that would automatically qualify her as a spinster. Fortunately, she was not quite there yet.

"Miss Taylor, it is very nice to see you again!" Preacher tipped his cap. He was genuinely pleased to see the lady. She was petite, blond, and immaculately kept up. She smiled easily and carried herself with confidence and charm. Although Preacher had lost his church in a dispute over the concept of free will before joining the Union army, the experience had not dampened his attraction to churches.

"I was disappointed that you left town without joining us for services on at least one Sunday," she said.

"Well, thank you, ma'am. I did go by there on a weekday before I left, hoping I might get to hear you play again." He smiled and nodded toward the white steeple visible over the storefronts. He viewed all steeples as white bridges to the heavens, even if they weren't always white.

Preacher started to doff his cap again in farewell and remembered his next mission. "Excuse me, Ma'am. I was just about to replace my old army cap. I wonder if I could impose on you to take a moment to look the hats over with me? Bronco bought one a couple of days ago, and I think I might get a warmer welcome around town if I did the same."

Miss Taylor beamed. "Why Mister Gracey, that may be the nicest invitation I've had all week. Not only is your current cap undignified, but it is also totally passé now that you are no longer in the Union Army. And while I am criticizing, I might suggest that the flowers sticking out of your pocket are a bit worse for wear as well." She smiled, slid her arm through his as she turned, and together they marched to the back of the store to the hat display. On the way Preacher quickly explained that the flowers were possibly the only clue to the disappearance of Mrs. Jordon.

"I just spent the morning looking for a match for them. So far, we have had no success at all," Preacher said.

"I'm sorry to hear that," Miss Taylor said. Her face was solemn. I have some cosmos flowers in my front garden but not the others you are carrying. I don't recall seeing anyone picking any. I wish I could contribute something, but I rarely stray more than several blocks from home. I can't come up with a single suggestion." Her face brightened. "I can suggest that you call me Miss Maggie." She smiled as she turned away and waved at the display. "So, to the matter of your hat. First, take off that worn-out rag you are wearing, and let's try on some of these." She plucked up a flat-brimmed hat with a five-and-a-half-inch crown, not bothering to check the size. Preacher bent at the waist so she could place the hat on his head. She stood back and laughed. "Oh, my! It looks like a large coffee cup sitting up there! You have a rather large head, Mister Gracey." Preacher grinned and bent down so she could sweep it off.

"And, I think something with a shorter crown would be better." She went through several hats and stopped at a tan extra-large wool felt hat with a four-inch brim and a four-inch crown. "If you can get this one on, I think it may be just right." She dusted it off a bit, as it appeared to have been in stock for a long time. Preacher ducked again. He felt it settle down snuggly just above his big ears.

"Feels right!" he said. He looked at Miss Maggie expectantly.

"Looks right." She nodded her head approvingly. "Just the hat for a minister of the gospel or any other respectable profession. Not too flashy, and not more than four years out of fashion." She laughed and then reached for a brush on the counter. "Let me dust it up a bit more."

After she finished, they proceeded to the counter. Preacher fumbled in his pocket for his money. He glanced around and noticed Miss Maggie looking through some scarves and ribbons in a display. "I appreciate you taking the time to help me out with my hat, Miss

Maggie. I wonder if you would permit me to express my thanks by purchasing one of those scarfs or other fancy doodads for you." He grinned. Somehow talking with this lady seemed to demand more formal speech than was typical for him of late.

Miss Maggie started to shake her head and then gave him a speculative look. "That would be very nice of you, Mister Gracey, but an inappropriate gesture toward a woman in the South." She pursed her lips together to signify mock distaste. "However, if you will promise me that you will come to church Sunday to witness how it looks when I'm all gussied up, I suppose I could consider it an incentive for you to attend worship and, therefore, proper." She grinned up at him.

"Yes, ma'am." His wide-gapped, toothy smile answered her. He waited while she went through all of the scarves and ribbons. Finally, she settled on a ribbon, and they continued toward the counter.

Preacher noticed a few suit jackets in passing as they moved down the aisle, but the selection looked skimpy. He made a mental note to come back the first chance he got. Something to match his new hat would be just the ticket. But, since he needed to get to the sheriff's office, he didn't stop to find out if they had his size.

Miss Maggie waited for the redheaded man to complete his purchase, placed the hat and ribbon on the counter, and stepped away so Preacher could make his purchases.

"Miss Taylor, back so soon?" The clerk looked up at Miss Maggie and Preacher out of the corner of his eye as he bent to slide a box under the counter.

"I came back in to help my friend, Mister Gracey, with his purchase," she said.

"Very nice ribbon, Ma'am. Is that for Mister Gracey as well?" They could tell that the clerk was teasing.

"Maybe," She laughed.

"Well, he is the second gentlemen to buy one of these today. And both of them are red." The clerk held up the red ribbon for closer scrutiny. "I wasn't aware that ribbons were in fashion for gentlemen."

"Which of my friends will be wearing the mate to my ribbon?" Miss Taylor asked.

The clerk frowned. "Well, I don't know the gentleman very well. He comes in very infrequently. He is something of a loner and lives out of town a bit. I don't think he is married. Perhaps he has a lady I am unaware of." He placed the ribbon in a small sack.

Before Maggie could respond further, the clerk turned to Preacher, who was counting bills. "Will you wear the hat out, sir?"

Preacher nodded, lay the money on the counter, and settled the hat securely on his head. He handed the small sack to Miss Maggie. "Thank you again, ma'am. Will you forgive me if I head over to the sheriff's office now?"

"Certainly. If there should be some way to assist you with your search, please let me know. I hope to see you Sunday, Mister Gracey." They walked to the entrance and parted ways.

42

Sarge turned his horse left down a secondary road. It had been many years since he was last in this area. After growing up near Titustown, Sarge had spent the next nine years in the Union Army. Sarge remembered enough to know that he was somewhere near the eastern boundary line of his designated area. He found random flower patches, both wild and domesticated but had seen nothing to match the flowers the three men had found in Emmy's kitchen sink. Sarge looked down at the limp sample in his vest pocket. He decided that some overlap of territory was necessary. He was determined to make sure he covered every road possible. Front yard flowers were available to both the house's occupants and passers-by. If the flowers he held came from a backyard, his mission could be doomed. If he found nothing during his search, all he could do was hope that one of his friends had enjoyed more success. And maybe they had! That possibility briefly tempted him to head into town to find out, but he made himself stay the course. Sarge's time in the military had taught him many things. Problem-solving was one of them; identify the problem, plan a solution, and follow-through.

His thoughts were interrupted by a motion far down the road. Giving it his full attention, he spied several men clustered together. Three mounted men were accompanied by two on foot. Their presence offered the promise of information. As he approached, he could see that the two men on foot were black. They had their wrists tied together. His jaw tightened.

One of the black men spied him and cried out. "Poppa Joe, look!" The younger black man pointed. "See the blue cap. See the blue cap, Poppa Joe." He was bleeding from his forehead. He looked like a man who had been pistol-whipped.

"Thank the Lord!" The older man called Poppa Joe was graying around his ears. He looked up at the mounted men. His expression betrayed his courage and a growing optimism against an undercurrent of fear.

There was an uneasy interplay among the riders. The three men moved their horses up to put themselves between Sarge and two black men. Sarge saw their hands touch the grips of their weapons. He knew from the hardness of their eyes that they needed little excuse to pull them. Finally, one of the men nudged his horse closer. "Howdy, stranger."

"Howdy." Sarge echoed the greeting and let it roll out with all the Georgia accent he could put into one word. "Those men were causing trouble?" he asked. He looked past the other riders toward the anxious eyes peering around the horses' hindquarters.

The three men smiled. Something about the way their eyes glinted beneath thick eyebrows and lips pulled back when they grinned told him they were likely kin. The closest man spit a stream of tobacco juice off to the side. He had an extremely weathered face and unkempt shoulder-length hair. There was a scar from the edge of his mouth to his right ear. His eyes fixed on Sarge's blue headcover. He seemed to weigh the southern accent against the cap.

"No. No trouble. We just don't let their kind run loose around here." The big man looked at his two friends, who nodded their heads in agreement. The wisdom of the statement seemed apparent to them.

"Why are they tied up?" Sarge's voice was neutral. The two black men were growing more anxious at the direction that the conversation was taking. Even the horses seemed to grow more skittish and danced a little, so the black men's heads were bobbing right and left around and between the hindquarters of the nervous horses as they sought to keep Sarge in view. Their faces had lost their brief hopefulness. Clearly, by his casual comments, the new arrival had the potential to be a collaborator with the white men rather than their savior. Even if his intentions were friendly toward them, they could do the math—three against one. From either perspective, their initial hopes were beginning to dim.

"Well, they was running loose. But, course, blacks ain't allowed to run loose in Georgia." The smaller man grinned as he spoke. He looked at the other two for affirmation, and they nodded in unison.

Sarge patted the shoulder of his mount to quiet its dancing. He thought a little perplexity was in order. "Any of you boys ever go to school?"

They looked at each other. Then, the two younger men looked at the bigger man for guidance as if the answer to the question came in the next grade after they dropped out.

The big man looked a little bewildered as well, then stuck out his chest. "Sure. I been to school." He looked at the two younger men. "I got past the fourth grade." He jerked his head toward the others. "They have less cause we was all pulled out early to work on the farm." Saying that seemed to turn all three men's minds back to the fact that Sarge was wearing a Yankee cap. Closer inspection would have revealed that most of the rest of his garb under his civilian jacket was Union army as well.

"So, mister. What's the deal with the cap? Did you take it off a dead Yankee?" He grinned.

Sarge reached up and gripped the little bill and briefly lifted the cap from his head. "Got it fair and square from Uncle Sam." He smiled. "Like a lot of men down here, I joined the army a long time before the war. When the shooting started, I decided to stay with the Union, seeing how I had pledged an oath to support the constitution. I guess some didn't take their oath as seriously as I did."

The talkative younger man scratched up under his hat. "I ain't had a lot of book learning, but I think you just now insulted Robert E. Lee." His eyes were quizzical when he looked across at the oldest. Then he turned toward the second young man who half-nodded agreement. Finally, he touched the butt of his gun. Sarge noted that he was left-handed.

Sarge pointed toward the black men. "You didn't answer my question about why they are tied up. Did you catch them in mischief?"

"Well, I told you they was running loose, and we plan to hang their asses as soon as we get to that tree over yonder." He pointed toward a field possessed of a giant oak tree.

"Sounds kind of excessive," Sarge commented. He directed his attention to the two black men motioning with their bound hands behind the horsemen's backs. His eyes narrowed. It took him a second to assess what they intended him to understand. Then he looked up at the sky. The weather was fair, with little wisps of clouds high in the heavens.

"It would be a shame for a man to die on such a beautiful day."

The big man spat again and smiled as if thinking Sarge referred to the black men, and then the possible threat seemed to dawn, and the smile faded. "You funnin' with us? Because if you are, we can hang a Yankee just as easy as these two run-aways." He looked at his friends for confirmation. They both nodded. Their tobacco-soaked teeth gleamed. A bit of tobacco juice slid from the corner of the big man's mouth.

"No. I'm not funnin'." Sarge leaned forward. His eyes were intent. "Now, you boys have a choice. I don't want to rush you into making this very important decision. Take time to think it over. You may even want to take a minute to talk about it among yourselves." Sarge's horse had veered a bit to the left. He paused for a second while he reined it around to face them head-on. "Are you going to do the right thing and let these men go?" He tugged his cap down tight on his forehead.

The men straightened in their saddles. It seemed that no complicated thinking was necessary.

"Hell, no!" The big man reached for his forty-four. The younger men were a half-second behind. Both black men brought their tied fists down hard on the haunches of the two outside horses. The horses startled into the horse in the center. With grim deliberateness, Sarge drew his weapon and put a slug in the big man's forehead. Simultaneously he spurred his horse straight ahead. The animal drove into the breach between the collapsing man and two remaining riders. As Sarge charged through the gap, he swung his gun to his right. The six-gun fired a second time, putting a bullet into the lefty's belly while he tried to move his weapon across his own body for a shot. The two black men scattered out of the way of Sarge's charging horse. Sarge quickly pulled up and reined his horse around. His third shot caught the outlying second-grader in the chest while he tried to get his horse turned around. Sarge pulled up short to take stock.

"I hate unnecessary bloodshed," Sarge commented as he surveyed the three bodies on the ground. "Best you grab those horses while you can," he said to the black men.

They both came out of their shock and chased down the animals.

"Now come over here close." Sarge pulled a knife from a belt sheath. Their eyes got wide for a moment, then they divined his intention and edged closer. When they held up their wrists, Sarge cut their bindings. "Are you men headed anywhere in particular or just scouting around?" He knew that some blacks were just trying to survive off the land in the confusion after Lincoln's proclamation and the war's end. That was very hard to do, given that two armies had been doing that very thing for better than three years.

They craned their necks around his horse and said the word almost in unison. "North."

"Do you know which way that is?"

They pointed.

"That's right. Check these men's pockets and see if they have any valuables. The guns are an iffy question. If you take them, you could make yourselves targets for carrying them and may have to use them. If you don't, you may end up wishing you had. Take your best guess which way to go."

The older black men bent over, pulled the forty-four from the big man's hand, and tucked it in his pants. "Maybe we'll take them and not let on like we have them." It wasn't a question, so Sarge let it pass without a response. The men found a little change in the pockets of the oldest rider. One of the small men had a beaten-up watch.

Sarge motioned toward the third horse. "Alright, I'd appreciate it if you'd load those bodies on that big chestnut. He can haul two of these men the short distance to town. Throw that little fellow up here behind me."

The two men did, as requested. The smaller man turned back toward him. "Why?"

"Why?"

"Why did you help?"

Sarge smiled grimly. "I met a man once who claimed the blue cap meant freedom. Let's just say everyone deserves a chance. In all honesty, this may be the only one you will ever get, even if you make it north. I suggest you ride at night and hide out during the day. There are plenty more gents like these three about."

Poppa Joe handed him the reins of the now-loaded horse. He offered the watch and chain. "Keep it. One more thing." Sarge took out his tiny bundle of flowers. "You men traveled down this road coming this way, right?" He motioned down the road. They nodded. "Did you see any flowers like this along the way?" Puzzled, they shook their heads in the negative. Then Poppa Joe pointed at the smaller cornflower bloom, now a very faded blue. "That house up the road had some of those."

"What about these others?"

"No, sir. I don't think so. Just the little blue one."

"Okay. Good luck to you." Sarge reached down and shook their hands. They were rough from labor. The men's faces were somber.

"Thank you, Mister," Poppa Joe said.

"God bless you, sir." The younger man touched his forehead.

Sarge nodded. "Now, get yourself out of sight." Sarge knew he couldn't show up at the nearby house with three dead men in tow. So he tugged the lifeless little man behind him forward a bit and pulled on the pack horse's reins before starting back to town. He'd keep the possibility of the garden up the road in reserve until he learned what Preacher and Bronco turned up. Sarge knew he'd have some explaining to do to Sheriff Beckett. But then the odds were pretty good that these halfwits were compatriots of John Coates. They'd not get much sympathy for that.

43

Sarah studied the details of the locked door. It opened inward. That put the hinges to the left with the pins on her side. There were three hinges; one toward the top, one in the middle, and the third close to the bottom. The one in the middle was the most convenient to examine. The door frame was cracked above and below the hinge from binding. After looking at it, she knelt and examined the bottom hinge. Then she pulled the chair over and set the back against the door so she could steady herself against the wall. The top hinge was a mismatch and looked older and more rusted. Sarah had never given the mechanics of a hinge a second thought. A plate was attached to the door's narrow edge that closed against the jam, and a second plate was attached to the jam itself. The pin kept all the loops in line and held the mechanism together. If she could remove the pins, it looked like the assembly could be separated, and she could pull the door inward even when locked! Then her enthusiasm waned. She had no tool and doubted she had enough strength for the procedure she envisioned if she did. She was shaking a little as he dismounted from the chair. She pulled it away and turned it around so she could sit and look at the door and reconsider how to proceed. Her reflection only lasted seconds before she was interrupted. First, she heard a rumble of feet in the hall. Then, she froze as she heard a key inserted in the lock. Before she could even stand, the door swung open. Elwood filled the doorway. He swooped down to pick up the chamber pot on his way and stood fully erect as he pushed the container ahead of him into the room.

Sarah was startled back in her seat. Her eyes were wide. Elwood beheld her sitting in the chair five feet from the door facing him with her hand to her mouth. He glanced around the room. He noticed the curtains pulled back from the window. Elwood closed the door and did a slow circle around her, looking at the room. He was suspicious. He moved to the window as if to ensure that it was indeed secure. She remained seated stiffly in the chair. He looked past the back of her head at the door and moved back to one side to address her.

"I brung you the pot," he said. He set it down as he sat on the edge of the bed and silently pointed toward the window.

"I was so tired of the gloom," Sarah said.

"Why are you sitting there like that?" Elwood tilted his head and looked past her toward the closed door.

"Silly, I was working on my posture." She smiled nervously. "Men don't worry about such things, but every well-bred woman spends some part of her day sitting very erect in a chair like this one." She illustrated her point for an instant, then popped up from her seat and scooted the chair over next to the bed. "Now you know one of my secrets! You have to tell me one of yours!" She put her fists on her hips and looked at him expectantly.

His face was blank with confusion. Sarah laughed. "Never mind, you can tell me later. Right now, I need to use that." She picked up the bucket and made a pushing motion on his arm.

Relieved that he was off the hook for a secret, Elwood moved toward the door. He stopped. "Oh, I brung you this." He handed her the sack and watched while she peeked inside.

"Why Elwood, it is beautiful!" Sarah put down the bucket, reached in, and extracted the ribbon. She held it to her hair. "And it's my color too!"

Elwood grinned. "I thought it would be." He glanced at the pot. "Well, I'll be going." Sarah heard the door lock behind him. She dropped the ribbon back into the sack and lay it on the table. She had never been as thankful that men couldn't read women's minds.

....

Sheriff Beckett tipped his chair back and looked up at Preacher in his new hat. The man's face was very expressive, as he could go from hilarity to somberness in an eye-blink. At the moment, he was going to great pains to tell the sheriff what he hadn't seen. The sheriff was having a difficult time feigning attention. He had gotten a report earlier from Fred Johnson, who owned the liquor store, that there had been a break-in the previous night. That and the reported firing of a pistol at the edge of town during the night was a reminder that John Coates was back. More of this kind of noisy outlawry stood a good chance of getting a rise out of the citizens on the subject of law and order.

So now he had to deal with a second local mystery. No doubt, Coates was hanging out with some of his thieving friends. The threat that such groups posed to the citizens of his county was high among his concerns.

"Spring is darn pretty in Georgia." Preacher said. He adjusted his new hat and sat in one of the desk's side chairs. "I did see some pretty flowers but not like these." He pulled the wilted blooms out of his pocket and twirled the stems between his fingers.

"Well, as if Mrs. Jordon's disappearance wasn't enough, we had a break-in at Thompson's Liquor Store last night," Beckett said. "John Coates returns, and we have a break-in. Think there is any connection?"

They were interrupted by Deputy Shires, who stuck his head in the door.

"Sheriff! Sergeant Jones is headed our way. He's dragging a horse packin' some bodies!"

The sheriff swore, tilted forward, and pushed himself to his feet. "Dammit! No more corpses!"

Preacher beat him to the door, pulled it open, and allowed the older man to stride through unobstructed. As the ex-Union soldier pulled up, all of the men exchanged looks. Sarge didn't bother to dismount. Instead, he leaned forward and pointed his thumb over his shoulder at the bodies piled on the trailing horse.

"Sheriff, where would you like these deposited?" He reached back and touched the one on his own horse. "There are three of them. These old horses would be very obliged to get some weight off." He stood in his stirrups for a second to stretch his legs. His demeanor gave no clue as to his own emotions. He waited.

"Dammit, Madison! Haven't we had enough killing?" The sheriff was ready to burst.

"Sarge, these men aren't by any chance Mrs. Jordon's abductors, are they?" Preacher asked the question with some enthusiasm, and Shires gave a gleeful laugh at the thought. The question jerked the sheriff out of his tantrum. He looked expectantly from Preacher back to Sarge.

"Sorry, no." Sarge shook his head. "I sure wish that was true." He looked back at the three bodies. "These three tried to drygulch me. There is an oak tree back a way that could have had me hanging from one of its limbs a little bit ago." He looked glum. "Sorry to throw some more bodies on you, Sheriff, but getting my neck stretched was going to interfere with our investigation." He looked at Preacher, and a smile briefly flickered on the edge of his mouth.

Beckett also caught the gesture before he stepped down to the street to see if he recognized any of the men. He noted that two of them did not have their handguns in their holsters. He surmised that they could have fallen out on the trip to town. They were all strangers to him. They were likely troublemakers just passing through. With any luck, he wouldn't have to answer to any local families. He stepped away and waved his arm down the street. "Take them down to Doc's office. Then get your ass back down here. I'll need a full report." He turned away and stomped back into his office. Preacher grinned and caught the door mid-slam. He and Deputy Shires followed the lawman inside while Sarge reined his horse around to follow the sheriff's instructions.

"Nice looking hat." Shires opined, looking at Preacher's purchase while they waited. The sheriff was back to fuming. As he fanned out some wanted posters and shuffled them back into a single stack, he muttered some obscenities. They heard hoofbeats stop outside a few minutes later, and the three men shifted around to face the door. It burst open with Bronco in the lead and Sarge close behind. Bronco was smiling.

"Bronco says he may have a lead," Sarge said.

Preacher jumped up and put his hand on his friend's shoulder. "Good man!" Deputy Shires' eyes shifted back to the sheriff, whose face was suddenly hopeful.

Bronco looked around the room at all faces, and his smile soured. "Well, I could have a lead, except the lady won't talk to me."

44

John Coates shifted in his chair when Elwood joined him on the back porch. "How's everything with the little woman?" After two days of positive reports from Elwood, Coates began to refer to Sarah as 'the little woman.' But, unfortunately, his sarcasm was lost on his cousin.

"Fine, I think." Elwood seemed deep in thought. "John, do you have any secrets?" He looked at the younger man with curiosity.

John threw his head back and hooted. "Why in the world would you ask me that? Of course, I got secrets. Everybody's got secrets." He shook his head in bemusement.

"I suppose." Elwood seemed to expect more information.

"Yes, you have secrets," John said. His cousin's face continued to gaze at him expectantly. The question on the heels of Elwood's time with the girl reminded John of how goofy some men got over a woman. "For example, remember when we was kids living over in Boonville, that time we castrated Beaver Daniels' prize bull? He was ready to kill over that bull. Then there was the time we snuck up on Patricia Smith, taking a bath on her back porch. Then, if you go way back, there was the time we killed Ralph Thompson's cat. Remember, we was playing ball at the schoolyard, and I spied that cat strutting around like he liked to do. You said Ralph was a bonehead because he wouldn't give you half his apple? Well, you took care of that cat, didn't you?" He grinned and looked at Elwood. He was smiling as well, and Coates laughed. "I bet you have a lot of secrets that I don't even know about, right?"

Elwood nodded. Other things had been coming to him while John talked. He wondered about which one Sarah Jordon would find the most interesting. He'd have to think on that some.

"In the meantime," John said, changing the subject. "There's been a little setback to my plans." Then, without waiting for a response, he told Elwood about his trip out to the Jones farm. The four-to-one odds were not what he had been expecting. "I guess you could say the three-and-a-half-to-one odds." John chuckled, thinking about Tom Jones and his amputated arm. Elwood grinned. That was a good one! Then, John told him that maybe he'd need a little help getting away with all that gold.

Elwood's smile faded. He was not interested in involving himself in any of John's schemes. He dropped his head. Just like always, here was John Coates wantin' to change the rules of the game. He looked at his cousin as he proposed how they could raid the Jones farm and get that gold together, and nobody would be the wiser. How he could just come back to his farm and settle in with the pretty girl in the backroom, and everything would be fine. Elwood shook his head.

"Nope." He looked at John, and his eyes were hard. "I ain't going to go raidin' Jones' farm. I ain't going to get killed for no gold that I ain't ever seen. I ain't going with you on this, John." He stood up, and for lack of anything else to do, he jumped off the edge of the porch and headed to the front of the house to retrieve his horse so he could lead it back to the barn to brush it down.

John Coates listened and nodded as if he understood. He had seen this side of Elwood before. Stubborn as a mule. Not only would he have to lead this mule to water, but he would also have to find a way to make him drink. John pulled out one of his stolen whiskey bottles. It was half empty. He gave it a shake, removed the cap, and took a long pull. The burn went all the way to the pit of his empty stomach. He studied the bottle. Maybe this bottle held the answer to his dilemma. Elwood was good with a gun, even when he was drunk. John smiled. Especially good when he was drunk! John had seen whiskey take away that little bit of inhibition that seemed to burden the other man when it came to killing. It was not an inhibition that he shared. But he cautioned himself; he needed to get Elwood just drunk enough and just mad enough to serve his purpose without jeopardizing the plan. So, there were two goals to be dealt with: a plan and a way to handle Elwood. He took another pull and grinned. It felt good.

Sarah Jordon sat in the chair and looked at the backside of the door to her prison cell. She had thought of the room in those terms from the very beginning. It was approximately eight by ten, close to the size of the cells in Sheriff Beckett's jail. She remembered her single visit back into the barred room to visit Bronco. It seemed like a lifetime ago. No, she corrected herself. It seemed like a different life altogether. It seemed like something she might have read in a book. She wouldn't let herself finish the thought to the point where she had started to say, "I love you," to the young man. That phrase was pushed back into a recess of her mind that she couldn't visit. With the memory, she thought of Bronco and Preacher and Sarge. They were gone now, and she could expect no help from them. Any rescue would depend on Sheriff Beckett, Pappy, or Cal Jordon. She marked Pappy off the list. He was laid up for no telling how long. That knowledge did not encourage her much.

She was in prison, the prisoner of a man who welcomed John Coates into his home! What could she conclude about a man who could do that? Welcome a man who killed for sport? Yes, Elwood Clemens seemed to be dutiful. He could feed her well, but she knew in her gut that she had not seen all of him yet. When would this friend of John Coates show her his other side? The thought sent a shiver through her as she looked down at her black dress. Sarah picked some lint from the sleeve. Elwood had stolen her out of her own home and rendered her unconscious. Then he had parked her here. She didn't dwell on why. Sarah thought she knew why. It was just a matter of when. If he turned amorous, her dilemma would be even more severe. If he became angry with her, how would he treat her? How might that happen? There were only three ways for her to respond to this situation. She would have to escape, or she would have to defend herself, or she would have to comply. The thought of the options filled her with deeper dread. The memory of a revolver thrust into her forehead ignited every fear all over again.

Sarah surveyed the room. Defend herself? With what? Escape? How? From her perch on the edge of the bed, she could see the bars through the dirty windows. Her eyes moved to the door. She needed a tool. She would require the use of some kind of tool to escape through one or the other. No, she needed a tool not only for escape but for defending herself. Her mind churned. Ironically, both seemed to rely on Elwood Clemens' unintentional assistance. How would she accomplish that?

45

Preacher and the other men questioned Bronco on his discussion with the widow Wood about the matching flowers. They all agreed that even though the lead was the best they had, there were no guarantees that it would pan out. Aside from that, there was the question of how to get Mrs. Wood to cooperate.

"Georgia Wood is a headstrong woman," Beckett said. "Once she sets her mind on something, it is not an easy matter to turn her around." He sat on the edge of his desk. "I can go talk to her and hope she'll see her way clear to tell me something." His voice sounded doubtful.

Sarge nodded. Deputy Shires looked at Bronco and shook his head. "I know her some. She is a friend of my mother's. We've butted heads a few times when I was younger cause she thought she had the right to order me around, and I ignored her. So, I don't think I'm the one that ought to go talk with her."

Bronco threw his hands up in disgust and looked around the circle of faces. His eyes lighted on Preacher, whose mouth showed a trace of a smile. "You have an idea, don't you?" The other men turned to follow his gaze.

"Well, I do. I have two ideas, actually." He looked at the sheriff. "How well do Miss Emmy and Miss Maggie know Georgia Wood?"

"Well, this is a small town. So, of course, everyone knows almost everyone a little. Georgia is a little older than Miss Maggie and some younger than Emmy. I don't keep track of who is close friends with who." He looked at Shires. "Deputy, why don't you go see Miss Emmy and tell her we have a possible lead. Ask if she has any particular kinship with Mrs. Wood."

Shires leaped up and headed for the door. He stopped. "How about I check with Miss Maggie while I'm out?"

Beckett nodded. "Good idea, and don't get sidetracked along the way."

Bronco was tempted to go Shires to maybe hurry things along. Mrs. Wood was his discovery, and he desperately wanted it to pan out. Responsibility for Sarah's disappearance still weighed on him though he couldn't put his finger on how he had created the problem. Even absent responsibility, her abduction brought its own dread over him. A week before, he had loved her enough to ask her to marry him. He convinced himself that her refusal killed that love. The fact that his mind kept dwelling on the subject did not reassure him that that was true.

Beckett's attention returned to Sarge. "Now sit down over here. I'm going to ask you questions. I want you to write down my question and then write down your answer. I'm tired of having bodies piling up down at Doc's office. The county's funds for burying the destitute are going to run dry. Couldn't you boys kill somebody with at least burying money on them?" He looked hard at Sarge. "Let's start with where you tangled with the latest three. Then, we'll talk about why."

Sarah heard the key in the lock. She sat up from her reclining position and patted down her wrinkled dress. From the slant of sunlight through her window and the beginnings of hunger, Sarah estimated that it was supper time. She had been able to discern raised voices earlier in the afternoon. It had not sounded friendly. Maybe Elwood would at least run John Coates off his place. Just the killer's presence nearby set her teeth on edge. But then she felt another chill. What if John Coates was the victor? In an instant between the insertion of the key and the door opening, revealing her captor's face, she felt the lurking fear that sometime, maybe this time, the door would open, and it would be John Coates holding the key. She shuttered to think of what could happen then.

"Howdy, Ma'am. I brung you your supper." Elwood held a plate toward her so she could see. "I made some biscuits and sliced up a pickle and fried some green 'maters. I kilt a couple of rabbits a while ago, so we'll be eatin' high tonight." He grinned and watched her expression.

Sarah looked at the plate appreciatively. "I do love fried green tomatoes, Elwood." She closed her eyes and breathed in the aroma of the rabbit.

Elwood grinned even more. "I thought you might."

Sarah's smile faded, and she looked down at her dress. She picked up a fold and let it drop limply from her fingers. She moved her hand to her eyes and seemed to wipe away a tear.

"What's the matter?" Elwood was taken aback that her disposition seemed to have taken an unexpected turn for the worse. He stiffened with anticipation.

Sarah looked up and met his eyes. "Mister Clemens, I've been wearing this same dress now for three days. I hate this black dress! All I can think of is poor Jimmy getting shot and the funeral." She looked away for a minute, and then, her gaze returned to him. "I need my other clothes, sir." She set the plate on the wobbly bed and stood. She crossed her arms and walked to the window, where the light was quickly fading. "I can't do this much longer without my things!" She whirled about so quickly that Elwood took a defensive step backward.

"Okay, okay! I can see what you're saying." His hands were up, palms facing her. "I'll see what I can do." He sidestepped to the door and hurried through it, then locked it behind him. For a moment on the other side, he paused and asked himself what had just happened. He felt the edge of rebellion rise deep in his mind. Then he shook it off and walked out the back door past his well-lubricated cousin and saddled his horse.

46

"So, what you're telling me is three men you had never seen before met you on the road and decided in the spur of the moment to hang you from a limb of the nearest tree?" Sheriff Beckett looked dubious.

"Sheriff, if you are asking me why they took an instant dislike to me, I only have one answer." Sarge swiped off his blue Union cap and threw it down on the desk. "That's it!" He looked around at the circle of faces and back at the lawman. "I don't remember so many low life's when I was a kid. I don't remember everyone being at each other's throats back then. This war has changed people, even supposedly decent people." He stopped and took a breath. "But from my experience with them, none of this bunch counts in the decent column."

"You saw how those farmers reacted when we showed up for posse duty!" Preacher said.

"Sheriff, it was three to one!" Bronco said.

The sheriff cut the men a look that said, *butt out!* He took a deep breath. "Alright, alright, alright." His voice was a growl. "I'll give you credit for the story, but I've got a feeling there is more than you're telling. So, if you think you got me fooled, just know it ain't totally." He picked up the blue cap and flung it back at Sarge. "Do us all a favor and follow your friends' example and go buy different clothes and headgear!"

The front door opened, and Miss Emmy and Miss Maggie entered the office, followed by the deputy. The men all stood.

"Sheriff, Deputy Shires says something might pan out with those flowers we found in my sink?" Miss Emmy took one of the offered chairs, and Miss Maggie took the other.

"Could be, ladies." The sheriff ran his hand from forehead to chin, then sank back into his chair. He quickly went over Bronco's discovery and the response he had gotten from Mrs. Wood.

"Thing is, we can't know until Mrs. Wood is willing to talk with us. Preacher thought that maybe a little persuasion from a couple of her friends might help ease the way." He looked at Preacher, who raised his eyebrows as if to verify the contention. The husky man's eyes were on Miss Maggie, who was nodding her understanding.

"Sheriff, Miss Emmy, and I would be happy to go out and talk with Georgia. We've known her forever. She is a fine respectable woman, and although losing her husband so recently still hurts her terribly, I'm sure she will tell us anything she knows."

Emmy nodded. "We should just go out there right now! Every minute is important. There is no telling what horrors poor Sarah is having to endure." Her eyes started to well up. Maggie reached over and patted her arm.

Sheriff Beckett took a deep breath. "That's fine. I'll take you out there." He rose from his desk and looked at the circle of men's faces. He pointed at Preacher, Bronco, and Sarge, "You boys go find something useful to do. Shires, you hold down the office. I'll get a wagon from the livery, and we'll head out to Mrs. Wood's place right now."

There seemed to be little for the group to discuss after the sheriff left to secure a wagon. Miss Emmy fretted, and Miss Maggie tried to console her. Shires couldn't leave the office to play pool, so he suggested a game of checkers. For lack of an alternative, Bronco agreed, and in a few minutes, succeeded in beating the other young man two out of three games. But his mind wasn't entirely on his game. Logically, Sarah's disappearance had no connection with their feud with John Coates. When she was taken, both they and Coates were a days' ride away. But having assumed responsibility for both Pappy and Jimmy, it was hard not to attribute some invisible connection with this new disaster. Again, his heart lurched a bit at the thought of her. She had lost none of her attraction to him. But she had rejected him, and he felt compelled to downgrade his concern to simple worry. While he sat playing checkers, was time running out? He ran that concern through his mind again and again as he captured Shires' pieces.

They heard the wagon out front. Bronco jumped up and opened the door for the ladies. After they helped the women board, they all stood on the walk and watched the wagon disappear into the gloom. Then their attention turned to another matter. Briefly, Sarge, Preacher, and Bronco discussed the wisdom of heading out to Tom's farm for the night. Bronco liked the idea of a free bed. Sarge and Preacher liked the idea of being close to the sheriff's office when Beckett returned. Recalling their jail stay in Barton City, they compromised by prevailing on Shires to let them spend the evening in the jail cells as they had done the night before for a small compensation. However, their first order of business was supper.

They took seats at the Lucky Star. In Miss Emmy's absence, the pretty new waitress took their orders. Preacher and Sarge noted that as pretty as the girl was, Bronco paid scant attention. They ate their food in near silence. There was a general feeling that something was about to spill. They just didn't yet know what.

47

It was dusky when Elwood started toward town. He knew that this was a risky venture. Just being seen in the general area of Mrs. Jordon's home before the discovery of her missing possessions could have regrettable consequences. Just being seen at all was unwise. He kept a sharp lookout ahead. Whenever he thought he spotted a rider, he reined off into the bushes until the traveler passed. He was almost inside the city limits when he spotted a wagon. His breath stopped when he caught a glimpse of a shiny badge on the driver's chest in the moonlight. The other two figures looked to be women. The light wasn't sufficient for him to make out who they were. Odd. Elwood clicked his tongue to urge his horse on. Putting distance between himself and the sheriff was a priority.

Elwood had debated on whether to bring the wagon or come on horseback. The wagon would hold more of Sarah's possessions, but it would also slow him down and be harder to conceal. He hardened his resolve. The little lady would get what he brought her and be glad to get what she got. Or else. At the same time, pleasing her was obviously to his advantage. He was expecting a reward for this little outing. There had been little in the way of physical contact before now. A touch of her shoulder against his, hands passing quickly against each other as he handed off plates of food and then received the dishes back, was the limit so far. His breath quickened at the thought. He tied his horse in the alley behind Miss Emmy's house. No one stirred, and there was no light in the kitchen window.

Elwood checked the door. Unlocked. He stepped inside and moved to the doorway that seemed to lead to the bedrooms. Sarah had told him that her room was at the front of the house. He dared edge up to the other door and listen for breathing. There was no sound. How could he be so lucky as to find an empty house! Clemens made sure the curtains were closed and lit the lamp. A strange room is eerie in flickering lamplight. He took no time to note the furnishings. He jerked off the bed cover and tugged the top sheet away from the foot of the bed. He immediately set to work. He opened the wardrobe and pulled the hanging clothes into a bundle, and threw it all on the sheet, hangers and all. Elwood emptied the dresser drawers in the same manner. He pulled the four corners of the cloth together and knotted them securely. With only a passing look around, he gathered the bundle up and headed for the back door. The sagging makeshift sack brushed across the dining table, dragging the table cloth half off as it passed. As he closed the back door behind him, gravity overcame the fabric's friction against the smooth table's surface, and it completed its slide into a heap on the floor.

48

John Coates waited till full dark to ride out to make a second survey of the Jones' farm. It would be ideal if he could catch Tom Jones alone and persuade him, through whatever means necessary, to disclose the location of his gold. John toyed with the idea of picking a time when no one was there to search the place himself, but to his mind, Jones must have a perfect hidey-hole. If all the searching by the Union Army for a stolen payroll box had not turned up Tom's gold stash, he would not have much chance either. Then it hit him that maybe Jones had a secret mine up on the mountain that was still producing! There was no telling how much gold there might be! At that prospect, a bead of sweat grew as it ran down his forehead. The three men John had spotted with Tom on his previous visit were not known to him. There was no way to know how capable they were with their guns. If they had spent time in the army and survived, it would be stupid to underestimate their abilities. Tom, alone without his intact right hand, would be easy both to intimidate and overwhelm. He just needed the three hired hands to take off long enough to allow him to confront the gimpy farmer.

There were lamps in the windows of the parlor. John secreted his horse behind one of the sheds and took out his bottle for a swig. There was a pile of spoiled hay close to the shed's entrance. He gathered several armloads and made himself a nest in the darkness with a view of the house. He sat down with his back to the wall to wait out the situation. He took another swig of whiskey and set the bottle out of arm's length. This was not the time to get soused. A few hours passed with infrequent interludes with the bottle.

Eventually, Coates tipped it the last time. A few drops slid down and nestled on the tip of his tongue. The man held the container up toward the overcast sky and caught the glow of the midnight moon. Yep, it was empty. He looked again at the quiet scene before him. From time to time, a figure passed before the parlor window. He wondered what the occupants of the house were doing to pass the time. Were they as bored as he was? Were they in the kitchen playing cards? John didn't have much use for cards. People had told him over the years that he didn't have a poker face. They said he gave himself away so badly that even if he had a winning hand at the deal, the best he could hope for was the ante money. Everyone would take one look at John's smug expression and fold.

He put the poker question aside and considered his situation. He was probably past the point where there was any chance of success tonight. If the boys inside got paid on Saturday, that would be when they'd head for town to enjoy a bottle. He squinted at the empty container in his hand and tried to read the label. No good. He pushed himself away from the ground, steadied himself on the corner of the shed, and mounted his horse. He'd pitch the bottle once he got away from the farm. Drunkenly, he grinned as he wondered how Elwood was making out with the "little woman."

49

Sheriff Beckett pulled the wagon up to the picket fence, set the brake, and climbed down. They all craned their necks to look around the immediate premises. They could see the faint shadowy outline of plantings in the flowerbeds, but the light was insufficient to make out more than that. The only sound in the darkness was the singing of insects. Emmy looked up in time to see some bats pass across the face of the waning moon. A lone lamp glowed behind a thin window curtain in the front room. The three in the wagon had only stopped for a few seconds before the night was disturbed by the baritone bark of a dog and scratching against the inside of the door. The ladies drew back. Beckett fingered his weapon. The volume was so great that it sounded as if the dog was almost on them. The curtain parted, and a woman's head appeared in the window. The door opened a crack. A shotgun barrel was thrust out and brought up to level. With a toss of its big head, the dog managed to shoulder its way through the partly open door and, in six long strides, was crouched at the gate with fangs bared.

"Who's there?" The voice was cautious but steady.

"It's Sheriff Beckett, ma'am." The sheriff stayed clear of the gate as the dog had taken to lunging against it as he tried to reach the intruders.

"Did you say, Sheriff Beckett? Virgil! Virgil, quiet down!" The dog looked back and reduced its bark to a low growl.

"Yes, ma'am. I have Miss Emmy and Miss Maggie with me. Could we talk with you for a bit?"

"Emmy, Maggie! My lands, what are you doing out here in the woods in the middle of the night?" The opening widened, and the woman withdrew the shotgun. "Virgil, it's okay. Come here, boy." The dog paused, turned, and headed toward her, suspicious but obedient, looking back at them over his shoulder. "You-all, come on in."

Each, in turn, the two ladies put a hand on the sheriff's arm for support and descended to the ground. The sheriff opened the gate, keeping a cautious eye on the dog, now panting at Mrs. Wood's feet. Maggie went down the walk first and stopped at the dog. "Oh, he is so big! The last time I saw him, he was just a little puppy." She patted the big head.

"Virgil is a big boy, all right. It's a good thing Oliver had him trained before he went off and got himself killed, or I wouldn't be able to handle him," Mrs. Wood said. "Come on in! I haven't had visitors out here in weeks. And I can't imagine why you'd be arriving by the light of the moon!"

Emmy laid a gentle hand on Virgil's big head in passing, and the heavy tail thumped against the floor. The ladies entered the parlor. There was a wool rug covering the center of the hardwood floor. Centered on it was a low table. A sofa and two chairs faced each other. A small table by the door held an oil lamp and some knitting needles and yarn. A small rocker and a hat rack completed the furnishings. There was a porcelain cross above the sofa, the only wall adornment. A pair of bifocal glasses lay beside a Bible on the low table.

"Please have a seat, won't you?" Mrs. Wood indicated the chairs and looked at the group questioningly. "I bought some tea at the store yesterday. It was just in. I couldn't wait to make a cup of the real thing. Besides cheating us out of our family members, that old war cheated us out of many other things. Can I make some for everyone?" She bent forward a bit and pressed her hands against her sides. She was surprised and briefly disconcerted before her natural civility kicked in.

The sheriff looked at the ladies and frowned. He was not interested in a protracted social call, yet he remembered Bronco's experience, and he didn't want to get off on the wrong foot. Finally, Miss Emmy settled the matter. "Oh, Georgia, that would be wonderful. I didn't know tea was back in the store already. I'll have to go by and pick up some for the Star." She looked at Miss Maggie, who feigned enthusiasm as well. The sheriff sagged into one of the stuffed chairs. Virgil, who had been ready to rip out his throat only a few minutes before, dropped slowly down at his feet and placed his muzzle on the toe of the sheriff's boot.

Rustling sounds came from the kitchen. They heard a lamp lit and a log inserted into the stove to ignite among the coals. In a couple of minutes, Mrs. Wood came out and sat in the remaining stuffed chair. "Well, it should be just a few minutes." She straightened her skirt around her. "I've been searching my brain trying to figure out the why of your visit!" She looked from the ladies to the sheriff. "Now, I think I have it. It's about that young man who was here earlier today, isn't it?" She looked at them, and before they could respond, she added. "He mentioned you, Sheriff, so I doubt you-all would be out here except for that." She finished by looking at each of them in turn over crossed arms, satisfied she had solved a mystery.

"Oh, Georgia, I am so worried about Sarah. Since you were in town yesterday, I'm sure you have heard about her abduction?" Miss Emmy placed her hands on her knees and leaned forward. "It has been three days now! She was so upset about that awful John Coates shooting Jimmy that, at first, I thought maybe she became disoriented and just walked off on her own. But when we couldn't find her, I was afraid that maybe he slunk back and took her!" She shuddered. "But we know now that he was over in Alabama when it happened." She took a breath. "We've searched high and low in town. No one has seen anything. We don't have any idea who could have done this." She pulled a handkerchief from her skirt pocket and dabbed her eyes. "Some flowers left in my sink are the only clue we have. Flowers of the kind that Bronco matched to those in your garden." She had to stop again.

Miss Maggie picked it up. "So, you see, dear, if you saw someone pick flowers from your garden, it could help get Sarah back." She searched her friend's face. "Did you see anyone around your flowers?"

Miss Emmy gasped out a final, "please!"

They all leaned forward and studied Georgia Wood's face. Silence. Her eyes darted from one to the other. Her mouth pursed. "Well, no, not exactly." She seemed to be weighing something in her mind. "Several days ago, Virgil and I were in the far back yard. He alerted me that someone was out front. He does that anytime someone comes by. Well, you saw him tonight. It doesn't often happen because we are so far out of town. It's usually just a rider or a wagon headed to town or back. You know, just my neighbor. I can't even say the time I'm remembering was the day you're asking about. They kind of run together, you know? Anyway, he took off around the corner of the house, and whereas I usually just have to look out the window when I'm inside. This time, as I said, I was out back, so I followed him around. By the time I got out front, there was no one there."

Sheriff Beckett leaned back and grunted. The two ladies sighed in unison, and then Miss Emmy put the handkerchief to her eyes and mouth and uttered a small sob.

"So, you saw nothing." The sheriff offered. Virgil raised his head alertly and looked toward the door as if responding to the conversation. In the awkward pause, the sheriff ran his hand over the animal's big head. The dog resumed his position at Beckett's feet.

"Well, I think I saw Mister Elwood Clemens off down the road in the distance with his wagon." Mrs. Wood said. "At least I assumed it was him. By the time I got my glasses on, the wagon was off a bit. But he comes by every once in a while. His is the last house on this road, and I would have no idea if he picked any flowers. It seems unlikely."

Sheriff Beckett chewed on that information while the ladies dealt with the niceties of shared tea. He understood that Miss Emmy and Miss Maggie felt obligated to visit with their friend, but he could only sip his tea impatiently and wait. Elwood Clemens? He hardly knew who the man was. He wasn't one to hang around the town's watering holes. Beckett had never had to interact with him at all. He was almost a shadow figure. And since Mrs. Wood had not seen him with flowers, this trip seemed to amount to a waste of time.

50

Elwood threw the sheet-encased bundle of clothes across his horse's neck and mounted. In another minute, he was headed back down the road he had just traveled. Though it was even darker now, Elwood noted that the white bundle almost glowed in the dark. He would have to be even more careful going back. He was anticipating with pleasure Sarah's reaction to having some of her things.

As he approached his neighbor's farmhouse, he saw a lamp in the window. As he drew closer, his blood suddenly turned cold. There was a wagon resting outside. It looked familiar. He could swear it was the same one that the lawman was driving earlier. He shook his head to clear away the fog of his anticipation of pleasing Sarah. There had been two smaller figures with the sheriff when he first encountered the wagon. He had surmised they were women. He had accepted that knowledge without pause then. Now, with the wagon parked less than a mile from his own house, everything about it took on new significance. Sheriff? Why would the sheriff bring two women out in the country in the dark of night? Was there some darker explanation than a mere social call to their being here, right now? He toyed with the idea of approaching the house to verify his suspicion. Then he remembered the dog. The big mutt made a commotion every time he passed by on the road. The day he picked the flowers for Sarah, he had heard the barking start up well behind him as he returned to town. He realized that if the animal sensed Elwood now, it could ruin everything.

Elwood shook his head to dispel the thought, let the reins lay slack in his hand so the horse would make as little noise in his passing as possible, and moved on. But, even as Elwood cleared the end of the picket fence, out of the faint glow of the lone lamp in the window, he couldn't let go of the notion that something was cooking.

Sarah wished for a book. When she had inquired of Elwood, he had looked at her blankly. He had no books. She thought of a newspaper. Was there a story in the local paper about her? What did it say had happened to her? Surely someone was smart enough to ask why she was missing? Thinking of these things made her feel even more alone. Sarah pressed her ear against the door. First, the heavy footsteps of Elwood Clemens echoed dully down the hall. Was he gone? Sarah put out the lamp. He could be just outside the house performing some chore. What about Coates? Her dread of encountering his vicious face made her shiver. She waited what seemed like an eternity for something, anything, to verify that she was alone. It was well past dark when a bit of motion caught her eye and sent her scrambling around the piles of clothes to the window. Barely discernable through the dirty glass, it appeared that John Coates was leading his horse toward the lane. Now was she alone? Was she finally alone? Her mind raced at the prospect. She relit the lamp. She looked back through the flickering light at the heavy door. It seemed impenetrable. Sarah had nothing at her disposal that could knock it down. She had nothing available with which to remove the pins. Sarah had nothing available to pick the lock! She turned back to the window. Past the reflection of the flickering lamp, she could still make out the vague shadows of bars on the other side of the glass. "Trapped! Trapped! Trapped!" Escape, considered through the lens of theory, had seemed like a real prospect until this moment when she thought that her two jailors could be gone. Now, with the human obstacles to her escape out of the way, the whole difficulty of the physical prison itself seemed to cut off the very air she breathed.

Sarah gasped, realizing that she had been holding her breath. She pulled the chair into a corner where she could look at both the door and the window from the same spot. Her eyes shifted from one of her options to the other. She looked at her old saggy bed. It rocked whenever she turned over in the night. The four corner posts shuddered so much in the joints when she moved that she had pulled it six inches toward the center of the room to avoid being awakened by the noise of the posts thudding against the wall when she moved in the night. Doing that had made the useable floor space even smaller. She rose resolutely from the chair, sat on the edge of the bed, and gently rocked herself. She looked around the room again. It was late. She was aware of the amount of precious time she had allowed to pass while she puttered around. She kicked herself that she had not already taken action. One or both of the men would surely return soon. The tiny ember of hope that she had nurtured for so long faltered. After all of her conjecture about rescue, she now knew that she was on her own. No one would come to save her, so she would have to rescue herself! The bed rocked under her, and Sarah tested the slack. Her plan seemed to materialize out of nowhere. She shook the bed some more. Suddenly an idea resolved itself. She had a plan! All she needed was another time alone. Next time she would be prepared!

51

It was getting late by the time Sheriff Beckett got the ladies back to town. He let them off at their respective homes and delivered the wagon back to the livery stable. All of the talk wore out his ears. Miss Emmy's repeated lapses into long rants against the gods, fate, and John Coates, and Miss Maggie's attempts to distract her had made about a dozen cycles by the time he got both of them out of the wagon. He just wanted to go home, but he still had to deal with the boys at the jail. Their horses were not visible at the hitching post. He'd never hear the end of it if he didn't let them know what a bust the night had been. He glanced in as he passed the window. The deputy was asleep in his chair. The three Yankees were not in view, which seemed odd. He was both elated that he wouldn't have to deal with questions from the three men and put off that it appeared that they didn't care enough to stick around to get his report. It was, after all, a clue one of them had dug up. He turned the knob noisily, which woke Shires. Beckett stalked across the floor and dropped into a side chair. The deputy made to get up. Beckett just motioned for him to keep his seat.

"Have you made rounds?"

"Yes, sir. Nothing's stirring." The young man yawned and leaned back in the chair. "So, did you find out anything?"

"Nope. Where are the boys? I figured they'd be here waiting for news."

"Oh, they are. They're back in the cells. When it got late, they wanted to be here when you got back, and I knew you'd want them to be here when you got back, so I told them to snag a bunk."

Beckett stiffened. "This ain't no hotel, you know." He started to say more but just waved toward the cells. "Well, get them out here."

"Yes, sir. They're paying four bits each, so it ain't free." Shires said defensively. The deputy opened the door to the cells and called out. "He's back!"

The three men filed in and took the remaining chairs. They were a chair short, so Bronco dropped down to the floor and leaned against the wall.

Sarge took one look at the sheriff and dropped his elbows to his knees, and supported his jaw with his hands. "Nothing?"

Bronco slumped. "Nothing?"

Sheriff Beckett gave them a quick synopsis of his evening. He was about to rise when Preacher tipped his hat back on his big head and eyed him quietly. "So, tell us about this, Clemens fellow."

"Nothing to tell. I've never had a run-in with the man. As far as I know, he hardly ever comes to town. Miss Wood had nothing negative to say about him. He doesn't hang out at the saloon." He shrugged.

"Clemens," Sarge said. "That's not a familiar name. When I left town, there were lots of Jordons and Whitesides and Becketts, but I don't recollect any Clemens."

Beckett shrugged again. "Well, he lives out at the end of Mrs. Wood's road, according to her. She describes him as something of a loner. She didn't seem to think there was anything significant about him. She said he's never shown any interest in her flowers. Her dog has a fit whenever he rides by, but that's it. He stood up. "I'm headed for the house. You boys make those bunks in the morning. Did

Shires already collect the rent? Well, I'll put it toward the burying of the three damn bodies you brought me today." He headed for the door. "One more thing, this ain't no hotel. Find yourselves someplace else to bunk tomorrow night!" The front door slammed shut.

"I'm ready." Sarge stood. He looked at Preacher, who had been mute through the sheriff's story. "You're awful quiet. You saving your two cents for Sunday church service?"

Preacher ran his hand over his forehead sleepily. "Maybe. Something's whizzing past my brain faster than I can follow it. Maybe I'll be able to keep up in the morning." He clapped Bronco on the back, and they all trooped back to the cells.

Deputy Shires opened the front door and looked out at the dark street. It was black except for a couple of businesses down the block. He had made his rounds earlier. He pulled his hat down tighter on his head, stepped outside, and closed the door behind him. Tomorrow was another day.

52

Elwood Clemens rode directly to the barn and put up the horse. It was late. He could see the light from Sarah's room, so he went to the window and tried to see inside. The girl was sitting on the edge of the bed. She was still fully clothed in the ugly black dress. He didn't think she had taken off the hideous garment since he had kidnapped her. Well, that was about to change. He hefted the bundle and draped it over his shoulder. He almost tapped playfully on the dirty glass but thought better of it. He didn't want to upset the apple cart by scaring her now. He sensed that he had scored a few points with the red ribbon. It seemed evident that these clothes could cinch everything. He continued to the front of the house and unlocked the front door. Apparently, John was not back yet. He tucked his bundle under his arm and thrust the key into the lock of Sarah's bedroom door. He was holding the bundle under his arm when he entered her room. Sarah jumped to her feet and squealed with anticipation. She had heard him coming down the hall and prepared the tone of her reception.

Elwood dropped the makeshift sack on the end of the bed and fumbled with the knot he had fashioned with the four corners.

"Oh, Mister Clemens! Let me do that!" Sarah brushed his hands aside and picked at the loose ends of the knot. It gave way quickly to her efforts. "Oh, you got almost everything!" she exclaimed. "Most importantly, you got my favorite things!" Her underthings were on top of the jumbled pile. She discretely pulled out a dress and lay it on top. "I can't wait to get this organized." She turned her head to face the man. She had his rapt attention.

"You are one purdy gal," he said.

Sarah felt her heart freeze. Her brain came to a complete stop for a blink. Then she regained her composure. "Thank you, Mister Clemens. You are very kind to go fetch my things." She cast her eyes down meaningfully. "But I am still in mourning." She fingered the sleeve of the black dress. "But I won't always be." She smiled at him, a fleeting reward for his efforts. "But now, where will I keep these things?" She surveyed the room. "We could put a rod across that corner for my hanging things. You were smart to bring the hangers." She gave him a congratulating look. "But right now, I am just done in." She indicated the chamber pot. "Do you suppose you could take that with you?" She yawned and touched his arm lightly with her other hand.

Elwood turned his head a bit to the side. She caught a glimpse of stubbornness. She feared that a hidden beast was lurking behind those eyes, and she dreaded the moment when it revealed itself. The notion gave her pause. If he refused to leave, they would be at a great divide. Would he force himself on her?

"Tomorrow!" Sarah cried. "Tomorrow, I'll take a bath and put on one of my clean dresses. I'll even let you pick which one! Would you like that? You can put up the rod! I bet there is a chest of drawers somewhere in the house that you could bring in here for me to put my other things in?" She tried to keep the desperation out of her voice.

Elwood took a deep breath. He straightened, and his head turned back toward her. The stubbornness was gone. Maybe she had only imagined the beast?

"I think I can do that." He eyed the pile of clothes. "That dress on top is right purdy. That is my choice!" He put his hand on the knob.

"Thank you, Mister Clemens," she breathed. "Thank you for everything." He nodded and closed the door behind him. There was a longer pause than usual before the key turned in the lock. Sarah wondered if the delay indicated Elwood's hesitation to leave or his inclination to return. Hope and fear followed one another in a heartbeat. She was suddenly afraid that persuading him to leave just then could cost her dearly tomorrow.

When John Coates approached the darkened house, he assumed that Elwood had arrived earlier. He took his horse around back and found the big man's horse in the pasture. John unsaddled and climbed up the steps to the porch to try the back door. He turned the knob, and it swung inward on rusty hinges. John had considered grabbing one of the bottles in the crate out back but shook off the notion. He needed sleep, not more liquor. Tomorrow would be a big day. If his guess was correct, tomorrow was Saturday. That meant that he would have to find a way to prevail on Elwood to accompany him to the Jones farm tomorrow when Tom's hands would be in town. Busy, busy, busy. He had no idea how to get Elwood turned around on helping out. The man was as stubborn as a mule. John kicked off his big boots and collapsed on the bed. He was asleep almost instantly.

Saturday morning, Sheriff Beckett found his uninvited guests still asleep when he arrived at his office. He let them be. He wasn't in the mood for socializing. His evening with the two ladies had tired him more than seemed possible. All the fretting and worrying was catching. They still had nothing to go on toward finding the girl. He started to enumerate all the negatives but pushed the thought aside.

It looked like the three Yankees were no more successful than he had been. Even the lead they had come to depend on appeared to have gone up in smoke.

Cal Jordon stuck his head in as he was about to go over to the Star. "Morning, Ben." He closed the door and dropped into the nearest chair. "Do I dare ask?"

Beckett motioned toward the door. "Let's head over to the Star and get some coffee. I'll tell you everything I know on the way."

Cal slowly got back to his feet. He recognized that the comment was not very promising.

"You boys headed for coffee?" Sarge emerged through the door from the cell room. They nodded. "I'll go with you."

"Sleeping in the jail now?" Cal nodded toward the door.

"Yeah, well, we had a reason last night. Or, at least we thought we did until the Ben got back from his little visit."

"Visit?" Cal looked over at Beckett.

"Like I said, I can cover everything on the way to coffee." The sheriff took his hat from the rack by the door and turned the knob.

It was quiet after Elwood took the chamber pot out to the backyard and returned it to its place outside her door. The night was undisturbed until Sarah heard the second pair of boots thump down the hall. She was sure it was John Coates. Sarah swung off the bed, relit the lamp, and went to the window. During her first inspection days before, Sarah had noticed that the single glass pane was loose. Decades of water coming off of the roof had disintegrated the glazing putty securing it. When she first considered her various escape possibilities, her original expectation was that the one she settled on would come into play when both men were gone. The option of a window escape might be accomplished by breaking the glass and fighting her way through the bars.

Elwood's growing edginess worried her. With both men sleeping nearby, she wanted to determine if it was possible to remove the glass without breaking it. It seemed a longshot, but the gleam in Elwood's eyes tonight sent a gut-wrenching sliver of fear through her. She had to calm her shaking fingers. She placed a hand against a corner of the glass and pressed steadily for a moment. Chunks of the outside glazing fell away from her movement of the glass. Her breath stopped. This experiment with the men nearby was a fool's errand! She could accidentally break the glass messing with it. Sweat beaded her forehead. She made a motion with the back of her hand to keep it from creeping into her eyes. She could imagine how the breaking glass would sound in the stillness of the night. *Stop!* Both men could be on her in an instant! She forced herself back to the bed. The presence of the men made any attempt impossible tonight. She feared one thing, Elwood Clemmons was likely going to want more than smiles and flattery tomorrow. She knew in her heart that he was expecting a reward. In averting his attentions tonight, Sarah had merely put off the inevitable. She shuttered. For a long time, Sarah lay and stared into the darkness. Finally, she slept. It was a restless sleep rocking her bed with every turn.

Sarah awoke early the next morning. She always woke well before Elwood brought in the chamber pot. Usually, she just sat and waited. This morning Sarah made her bed and spread out her things in preparation for his return. She selected the clothes she wanted to wear. She arranged the dress so that it covered her underthings. The red ribbon lay across the bodice of the dress. She thought of the ribbon as icing for Elwood. She was looking for anything to distract him.

There was the familiar thumping in the hall, the key in the lock, and then the big man filled the doorway. He picked up the pot and set it inside. He had that gleam in his eye that Sarah so dreaded.

"Elwood, do you have a tub for me to use for my bath?"

"Well, there is an old tub on the back porch," he said.

"If you would please heat up some water and fetch in that tub, I can finally clean up before I put on the dress you picked out for me." She stood and faced him head up, shoulders squared.

Elwood looked at her, to the bed and back. "Alright." He thought he detected a bit of defiance in her eyes that he had not seen before. That was a puzzle. It wasn't what she said but the way she said it. He closed the door. As he wasn't going far, he didn't lock it. In a moment, he was back with the tub. He set it down against the end of the bed and went back into the kitchen to heat water.

Sarah heard the pan land with a clatter on the stove. Water splashed, and in a few minutes, the door opened again. He brought in a full bucket of water for the bath. He went away and returned with a second bucket. In a bit, Elwood brought in the pan of steaming water and added it to the water in the tub. Then he straightened up. Elwood eyed her and the clothes on the bed as he was still puzzled over the defiance. He looked back at Sarah. She was standing as tall as her diminutive figure could manage. Her clenched hands were on her hips.

"Thank you, Mister Clemens," she said with finality. She glanced at the clothes and back at him. Elwood's eyes followed and settled on the red ribbon. He nodded and backed out the door. The key turned in the lock.

53

Sheriff Beckett filled Cal in on his trip to Mrs. Wood's house the previous evening as they walked to the Lucky Star. The three men shuffled to the back of the eating area and took seats. In a moment, Miss Emmy joined them. She was in a tizzy.

"I'm glad you're early." She sat, her face drawn with anxiety. "Someone was in the house last night." She shivered. "I don't know if they came in before I got home or after. I was so worn out that I went straight to bed. This morning I was getting ready for work, and I noticed that the linen table cloth was in the middle of the floor. That made me check on Sarah's room. My heart just lurched. Just to think how wonderful it would be if she had found her way back! I always check it every morning just to make sure all of this isn't just a bad dream, you know." She looked at the faces around her.

"Sarah's clothes are gone! Her wardrobe is empty. Her drawers are empty!" Emmy's eyes were red. She was wringing her hands a bit, and when she realized they had noticed, she put them in her apron pockets, but after a moment, she pulled them out again and continued.

"It had to be before I got home because I didn't get a wink last night," Emmy said.

The men were stunned. Her words came out in such a burst that none of the three could think of anything to say.

Cal finally slammed a hand on the table. "That is the damnedest thing I ever heard! While we're trying to figure out who took Sarah, the man comes right into town and makes off with her belongings? He came into town right under our noses!" He looked at Emmy. "What time did you get in last night, Miss Emmy?"

"Well, Ben, let me out at my house at close to ten o: clock." She looked at the sheriff for verification.

He nodded. "We were gone for a long while, what with the trip out, the chitchat, and the trip back. So there was better than a two-hour period for the theft to happen."

Emmy said, "I so hoped that Georgia would be able to tell us something useful." She looked at Sheriff Beckett as if he might know something new.

I was feeling kind of hopeful myself," the sheriff admitted. "But she didn't see anything useful. So we're back to square one. Could you bring a pot out? I expect the other boys will be here in a little bit?"

Cal looked befuddled. "Seems like a longshot for sure. Flowers aren't exactly rare in Georgia this time of year. Just because Georgia had some to match the ones in the sink didn't guarantee she is the only one in the county who did. Why the man could have been collecting flowers from several places on his way to Emmy's house!" He looked at Sarge, whose set jaw and eyes gave him pause. Then Cal nodded his grudging acknowledgment and continued.

"Okay, I can see that it's the only lead you had, and you had to follow up. But now that it has petered out, have you got any new ideas?"

"Well, while we were all being so gloomy, I just had a thought that's got me celebrating," Sarge said.

"Celebrating?" Cal looked from Miss Emmy to Sarge.

"Yes. We might not have discovered who took Sarah last night, but we found out that we're still looking for a live girl! The stolen clothes prove that!" He raised his eyebrows and looked from one downcast face to another.

"Dammit, that's true! Cal said. Emmy's face lightened for a moment and then resumed its mournful expression. Sheriff Beckett blew on his cup's contents and took another sip. He knew that even if Sarge was right about the missing clothes being a good sign that Sarah was still alive, but without a break, they were no closer to finding her. That was the ultimate problem.

54

Saturday morning, John Coates awoke at the shrill, high-pitched cry of a woman's voice. His head was buzzing from the whiskey he had imbibed the night before. He put his hand over his eyes and tried to make sense out of the doings down the hall. The heavy doors of his and Sarah's rooms were muting much of the sound, but the piercing cry of anguish made it clear that something painful was definitely in progress. Other people's pain always energized John. He threw his legs off the bed and reached down to pull on his boots. He entered the passage, and half reeling, worked his way down the narrow hall. The volume of screams grew in intensity with each step. Finally, he threw open Sarah's door.

The girl was lying on the floor in a pretty floral dress with a white lace collar—her forearm over her head in a defensive position. The black dress was lying in a wad on the bed. The arm already had two welts almost through the skin. Her contorted face revealed tears and pain. When she spied John Coates, her screams died in her throat.

Elwood's black wool-covered jaw clenched. His right hand held a belt on the buckle end. In the other, he held his old floppy hat by the brim. He swatted the hat at her catching the swelling, unprotected forearm in the arc of the blow. His face twisted with renewed rage. John looked from Elwood back to the girl. She was terrified, but now her gaze was on him rather than her assailant. He wondered what she was looking at and decided that she was staring at his clean-shaven face. He realized that she could be surprised that he had appeared at all.

"What the hell." Coates' head swiveled between the two.

"She's complaining!" Elwood yelled. He stomped both feet angrily as if beside himself. "She's complaining! Remember what my pa used to do when my ma complained?" He held up the belt for Coates to see. "He always said he could take a lot, but he could not abide complaining from his woman. Well, I won't abide complaining either." He looked back at the girl, who surprisingly was still staring beseechingly at John.

"What did she say?" Coates' eyes took in the change of dress and the recently washed hair. The tub of water seemed oddly tranquil at the foot of the bed amid the uproar. Coates was baffled.

"I told her she looked real purdy in the dress I picked out, and she said it was a shame to waste it sittin' in this room." He looked around. "Waste it? How is it wasted? I'm here, ain't I? I spent the last three days courtin' her, and she thinks getting fixed up in here for me is wasted?" He slapped the hat back on his head and hefted the belt as though he was considering another blow with it.

"Whoa." John Coates' brain shifted gears, and his eyes brightened at the possibilities Elwood's ire presented. He had not seen his cousin this aggravated in a long time. He had not been privy to his uncle's whippings of his Aunt Jane. Even though she was his father's sister, no word of such treatment had ever escaped this house as far as he knew. Or perhaps, neither his old man nor Uncle Rufus gave a care? His aunt had been pretty docile, as far as he knew, except for demanding good locks and bars on the windows. Then he had another thought; maybe it wasn't his aunt who wanted bars on the windows? Perhaps this scene was an example of why the house needed bars? He passed over the implications as the bud of a new idea blossomed in his brain. He nodded.

"I can see what you mean, Elwood. You go to all the trouble to fetch her stuff." He waved his hand toward the sorted clothing. "You risk life and limb going to her house, in the dark of night, right under the nose of the law, and she complains that it was wasted? That is for sure pretty willful."

Sarah watched this exchange and cringed. Elwood could add to the stinging welts on her arm at will. It would already be even worse, except for her quick evasion and John's arrival. She frantically searched her memory. Had she been as blatant as Elwood seemed to think? She had merely been setting the stage for him to think about fixing up the place some so that she could send him off for supplies, and she would be alone one more time. Her comment had seemed so innocuous. She was shocked that she had accidentally pulled a trigger that she had no idea existed.

She stared up at John Coates. For just a moment, Sarah had hoped he would defuse the situation. The hooked nose, deeply recessed eyes, and stained teeth seemed even more prominent without the beard's camouflage. As unexpected as Elwood's interpretation of her words was, John's fanning the flames was just as disturbing. What was he up to? She wondered with a new spurt of fear how the man would use this. The possibilities gave her a shiver. She couldn't let a chance to clear this up go by without at least some attempt.

"I didn't mean to complain. I was just going to say that with a little work, we could fix up the house. Some cleaning, maybe wash the windows, even some paint and new wallpaper could make a world of difference."

"Oh yeah?" John Coates narrowed his eyes. "Well, it isn't your place to come into a man's home and start telling him what he ought to do. I agree with Elwood. You was complaining!" He looked at his cousin, and they nodded their heads in mutual agreement.

"For one thing, it takes money to fix things up like you want. Right, Elwood? Does it look like we are made out of money? No! You was complaining about something Elwood can't help. That's wrong!" He grabbed Elwood by the crook of the arm and made to lead him out. Elwood shook off his hand.

"I have a good mind to whack her again!" He said the words as he let the belt swing loose. Sarah threw up her other hand to protect herself.

"Well, maybe you should wait on that." Coates grabbed the free end of the belt and got up close to Elwood's ear to give him a few words of wisdom. "Though I agree with you about this entire situation, you need to be careful. If you accidentally whack her across that purdy face, you'll ruin her forever." He stage-whispered the warning. Sarah reflexively touched her face and then put her hands down long enough to scoot backward a couple of feet across the floor. "One rule with purdy women you should always remember is don't mess up their faces. Time will do that soon enough." The man said this as if it was a time-honored bit of wisdom, passed down between menfolk from generation to generation. He continued. "Let's go out on the back porch, and think of how we can fix this situation. If we can't come up with anything, you can always come back in here and swat her again. What do you say?"

John jerked the end of the belt out of Elwood's hand, and holding the doubled belt in two hands, gave it a ringing pop. He grinned callously at Sarah's involuntary cry. In the close confines of the room, the sound was as loud as a rifle. Elwood was still angry, but his cousin's advice was making its way through his brain. He was so full of righteous anger that there were almost tears in his eyes.

Elwood couldn't forgive having done so much to please her, and now this! He grabbed the belt back and let the belt swing free just to watch the girl's expression. The moment of decision hung in the air for a moment. Then, finally, he nodded at his cousin and turned toward the door. John followed him out with a smirk crossing his face. He couldn't remember when he had been so lucky.

55

Saturday morning. When Pappy gingerly made his way through the door of the Lucky Star, the men were still sitting dejectedly around the table. Pappy was walking slowly with a stiff arm pressed gently against his injured side. He allowed himself a groan as he dropped as slowly as possible into the chair Cal pulled over from another table.

"I have some advice for you, young whipper-snappers." He looked at the others and grimaced. "Don't get shot!" He ran his forefinger across his mustache. "There is no such thing as a good place to get shot!"

Several of the men chuckled appreciatively. His comment was the one bit of levity they had available to amuse them. Miss Emmy poured the old man's coffee. Sheriff Beckett was about to make a retort when the door swung open again, and Bronco and Preacher charged into the Star in a manner that telegraphed urgency.

"Guess what!" Bronco pulled over another chair, turned it around, and straddled it. He laced his arms across the chair-top and looked back at Preacher. "We know who abducted Miss Sarah." He made an underhanded waving motion toward Preacher as if to say, "lead on." Preacher didn't bother to sit.

"Guess who bought a red hair ribbon at the general store yesterday." All he got in return were blank looks. Cal looked around and could only manage,

"Why?"

"Okay, let me put it another way. Guess who, for certain, picked the flowers we found in Miss Emmy's sink." He got more blank stares. Their expressions reflected that the men had already determined that the flower lead for which they had so much hope was a dead end. Preacher swore under his breath, swept off his new hat, and then settled it back on his head. He seemed determined to try one more time.

"Okay, here is the situation. Yesterday I went by the general store and bought this hat." He doffed his purchase. "I also bought a pretty red hair ribbon for Miss Maggie, who took the time to help me pick out the hat. When I paid for my purchases, the clerk mentioned that another gentleman had also bought a red ribbon. Miss Maggie inquired as to who the lady recipient could be. The clerk said he didn't know who the lady was. He said the man who made the purchase was an infrequent customer and a loner. So Miss Maggie and I left the store without thinking anything more about it." He looked at Beckett. "How was it that you described Elwood Clemens? You called him a loner. Remember? Well, that struck me last night, but I was too tired to put it together."

The sheriff nodded, but his face still didn't register a connection.

"Well, Bronco and I just stopped by the general store. The clerk says that the man who bought the ribbon was Elwood Clemens."

There was a long moment while Preacher and Bronco studied the other men's faces. Then, slowly the light dawned, and the sheriff's face perked up.

"Elwood Clemens, who lives down the road from Mrs. Woods, picks flowers for himself? No! He picks flowers for the woman he is going to kidnap. Does he buy a ribbon for himself? No, he buys a ribbon for the woman he has already kidnapped!" Ben jumped up and made for the door. "Boys, get your horses! I'm going down to the pool hall and round up my deputies!"

Pappy raised his hand and waved for attention. "Hold on! There is another twist in this here story you boys don't get." He frowned. "While we're playing guessing games, who is the varmint we've been wantin' to find? The man who has probably been hiding out close by, and we haven't had a clue where?" The men stopped in their tracks and grunted a collective "Coates?"

Pappy twisted around to face them and grimaced at the tweak in his side. "Elwood Clemens is a cousin of John Coates!" Pappy held his side and waited for their lights to come on. "If one of you had mentioned Clemens earlier, I could have told you that little bit of information the day Sarah got snagged."

Miss Emmy started up. "His name just came up last night talking with Georgia Wood." Her face turned gray. "So. You think Sarah is in the hands of John Coates?"

Pappy's face was somber. "That sure, seems likely now, don't it?"

56

Once John got Elwood out of the room and waited for him to lock the door, John pushed him roughly toward the back porch. It took longer than it should have. Halfway down the hall, Elwood had second thoughts about leaving the girl without giving her another whack. It was like he couldn't get the girl's words out of his head. So, even after they got out the back door, he had a change of mind and made an effort to turn around and confront the thankless wench again.

"Elwood, what you're thinking ain't the answer," Coates said. "She was unrespectful. I'll give you that. She deserves a good whippin'. I'll give you that." With those words, it took all of his strength to push the man down in the cane-bottom chair. He stood over him and stuck his finger into his chest. "But listen to me, El! Listen! Whippin' her with your belt ain't going to cure the problem, is it?"

Elwood looked at the finger and up into his cousin's eyes. Elwood squinted, and the pupils the other man could see beneath his drawn brows were black. Red veins crisscrossed the little bit of visible white in a lurid pattern.

"I bet my belt can stop the complaining and unrespecting." He made another motion to rise.

"No. It might make the little lady hold her tongue, but it won't keep her from thinking it." John pushed his cousin back down and tapped his own forehead meaningfully. He reached over and pulled a bottle from the crate, and removed the cap.

"You need a swig of this." John took a draw and passed the bottle over. Elwood took some and then shook his head before taking another. He handed it back and leaned his chair against the wall as the alcohol burned toward his stomach.

Coates couldn't believe his good luck. He had pondered for two days on how he would get Elwood lathered up, and the little gal had done it for him in just a few seconds. Now he needed to turn all that rage into something positive.

"Listen, Elwood." Coates grabbed the big man's shoulders and tried to shake him some. "The way to fix this is called gold!"

Elwood peered up at him. The whiskey was already affecting his brain. He liked the feeling and grabbed the bottle for another gulp.

"Gold?" He kept the bottle and wrapped his arms around himself. "What are you talking about?"

John pulled the other chair close. "Today is the day, Elwood. This is Saturday. I already told you Tom Jones has got gold out at his farm. His men will head for town to get liquored up. He will be alone with all his gold. All we have to do is ride in there and take it!" He made it sound so easy that for just a minute, John himself wondered why he even needed Elwood at all. Then he remembered that no matter how easy it seemed, he needed someone to back him up. He knew from recent personal experience that any little thing out of line with the plan could throw the whole shebang out of whack. An unexpected trip-up needed a little backup to right the boat.

"Listen! We go out, grab Jones' gold, and I take off for New Orleans. You come back here a rich man! What can you do then? You can get this place fixed up. You can buy the little woman some fine clothes. All women appreciate nice things, cousin. Did that dress the little woman has on right now cost a pretty penny? You bet! The more fine things you can buy her, the more she will appreciate you.

The more she appreciates you, the less she will want to unrespect you! Are you hearing me?" He looked at Elwood closely. He thought he saw a little light come on in his eyes.

Elwood nodded. A bit of a smile exposed the gap created by missing eyetooth as he lunged to his feet. He squinted at his cousin as he took another swig of the whiskey. Then Elwood put his hand on the grip of his six-gun. "I'm ready."

"No, you ain't," John said. "If you expect to come back here afterward, you need a disguise like I've got. Take a minute and shave off that beard. That way, if anyone sees us going or coming back, it won't matter. Then, when it's over, you can come back here and lay low while it grows back. "Of course, we could just shoot Jones cold." Elwood frowned at that last comment. Coates pulled out his Danish chaw and let Elwood bite off some to distract him before he shoved him into the kitchen to use the razer.

57

Sarah lay still for a moment, dazed at the turn of events. She listened for the inevitable click of the lock. Sarah felt relief flood over her. As long as the two men remained on the other side of that door, she was safe. She examined the welts on her swelling forearm. Elwood had dealt her a couple of vicious blows. There were little tears in the skin, where clear liquid and some blood had started to ooze to the surface. She flexed her wrist to see if the blows had broken her arm. A swelling redness now surrounded the welt left by the belt's edge. She pushed herself off the floor and stumbled to the bed, where she located a handkerchief among her things to wipe her eyes and blow her nose. She stood straight and took a deep breath. She swung the arm about a bit, hoping to dry the oozing. As painful as the contusion might be, she had again escaped a full assault. There had been a leering quality in Elwood's face when he caught sight of her in the clean dress. She had been ogled before at the Lucky Star, but there the men had felt restrained by the public place. She was bitterly aware that there was nothing to hinder Elwood here. She examined the arm again. There were no medical supplies with which to treat it. She stared at the door, waiting. For a long while, she could hear nothing.

Suddenly, her heart leaped again. There were footfalls in the hall. The door rattled as the big man lurched against it. She could see the shadow of his feet in the gap at the bottom. He was speaking very loudly through the door. "I'm going to take care of this." Sarah thought that he sounded half drunk. Her heart began to pound at the realization of his mental state. She clutched the pillow and held it before her with her uninjured arm.

"John and me got plans," Elwood yelled. He pronounced the words slowly, but they were oddly slurred. "We're riding out right now. We're going to take care of everything. Then, when I come back, I'll be rich." He paused, then slammed his hand against the door for emphasis. "We'll be rich." The door rattled again as he jerked his hand back and walked back down the hall. A few minutes later, there were voices outside her window. At first, she was frozen in place, then ran to the window and stood to the side out of sight. Her heart still pounded as she watched the men's matching red-shirted backs ride away.

Sarah didn't even wait for the dust to settle in the lane. She had a plan! Immediately she ran to the head of the bed and grabbed the top of the outside bedpost. She had a plan and now was her chance! She forced the big post back and forth, rocking the bed from side to side. It gave a little, so she rocked it again but couldn't gain any more. It seemed to have reached some invisible obstacle. Panting, Sarah tried again. No progress. Her brow furrowed. Fear ceased her again. She had no idea how long the men would be gone.

Sarah pulled the bed further away from the wall and tried the other post. It, too, seemed constrained by some obstacle. She turned the bed on its side as a last resort, dumping the mattress, clothes, and pillow to the floor. It lay sideways like some stiff-legged animal. She stood on the bottom post and levered the top post upward. Nothing! She knelt a bit and put her shoulder under the top post. Using the strongest muscles of her body, she thrust with her thighs against the bottom post. For a long moment, she strained. The edge of the top post dug cruelly into her shoulder. She grabbed the pillow and put it between her shoulder and post for a cushion to ease the pain. It wasn't enough, and pain imposed by the obstinate post shot through her anew. She cried out in frustration. She gathered herself for another try. Then with no warning, the post came free, revealing a long connecting spike.

She didn't take the time to catch her breath. The fear that time would run out seized her. She carried the post to the window and thrust the top end into the glass. It shattered with all the clamor she had feared the night before. But now, she assured herself, it didn't matter. Glass was strewn both inside and outside by the impact. Sarah reached between two hanging shards and pushed at one of the bars. It was loose! She knocked out the remaining glass, placed the post between the first bar and the right side of the window, and leaned into it. One end of the bar came away, taking shreds of weathered wood with it. She grabbed the loosened bar with her hand and worked it back and forth until the wood at the other end gave way.

Through a system of butting the end of the bedpost against each of the remaining bars, then levering the loosened bars out of the way, she made an opening large enough to climb out. She ran to the pile of discarded old lady clothes and gathered an armful. She wrapped the bundle in the black dress and spread it across the ledge of the window to ease her way over the remaining nail head and shards of glass. She gathered her skirt about her, sat on the discarded dresses, swiveled around, and dropped into the high weeds. She was free! But could she stay free? She hurried to the front of the house and looked up the lane. It was her first opportunity to learn that Elwood's farm was at the end of the road. No one was in sight. But since the lane was the way Elwood and John had gone, it would be their return route and was to be avoided. She looked east and noted that the tree line past the house's neglected field ran roughly parallel to the road. That seemed to be the only exit available.

58

Sheriff Beckett's posse made good time riding toward Elwood Clemens' farm. The news that John Coates was probably there also added to the churning in the sheriff's belly. Foremost in his mind was Sarah Jordon. The fact that either Elwood Clemens or John Coates had stolen her clothes the previous night encouraged the hope that she was still alive. That she had been in their hands for four days could be a prelude to a tragic revelation when they arrived. Catching the two men would be a feather in his cap for sure. He looked around at the other riders. Each face suggested that the men accompanying him had made the same calculation. They were only a little over a mile from the turn onto the road to Clemens' farm. Yet, all of them felt the weight of time working against them. The dread was building.

"Dang, that must be them!" Bronco was the first man to catch sight of the two riders ahead of a small cloud of dust from the direction of Elwood's farm. For a moment, both groups of riders continued full tilt toward each other. Bronco strained his eyes, trying to make out the men's faces as they neared. His keen eyesight alerted him to the fact that the lead rider clean-shaven jowls. "Looks like Coates has shaved off his beard." He yelled the words and touched his own chin with the back of his gloved fist. They watched while the two oncoming riders suddenly held up and reined about sharply.

The two men's reaction seemed to affirm that Bronco was right. Then, as the two riders' dust overtook them, they wheeled about and headed back up the road in the direction from which they had come.

"That's them, boys!" Beckett yelled. The men spurred their horses in hot pursuit.

Sarah felt the limbs of saplings and brambles snagging her dress as she entered Elwood's overgrown field, heading toward the edge of the deep woods. After several years of neglect, the field had already started the process of reverting to its natural state. That process was most pronounced at the varying boundary line with the forest

She knew that she had to stay deep enough to remain hidden from John and Elwood should they return via the road. She looked down at the colorful fabric. As good as the bath and clean dress had seemed when she emerged from the tub pink and silky, she wished now that she was still wearing the ugly black garment to better blend in with the shadows and dark vertical columns of oaks and pines.

It was unseasonably hot and humid. How far would she have to go? Sarah had been unconscious and blindfolded during transport to the farm. The road itself was the best clue as to the direction of civilization. She could see that venturing deeper under the high canopy could afford few obstacles but also put her so far out of sight of the road that she might miss any possible assistance.

After difficult headway along the boundary line, she was now even with the back of an abandoned house with a caved-in roof. She wondered how far it would be to the next house. Then she heard the sound of riders. She automatically crouched, and her heart raced. There on the road were the two figures she most dreaded. Even at a distance, she could just make out their matching red shirts. Elwood Clemens and John Coates were riding hard back to Elwood's farmhouse. Their horses were wild-eyed as the men spurred them onward. What was happening? Sarah cringed. When they got to the house, Elwood would immediately see the broken window and know she had escaped! Once they passed, Sarah hurried forward and caught sight of another farmhouse far across the field close to the road. Then there were more horses on the road! She spied the figure of Sarge immediately. As she stood open-mouthed, she identified the sheriff and Preacher and Bronco! Bronco and Preacher were wearing civilian hats, and that had thrown her for an instant. There was Cal! The sheriff's two deputies! Before Sarah could react, the men pounded by and down the road hard on her captors' heels. Sarah could feel a great relief wash over her. She would head across the field to the road and the farmhouse. She was exhausted from her exertions, but she was safe!

Sarah's sense of relief was short-lived. As she started across the narrow field toward the road, Sarah heard a disturbance to her left. She looked around and was startled to see a horse and rider riding toward her in the middle distance. Was that possibly one of the last riders she had just seen on the road? No, the man was clean-shaven and wearing a red shirt. It had to be John Coates, the man she feared most in the world. The rider was hindered in his travel by saplings, brush, and a fence line just as she had been. But Sarah knew from her own experience that the fence was down at numerous places. So she picked up her pace and waded her way through tall grass.

Sarah stumbled and cried out in frustration and glanced back again. She caught the movement of the rider in the corner of her eye. He was now moving parallel to the fence, heading toward the wood line. She knew he was looking for a route for his horse. She knew that he wasn't far from the opening he was seeking. Should she try for refuge back in the forest or keep running for the road? She felt like a squirrel caught in the path of a wagon trying to decide whether to run right or left! The shortest route to the next house was to get to the road as quickly as possible. She negotiated a low area of the field and ran clumsily through the shoulder-high weeds toward the road. No one else was in sight. It looked like the only chance she had. Sarah wondered what had happened to all of the riders who were supposed to rescue her. She held up her skirts and ran as fast as she could. She knew that if John Coates wanted her dead, she was presenting the perfect target.

59

John glanced a little to the left, where Elwood's stronger horse was beginning to pull away. The man bared his teeth. The worn bandana he wore to disguise himself was streaming straight back in the wind. Behind them were at least half a dozen riders. Clemens and Coates passed the closest neighbor's house. The big dog who had barked lustily as they passed only a few minutes earlier was no longer in sight. They passed the abandoned house, and in a matter of seconds, they approached Elwood's lane.

The two men turned into the short wagon track and rode hard toward the house. Coates thought their best chance to escape was to ride straight into the vacant field behind the house and split up. One could take the back way to regain the road behind the riders using the outbuildings and overgrown bushes as cover. The other could head into the forest to one of the logging roads that laced the area. If they were lucky, the posse would waste some time assuming they were going to hold up at the house to fight it out. Elwood was now just ahead of him. The big man was veering off to the left toward the front porch.

"No!"

Elwood looked back at Coates, who only had time to point ahead where he could see the broken window. As the two men sped past, Elwood cursed in recognition.

John figured they'd have a chance if they could just get out of sight of the lane before the posse made the turn. He grimly smiled as the thought struck him that having Elwood's horse parked in front of the building might have helped mislead the posse. He cursed himself for not thinking about that earlier.

So far, no one had fired a shot. As soon as John and Elwood made the field, John motioned which way he would go and pointed the way for Elwood.

The other man didn't bother to respond. He took the designated route. Just as they hoped, the last two riders of the posse disappeared behind the grove of trees just a half moment before they set out. Coates spurred his horse again. The animal was wheezing a bit. He wished he still had the fine army horse he had stolen at Carson's Junction. The going was not as easy as he had hoped. The field he was crossing was full of scattered thickets of brush and thorns that required his horse to dodge among the obstructions. That slowed his pace, but he realized that the more the small trees and brush he put between himself and the posse, the better his chances. He looked over his shoulder. Elwood was no longer in sight, nor was the posse. The way to escape looked clear.

Elwood could only think of one thing, Sarah. He could feel himself sobering up in a hurry. His rage grew with every stride of his horse. Matching his anger toward her was his anger toward his cousin and himself. Despite knowing John since infancy, he had agreed to let him hide out at his house and then decided to pull a robbery with him. Just the thing he had sworn he wouldn't do. Whatever happened next, the blame would be on himself. The broken window was proof Sarah had escaped! Elwood swore again. He could not fathom riding away without the girl. Which way would she run? He felt his ire rise. First, she had complained, and now she had run. After everything he had done over the last week toward courting her. This was just more unrespect! There was a price to pay!

As Elwood stewed, Coates overtook him and pointed out the options. Elwood made his decision and urged his horse on. Somehow, he'd teach her a lesson for sure. As he rode away from his house, now overrun by the posse, he realized there could never be anything there for him again. There was no going back.

60

Bronco, Sarge, and Preacher reined up at the front of Elwood's house and dismounted. Bronco and Preacher clambered up on the front porch and peered into the house and down the hallway. Sarge went around the left side of the building and moved slowly toward the back porch, searching for a sign of occupation. There was a yell from one of Beckett's deputies from the other side of the house. "This window is broken out!" Bronco and Preacher eyed each other. Cal came around the corner with his weapon still drawn.

"The window is busted out. It looks like Sarah may have escaped." He looked around the yard. "But where did she go?"

"What about John and Elwood? Preacher said.

"They could have let the horses go and be hunkered down," said Cal.

Sarge returned and took a position on the other side of the doorway. He stuck his head in the entrance. "Give it up, Coates, Clemens. You are surrounded." There was silence.

"Suppose they could have kept on riding," Bronco said.

Sheriff Beckett motioned his two deputies toward the barn. "Let's have a look around all the outbuildings." The group headed off with guns drawn.

"Let's search the house before we go tearing off looking for ghosts," Preacher said. He was unconvinced the men were gone.

The house felt empty, but taking off without a search seemed wrong.

"Good idea!" Sarge stepped into the hallway. Preacher and Bronco were right behind him. Cal was about to follow the men when his visual sweep of the surrounding area caused him to notice movement through the trees far out in the field. He strained to make it out. Yes. Someone in a brightly colored garment was running from right to left toward the road. It could be Sarah! Then closer to him and to the right of Sarah, a horseman emerged from behind a clump of saplings. But the horseman was riding left to right. He shook his head. It didn't make sense. Cal stuck his head in the doorway. "I think I see Sarah and Coates out in the field." He ran to his horse, Moon, mounted and headed down the lane toward the road without waiting around.

Desperate, Sarah was in a blind run. The house! The house! The word was screaming through her head. She dared not even take a moment to determine how close her pursuer was. The dread propelled her faster than she had ever run before. The backs of her hands and fingers holding up the hem of her dress to avoid tripping were taking the brunt of the punishment from passing brush and weeds as she scrambled across the field. Beneath the gasps was the silent cry of one who knows they are prey. She did not look around again. She did not have the energy to do more than run.

Then she heard uneven hoofbeats on the road behind her as a horse leaped from the field across the bar ditch. The house with the picket fence and a flower garden grew closer, but was it close enough? Now, above it all, she heard a laugh, loud and half-crazed! It froze her heart. The hoofbeats were almost on her. They grew louder as she neared the only shelter in sight. Then a wicked blow from the charging horse's shoulder threw her half off her feet and into the gate. As she staggered, the man grabbed a clump of her hair and pulled her upright before she could tumble to the ground.

"Now, what do you think you are doing out here in the middle of the road?" He laughed without amusement. For the moment, he seemed to have forgotten that he was himself, in a race for his life. Despite his grip on her mane, Sarah slumped forward with her hands on her knees. Her panting matched that of the horse wheezing over her. She felt the heat and smelled the lather that was thick on the animal's neck.

Exhausted, Sarah was numb to the pain that the man was so ecstatically attempting to inflect with his grip on her hair. It was no match for the perpetual pain she felt from that moment on her Aunt Emmy's porch. Then, in memory, Sarah felt the thunderous blast of a six-gun again. She watched as Jimmy Jordon was propelled forward out of the swing to sprawl face-first on the floor. There was Pappy's revolver in John's hand, thrust against her forehead. Sarah's legs gave way. Her hands slipped from her knees, and she dropped to the ground leaving severed strands of her dark auburn hair in the angry man's grasp. For a moment, he held it aloft, inert with surprise. Then he opened his hand and flicked his fingers to release the clumps of hair to be blown away in the wind. His hand pulled his revolver from its holster.

A shotgun emerged from the door. A solidly muscled mixed breed brindle-coated dog lunged through the opening and off the porch. When the dog reached the gate, the big animal stopped long enough to sniff the hand of the fallen woman through the pickets. Though exhausted, the horse shied.

"Mister, if you so much as move a hair, I will fill you with buckshot." Mrs. Georgia Wood cocked the hammer. "Drop the gun!" The man hesitated.

"That is not a suggestion." Georgia moved through the door to the step. He knew that it would be impossible for her to miss at such a close range. He slowly let his arm drop to his leg but hesitated.

61

Cal Jordon reached the road and pulled up. His look back told him that the two deputies had edged past the rear porch and were still moving stealthily toward the barn with guns drawn. Their backs were to him. Sarge, Preacher, and Bronco had not yet emerged from inside the house. Cal looked down the road and spotted the brightly colored figure of Sarah in flight. He clucked to his horse and headed toward her. Cal had gone only about fifty yards when the horse and rider he had observed in the field earlier jumped the bar ditch well ahead of him and took off in rapid pursuit of the woman. Cal urged his horse on. He couldn't recollect seeing the man before but remembered that Bronco had called attention to his shaved face. He knew that the stranger was John Coates, the killer of his son.

That was all he needed to know. He watched as the man overtook Sarah, and after a moment of holding her upright by her hair, let her slump to the ground. Cal's six-gun was in his hand, but he stayed himself. He would hold his fire unless the man prepared to use his gun. He felt the blood lust flood over him like a hot blanket. He wanted more! He wanted to see the fear in the man's face when he put the barrel between his eyes. He imagined the concussion of a bullet fired at point-blank range! But all of that had to wait until he found out the answer to his singular question of why?

As he drew closer, he realized that a woman on the porch had Coates in her sights. From that distance, the weapon looked to be a shotgun. He said a silent prayer that she wouldn't need to pull the trigger. That was for him to do. Now he was close enough to hear her command that Coates drop his weapon. Hesitating a moment, the tall man slowly let the gun drop to his thigh as if to obey but then seemed to hesitate. But Cal was on him.

In the confusion of Sarah's fainting, the shouted commands from the woman, and the barking dog, the man had not heard Cal's approach. "Do it." Cal Jordon stuck the barrel of his six-gun into the outlaw's ribs.

The three men inside the house heard Cal call out something while surveying Sarah's room, but they couldn't make out what he said. It didn't take them long to take it all in. The bed was lying on its side. One of the corner head posts was lying close to the broken window. The girl's scattered clothes proved she was in a hurry. Preacher and Sarge looked at Bronco, who was eyeing the bathwater and the clothing spread on the window sill. There was an intimacy suggested here that made the three men cringe for Sarah. None of the men knew how to interpret, much less comment on the scene. Finally, after a second, Sarge spoke up.

"Let's move on." The other two men nodded. The three emerged from the front of the house and looked around for Cal Jordon. He and his horse were no longer in sight. The sheriff approached. His deputies were still nosing around the distant barn.

Sarge looked at his two friends. "Do you think he played his 'little loop around behind' game again?"

"Dang!" said Bronco.

"Did you see which way Cal went?" Sarge asked the sheriff.

"Yes, Cal hightailed it down that way," Beckett said. He motioned toward the lane leading to the road.

Bronco looked at his companions. "I bet he's on to Coates!"

Alarmed, Sarge and Preacher nodded. The three men ran to their horses and mounted. They knew that John Coates was capable of anything. The sheriff drew his gun and stepped through the front door. He wanted to make a last sweep of the interior of the house for his own satisfaction.

62

Approaching from the rear, Cal jabbed the barrel of his forty-four deeper into the rider's ribs. The man jumped and champed down harder on his chaw. The two were now only three feet apart, and their proximity eliminated the shotgun as a threat. Mrs. Wood immediately recognized that.

"Cal, get back!" Mrs. Wood hurried forward off the front step in a panic, trying to narrow her gun's shot pattern. She squinted. "Who is he?

"John Coates, ma'am," Cal shouted.

Cal sensed that Coates was prepared to take his chances. He was not surprised when the man slipped his finger inside the trigger guard and turned his weapon toward him. He only made it halfway. Cal's forty-four barked, and the slug caught the man's forearm from only a foot away. He cried out as a small bit of flesh just below the elbow disappeared in a red mist. The man released his weapon, and it bounced against his leg to tumble to the ground. His eyes took in the bubbling hole and newly exposed bone. The injured man grabbed his arm as he lurched out of the saddle. He tumbled head-long and landed on his shoulder, only four feet from Sarah, whose face was turned away as she clung to the gate. Virgil, now thoroughly aroused, howled fiercely.

Cal dismounted as quickly as his sore leg permitted and kicked the gun out of reach. His face and neck glowed almost as red as the blood spilling across the fallen man's lap. He looked down at his son's killer and asked the question that had eaten at him from the first news of the shooting.

"Why?"

The man leaned against the fence with his back to Sarah, who lay dazed and panting. He was bleeding profusely from the severed brachial artery just below his elbow. His face was white and grim. Blood was coming in spurts with each throb of his heart. His hand was lathered in blood as he held it across the wound, and a little splashed and dripped from his chin. Cal could readily see that the man would bleed to death if not assisted. However, Cal was not ready for that yet. He swore, holstered his gun, and pulled his scarf from around his neck. Cal quickly tied it as snuggly as he could around the bleeding arm just above the elbow.

"Don't you die on me, you son-of-a-bitch!" His eyes caught on a nearby stick. He jabbed it between the arm and scarf and gave it a wicked twist. The man cried out as Cal gave the tourniquet another half turn. The spurting blood stopped. Cal grabbed the man's other wrist, pulled his hand across his body, and slapped it against the tourniquet. "Hold it there," he commanded. He glanced over at Sarah, who was coming out of her faint. She sat up, disheveled and fearful, and scooted to the left, further away from the blood-drenched ground.

Georgia Wood hushed the dog, who was still howling in the aftermath of the shooting.

"Why!" Cal shouted the question again. "Why did you kill my boy?"

The injured man's hooded eyes looked down at the wounded arm and seemed to freeze in place. The face was white. Cal slapped him hard. He felt some of the blood cling to his fingers. He repeated the word.

"Why!"

The dark eyes lit up after the insulting slap. The man glared up at Cal, who was vaguely aware that more horses were arriving. Bronco, Preacher, and Sarge were out of their saddles before the animals came to a complete stop. They pushed their way past the two men's horses and halted at Cal's shoulder.

Cal put the barrel of his gun against the clammy forehead. He could feel the knot of rage in his throat. His heart was crying for blood, and with single-minded intent, he pulled the hammer back.

"This is your last chance!"

"Cal." The big man felt Preacher's hand on his shoulder. He shook it off.

"Get away," he whispered.

The man on the ground looked at Cal with confusion as if the question didn't register at first. Then his eyes cleared long enough to respond. "Jimmy was in the wrong place at the wrong time." The lips attempted to smile as if finding humor in the words. His bloody fingers still held the tourniquet. The eyes squinted, and his teeth showed yellow against his white lips as he coughed out the remains of his Danish chaw. The hollow eyes traveled a blurred circuit around the uneasy group of faces.

Sarah's eyes were closed, and her hands were pressing on each side of her face to protect her ears from the anticipated blast of Cal's six-gun. Even though the man was disabled, having John Coates so close filled her with fear.

The bleeding man cricked his head around and peeked at her for a quick moment. He looked back at Cal, then glanced up toward Bronco. "I saw it. Well, yah might call it a accident."

Cal Jordon was incredulous. "You lying Bastard! Killing my boy was no accident! Nobody walks up and puts a bullet in the back of a man's head by accident! Tell me the truth! Why?"

"Cal," Preacher spoke, his voice insistent.

"Why won't he tell me the truth?" Cal glanced around. His eyes were wild with grief.

"He did, Cal," Bronco said.

Cal looked away from Preacher toward the voice. "No!"

The young man nodded as he took a step toward Cal and wiped the tears from his eyes.

"He is telling you the truth."

"Cal. Listen to Bronco," Preacher said. "You don't want to do this. Not because he doesn't deserve it, because he does, but because you don't deserve to spend the rest of your life knowing that you killed this skunk in cold blood."

Cal shook his head. He noted that the grounded man was starting to shake a bit from shock. "Don't you die on me yet, Coates!" He slapped the man again.

The wounded man took a deep breath. He gave the stick a bit of a twist himself to tighten the tourniquet and winced. He looked up at all the faces and spoke through teeth beginning to chatter. "I ain't going to die till I'm ready."

Cal's gun was steady while he wrestled with Preacher's words. Then, finally, he shook himself and took a step back to relieve his aching leg. There was finality in his voice.

"No! You're saying my boy died for nothing?"

"Please, Cal!" Sarah's voice was barely above a whisper. The truth of Preacher's words had startled her. Cal was about to commit the irrevocable act of murder. She realized that this didn't end here. If he killed Coates, the consequences would follow him to his grave and deepen her guilt for starting this horrible chain of events. Averting that tragedy was the only way she could atone for her sins.

She lurched forward on her knees, away from the fence a bit. Her voice was pleading. "Please don't do this!"

Seeing her anguish, Bronco cut her off. "Cal, Coates was after me, not Jimmy. He was angry because of what happened in Alabama and Carson's Junction. He wanted revenge because he blamed us for his spoiled plans." Bronco looked at Preacher and Sarge while he paused to let his words sink in.

"I was at Emmy's house earlier when Coates tried to ambush me. But Sarah and Pappy spoiled that plan, and Pappy took him off to jail. That's when Pappy got shot. So it makes sense that John came back to take a second try at me, but I had already left, and John mistook Jimmy for me when he shot him from behind."

"You and Sarah?" Cal tried to follow it.

"Bronco and I became friends," Sarah said. She glanced at the back of the dark man's head. "He knew that, and that's why he showed up at Emmy's to find Bronco!" She was blind from the tears streaming from her eyes as she recounted the moment when Coates shot Jimmy from behind. "He thought he was shooting Bronco!"

Now Bronco took another step closer. His tone said more than his words. "I'm sorry, sir. I didn't think Jimmy was coming back. Lots of times since then, I've thought about how I maybe should have been the fella in the swing." He looked over at Sarah and back into Cal's bleak eyes and swallowed back his regret. "Sarah told me all along that she was waiting for Jimmy. She told me all along that she wanted him to come home."

Stunned, Cal still couldn't put it all together. He stepped back a pace and unconsciously flexed his sore leg.

Preacher used the moment to step between Cal and the wounded man. His face was solemn. "Cal, you have heard the truth. I can't let you turn yourself into a killer. You'll have to shoot me first. I don't think you'll do that." His big jaw jutted, and he reached for Cal's gun.

The gun shied away from Preacher's hand. The words of Bronco and Sarah churned through Cal's mind. He glanced at the young people now searching his face with imploring eyes as everyone seemed to be holding their breath. He looked at Sarge, taunt and solemn. His eyes went back to Preacher, and finally, he nodded. He swung the gun away. Preacher reached over to take it and stepped to the side.

While Cal wrestled with his decision, the fallen man looked up into the eyes of the bereaved father and then away. He had reached the point where conniving and lies were no longer viable strategies. He had reached the point where gold no longer held wonder.

There was a shudder from the fallen man. He licked his pale lips, perhaps searching for a last taste of sweetness from the Danish tobacco. He glanced back at Sarah. The vivid welts on her arm caught his attention. He motioned Cal closer and used his last breath to whisper. "She was complaining." Then he tilted his head up. He gave the ex-Union men standing over him a look of disdain. "Damn all Yankees!" He said the words, and his head turned a bit to the side and seemed to be starring askance into the forest of legs. Cal noticed then that the puddle in his lap had spread. As the mystery of Jimmy's murder was revealed, Elwood had allowed the tourniquet to loosen. He had indeed decided when he would die.

While Elwood Clemens pursued Sarah across the field, John Coates' horse weaved around the bushes and brambles as he crossed the field and rode hard toward the timber behind Elwood's house. Both he and his cousin had spotted Sarah in the colorful floral dress far across the way, and Elwood had chosen to pursue her. John watched that drama play in his peripheral vision for only a moment. Soon he was deep in the pines and oaks, searching for a trail to a logging road that would lead him away. John perked his ears for the report of a weapon. In but a few minutes, it came, faint and singular. He smiled and spat out his Danish chaw. He reached into his inside pocket for the packet of chewing tobacco. His supply was dwindling. He was a little sorry he had shared it with his cousin. He did not know who fired the weapon or who received the pain that it probably inflicted, and he didn't care. It could have been any of the three men he despised. It could have been the useless girl. Maybe it was Elwood? He didn't care. It was enough to know that it was someone other than himself. He had other fish to fry and gold to acquire in any way necessary.

63

Sheriff Beckett and his deputies rode up just as Cal allowed Preacher to take his six-gun. The lawman walked up to the body, sprawled against the peeling fence. Beckett looked at the circle of faces and saw that Preacher was holding Cal's gun. He reached for it and raised the barrel to his nose.

"Okay, let's have it. What happened here."

"Cal got the drop on Coates. Coates made his play and got shot in the arm for his trouble." Sarge shrugged. His voice was matter-of-fact." Cal put a tourniquet on Coates' arm to keep him from bleeding to death. Coates was supposed to hold it tight. But, thinking about it now, I suspect he loosened it himself to avoid the rope." He looked around at the others. "Is that how the rest of you see it?" Everyone nodded. The sheriff cupped his chin between his thumb and fingers and noted that Mrs. Georgia Wood was standing behind the fence with her dog.

"Is that how you saw it happen, Ma'am?"

Mrs. Wood reached into her apron pocket and belatedly put on her glasses. She shifted the shotgun from one hand to the other. "Exactly like that, Sheriff. If Cal hadn't winged him, I would have blasted him with this. I couldn't have missed him even if I weren't wearing my glasses".

Sheriff Beckett looked down at the dark, bloodied visage. The man's head had fallen against his shoulder as life left him. John Coates still looked foreboding even without the beard, with his black, unseeing eyes, dark brows, and serpent's tooth. He turned once again to Mrs. Wood.

"Sorry, you had to see all of this, Ma'am. I hope it won't set you back too much." Cal reached over and put his hand on Bronco's shoulder for additional support. If you and Preacher hadn't stopped me, we would have had another murder."

Sheriff Beckett turned to deputy Shires. "Load this pile of crap on his horse. Let's get this show back to town." He watched Shires and Boggs pick up Coates and throw him across his nervous animal.

Georgia Wood stepped closer and opened the gate to help Sarah to her feet. The dog put his muzzle against the lawman's leg for the sheriff to stroke. The sheriff bent over a little to lay his hand on Virgil's head.

"Sheriff, I think you have won Virgil over. You should come by sometime and say howdy."

Beckett pulled his hand back and colored a bit. "Thank you, ma'am. He is right friendly once he gets to know you." He turned to see if the body was loaded and tied down. "Alright, let's get going."

It was a solemn parade when the sheriff and deputies returned to town with the body they thought belonged to John Coates. It was Saturday, and the streets were busy with farmers and their families. The hitching posts were thick with horses. The news of the posse's return spread ahead of the riders. The blood and gore were evident and much remarked on as they rode to Doctor Jenkins's office to dispose of the body.

Sheriff Beckett noted the crowd with a mix of satisfaction and concern. The word would travel around the county that he had saved the damsel in distress and brought in Jimmy Jordon's murderer. Ben couldn't think of a way for that part to turn out any better. But then he concluded that word would also go out that the girl's abductor was still free. Were other women in danger? Would Elwood Clemens hang around or try to escape the county? Well, at least, he wasn't a murderer yet!

And the lawman was satisfied that the Yankees wouldn't hang around for long. Maybe soon, very soon, he'd have his quiet little town back. Sarge, Bronco, and Preacher rode in at the tail end of the parade, giving the sheriff and his two deputies their moment of glory.

Cal and Sarah were aboard his horse between the two groups. Cal, though still heavy of heart, rode erect and with a sense of serenity in the knowledge that he now knew the why of his son's death. Though proud of Jimmy's war service, Cal took more pride in his boy's long walk home. It was just as heroic to his father's mind. It occurred to him that the best that could come of war was the knowledge of duty done, whether in victory or defeat. That thought brought some solace. And just as comforting was the knowledge that his son had not died the victim of another man's personal hatred for him. The two dismounted, and Cal briefly hugged Sarah's shoulders. Then, as he turned away, his thoughts shifted to his near murder of the outlaw. That act would have been a brutal betrayal of everything he believed. Cal left Sarah in Aunt Emmy's good hands and started walking his horse toward the sheriff's office to make his official report. The three ex-Union soldiers were just ahead of him. For a moment, Preacher's form lined up with the soaring spire of the Baptist church over on the next street. That nudged Cal's mind in a new direction. In a moment of clarity, he realized there was something else that he needed to do.

Preacher also noted the spire of the baptist church over the nearby rooftops. He had a deep appreciation for the little bustling town. He felt at peace, although his calling always nudged him a bit whenever he saw a church. It looked like they now could resume their journey toward New Orleans.

After their brief visit with Sheriff Beckett, the men delivered their horses to the livery stable and checked into a hotel room. When they strolled back down to the Lucky Star for coffee, they found Pappy sitting in his familiar place. They took seats and received Pappy's congratulations and thanks. Miss Emmy took their orders. Surprisingly, she leaned down to hug each man in turn.

"I want to thank you, men, for what you did," she said. She straightened up and laid her hand lightly on Bronco's shoulder. "My sweet niece assures me that Elwood Clemens never laid a hand on her except one time with his belt. I am thankful for that, but the thought of him whipping her makes my blood boil." She wiped away a stray tear as she voiced her one remaining fear. "Do you all think there is any chance he might try taking off with her again?" For a moment, there was panic in her expression. The men looked at each other and shook their heads in unison, for the notion had not occurred to them. Her face relaxed.

"Anyway, after some rest, I'm thankful she will be herself again." She patted Bronco's shoulder and headed back to the kitchen.

The men discussed the day's events for a little while until Preacher glanced at the other men. "Everything considered, we all have a lot to be thankful for." The other three nodded in agreement.

"You boys going to be ready to ride tomorrow?" Sarge looked around the table.

"Well, not tomorrow." Preacher said. "I kind of promised Miss Maggie that I'd show up for services tomorrow. Let's plan on Monday."

Sarge and Bronco nodded. After finishing their coffee, the men walked out and surveyed the street. "Nice town," Bronco observed. He stretched and thought about his options. "I could go over to the jail and beat Deputy Shires at checkers again." He looked to see if anyone had a better idea. The other two men shrugged.

"I think I'll ride out to the farm for a final check on how Tom is getting along," Sarge said.

"I think I'll amble over to the church. Maybe I'll catch Miss Maggie practicing tomorrow's hymns." Preacher touched his hand to the brim of his new hat and stepped down from the walk to cross the street. When Preacher reached the church, he could see several horses and wagons pulled up out front. There seemed to be a meeting underway. He sat down on the step and waited.

Thirty minutes later, the piano music started up, and several men started coming out the door. Cal Jordon was in the lead. He threw his arm over Preacher's shoulder and started introducing him to the other men. Preacher was surprised when he heard the nature of the meeting the men had just completed.

For an hour, the men stood in a circle and talked. There were questions and nods. The demeanor of a couple of the men seemed a little half-hearted at first, but as the discussion continued, they eventually nodded in agreement. Finally, there was handshaking all around, and everyone departed, leaving Preacher alone.

He entered the sanctuary and sat in the second-to-the-back pew. Miss Maggie looked over and gave a little wave and smiled. Then, after beating out a couple of songs on the piano, she stood, pushed the stool back, and came over. "It turns out that Cal Jordon wanted you in church tomorrow, as much as I did," she said.

Preacher grinned. "I'm kind of overwhelmed that the two of you care so much for that to happen," he admitted. He looked at the angle of the light through the west windows and then down at his worn army duds. "If I'm to make my first appearance in church tomorrow, I better get some suitable clothes. Would you, by chance, have the time to help me with that?"

Miss Maggie smiled. "I'd be delighted, sir." She paused. "I know just the person we need for a second opinion. Let's go by the Lucky Star and see if Emmy can get free long enough to help out."

64

Preacher, Bronco, and Pappy regrouped and were eating their lunch at the Lucky Star. Miss Emmy's helper had just delivered three plates piled with ham, okra, cabbage, and new carrots.

"Preacher, are you sure about this? Seems real sudden," Bronco proclaimed a bit crossly.

Preacher was apprising the two men of his afternoon shopping activities and why they were necessary. "I admit that," he said.

"But what about New Orleans?" Bronco cut off a piece of ham and paused the fork for a moment before he filled his mouth.

"Well, Bronco, I guess the short answer is I won't be going with you." He looked a little deflated for a second. But his joy returned in a rush, and he smiled. The Lord had given him a new assignment as pastor of the Titustown Baptist Church. He couldn't hold a solemn expression for long with that thought on his mind. "I seem to remember when you were thinking about sticking around here for a while yourself, Bronco." He looked over at the younger man through his bushy eyebrows.

"Well, yeah. I guess that's so." Bronco agreed. His discontented expression did not change, though his eyes showed that he recognized the validity of Preacher's point.

Pappy's eyes moved to the door. Sheriff Beckett was coming in the entry and appeared in a hurry.

"Good, you're still here," he said.

"Just having some supper," Bronco said. "We aren't leaving till Monday. Preacher is preaching at the Baptist church tomorrow." Bronco enjoyed being the bearer of news and doing so now perked him up some.

"Well, okay." Beckett wasn't sure exactly what all that meant. He had his own news, and the ramifications of what Bronco said didn't fully gel. "I wanted to catch you boys before you headed out. John Coates is still on the loose." His eyes went from one man to the next, watching the perplexity register on each of their faces.

"Huh?" Bronco and Pappy said together.

"What do you mean?" Preacher was the first to recover enough to make a complete sentence. He arched his eyebrows and straightened up in his chair.

"I mean, the man who died this morning was Elwood Clemens, not John Coates. John's cousins, Schooley and Barney, were back in town and heard we had John over at docs. So, they went in to verify the news and claim it's Clemens' body in Doc's back room rather than John's. I didn't believe it at first, but they showed me how Clemens has these warts up his neck and the side of his face, and they say John doesn't." Beckett pulled off his hat and ran his hand from his forehead to his chin. "Dammit!"

"Wait a minute," Preacher said. "Surely, Mrs. Wood could tell the difference. They're neighbors. She was right there when it happened."

"Yeah. Mrs. Wood would have to know which was which," Bronco said.

Pappy nodded in agreement. "Are you sure those rascals ain't trying to pull something over on you?"

"I thought about that," Sheriff Beckett said. "Then, I remembered how Mrs. Wood's eyesight is so poor. She mentioned it while I was at her house last night with the ladies and then again this morning right after the shooting. I reckon she couldn't see Clemens clear enough without her glasses to tell the difference."

"Well, they were both freshly shaven and sure looked different than they did with beards, but still," Bronco said.

Preacher stood up. "I've got to see this for myself."

"Me too," said Bronco.

"Yep." Pappy started to stand up and then thought better of it. "You boys, hurry back and let me know what you find out." He rubbed his sore ribs. "This does boggle the mind." Sheriff Beckett nodded and rose to his feet.

"I'll walk you over, but I've got a feeling this is on the up and up. Dammit!"

65

The man was tall and lean. Tom Jones did not recognize John Coates at first. John wore a wide-brimmed hat, a red shirt, and dirty trousers. His manner was typical for a southerner. He sat loose in the saddle upside Tom's front porch, with a chaw in his cheek. Tom's first thought was that the stranger might be looking for work. That changed when the man spoke. "Good mornin'. Hot, ain't it? I reckon it's almost a hundred degrees." The man grinned and pulled a dirty bandana from his pocket to wipe his face and neck. The sound of whiney drawl and the sight of the yellowed teeth sent a chill that stood the hair up on the back of Tom's neck. It took but a fraction of a second for the reason why to register.

John Coates looked different than he had the last couple of times he had seen him. Though Tom had been under the influence of laudanum when last they encountered each other, he couldn't forget that voice. He noted that the heavy beard that had fluffed out a bandana mask back then was now missing. This man had recently shaved his jaw and upper lip, as betrayed by the pale skin, three shades lighter than the rest of his features. He was sure that this was the taller of the two men who had attempted to break him out of jail. But he wasn't a friend. The thick eyebrows perched crudely over the dull blackness of deeply recessed eyes. The hawkish nose, thin lips, and yellowed, fang-like eye-teeth made him an easy man to remember from their time in jail the week before. The mouth carried a permanent sneer except when he grinned. A bulge revealed the remains of a chaw in one corner of his mouth. According to the last report, Tom had heard, John Coates had left the county headed west. But the voice was unmistakable. So much for the reliability of reports.

"Morning," Tom said. With his quick recall of the recent past, Tom suddenly felt naked without his weapon. He instinctively touched his ribcage with the truncated nub of an arm. Then, he took a casual side-step toward the door. His holstered six-gun was lying on the table inside. He seldom wore it since his return after being wounded. His eyes fell on the man's snakeskin boots. They clinched his identification. Yep. It was John Coates.

"I bet your hands went to town, it being Saturday." John stretched leisurely in the saddle and looked around. Tom noted that the man's hand stayed close to his six-gun.

"Expect them back soon." Tom lied. He took another step backward toward the door.

"No matter." Coates noticed Tom's movement and completed his visual surveillance of the surrounding area. He pulled his sidearm. "I won't be here long."

"What's this about?" Tom lifted his chin in defiance.

John dismounted and stepped up on the porch. Confident in the advantage his two arms and six-gun provided, he pushed Tom Jones roughly around, so his back was to him. Then, to erase any doubt Tom might have about his position of dominance, John kicked his legs out from under him. Tom sprawled toward the doorway. He swung his arms wildly, trying to regain his balance before he landed on his good left arm, belly-side down. As Tom managed to get back to his knees, Coates brought his six-gun level with his nose. "You will lead me to your gold mine, or I'll plug you right here and now."

Tom, jolted by the man's knowledge of his gold, looked into the man's eyes and believed him. Sweat gathered on his forehead. The reference to a mine gave him an idea of the limits of the man's knowledge. Tom desperately needed the big poke of gold he had received from Madison to put his farm and sawmill back on a profitable footing. He swore silently at the useless right arm. Tom got his legs under him and took a deep breath. He studied the barrel of the six-gun four inches away.

"Sorry to disappoint, but there is no mine," Tom said evenly. He was unsure if feigning ignorance of Coates' identity could give him an edge, but he couldn't see it would hurt. Tom tried to guard himself against another blow once he regained his feet. He searched the man's dark eyes for some sign of intelligence or humanity. Instead, all Tom could detect was callousness and cunning.

Coates smiled. "You've got gold, all right. This place is not a poor man's house." He stepped a pace to the right, pushed the door open, and spotted the six-gun on the table. He reached inside, plucked it from the holster, stuck it in his belt. Then he motioned for Tom to follow him in. He glanced around the large parlor. Tom's eyes followed his. Seeing the room through this killer's eyes brought a different perspective. The oil portrait of his mother, an attractive lady, had been returned to its place over the fireplace. But the furniture was worn and the floor scuffed. It indeed was not built by a poor man. But the signs of wealth that John Coates was pointing out were no longer accurate indicators. They were from a time before the loss of his brother's help, his three slaves' disappearance, and before the war interrupted his farming and lumber business.

Now, John needed Tom alive until he divulged the necessary information. John could see only one solution. "You can give it up now so that I can move on, or I'll have to sweat the information out of you." He shrugged to indicate it made no difference to him. In truth, inducing pain was a prospect that usually gave him a welcome sense of anticipation. But at present, his past sins kept him looking over his shoulder. He waited a moment, but Tom did not respond.

"We're going to the barn," he announced. He pushed Tom's weapon farther under his belt and retreated out the front door. He waved the gun for Tom to follow.

"What's in the barn?" Though concerned, Tom was thankful for a brief respite. If he could buy a little more time, there was a chance he could outsmart Coates.

"Some persuasion," Coates replied. "If I truss you up by your heels on that block and tackle out there, you will be talking like a jaybird."

"Persuasion only works when the information exists. There is no gold mine." Tom said. He felt that chill again.

Coates smiled and shrugged. "Suit yourself. It don't matter; I'll enjoy it either way. Let's get going. I'm looking forward to it."

"I don't know where you got your ideas about a gold mine, but the only gold around here was placer gold panned by my father back when I was a boy. And he only panned when he didn't have farm work to do." Then, playing for time, Tom looked at John over his shoulder. "Where did you get your information?"

"I'd say I have a pretty good source. Your brother and his two Yankee-scum friends ambushed my two cousins and me over in Alabama. While they thought I was unconscious, the one called Bronco mentioned they was coming here for gold. So now I'm here for some too."

Tom feigned a laugh. "Well, that's where you got off the track. As I said, my father did a little panning. The gold you are talking about was collected by him over several years. He kept it here in some hidey-hole for my brother, Madison. When my father died, I inherited the farm, and Madison inherited the gold. But you're way too late; Madison took it with him when they went off tracking you." Tom looked back over his shoulder and waved his single arm over his head. "Goodbye, gold."

Coates felt his ire rise. Tom seemed to be toying with him. He turned his pistol around and gave Tom a hard blow to the side of his head. It was not hard enough to knock him out, but John thought it would be enough to take the jesting out of his voice. Tom reeled and went to one knee before he caught himself. He used his good arm to push himself back to his feet. Coates watched the man struggle. He had no time to waste. John hated to admit it, but what Tom was saying had a ring of truth. If he stuck around and a posse showed up, he'd be in a pickle for sure. It looked to be time to put the one-armed man out of his misery. Coates raised his weapon once again. This time it was pointed at Tom's head. "I'm tired of fooling with you!"

Sarge rounded the curve in the lane just in time to see Tom receive the blow to the side of his head and tumble to his knees. There was a finality to the attacker's action, and the position of his gun pointed at Tom's head filled Sarge with instant alarm. He instantly recognized that he had but seconds to act. Sarge grabbed his rifle and aimed high toward the barn. At that distance, Sarge knew that if he targeted Coates, he was as likely to hit Tom.

At the crack of the rifle, there was a brief moment before Sarge saw a reaction. Then Tom, who had been struggling to right himself, hit the dirt. John turned his weapon away from Tom toward Sarge and fired twice. They were hurried shots at too great a distance, and Sarge didn't even hear them pass. In response, he grimly spurred his horse directly toward the man. Sarge's eyes were slits against the wind, and the front of his Union cap pressed against his forehead. Sarge realized that somehow, as unexpected as it might seem, the man had to be Elwood Clemens, and for some unknown reason, he had been planning to murder Tom.

But then the man seemed to forget Tom. He turned tail and ran for the interior of the barn. Sarge pressed his advantage, and his horse thundered toward the pair. Tom was still lying on the ground. As John darted across the barnyard, he turned his weapon toward Sarge again and got off another round. It went badly astray as the man in the Union cap charged forward.

Sarge raced straight into the gunfire. His eyes were hard, his face set in deadly purpose. His immediate concern was giving Tom time to seek shelter. And he was determined to finish this thing. He fired toward the man he thought was Elwood once more and motioned with his rifle for Tom to run. As he passed Tom in his approach to the barn entrance, Sarge discarded the rifle and drew his handgun. Tom staggered to his feet and ran to get behind a nearby tree.

"It's John Coates," Tom shouted at his brother as he galloped past.

Sarge went rigid with that news. He saw Coates respond by briefly turning his weapon toward Tom again, but then he turned it back to shoot toward Sarge. With Tom's words and the sight of John's lean form running awkwardly in the snakeskin boots, suddenly everything Sarge thought he knew shifted. Sarge fired as John ducked into the barn. Sarge's horse charged in after him.

For a second, John stared down at the weapon he held and wondered how many cartridges were left. He realized he was hurrying his shots. His eyes swept the interior of the barn for better cover. Sarge was almost on him. Coates spied the ladder to the loft and ran for it. He was four rungs up before Sarge came through the barn's entry. Sarge reined up with his gun only inches from Coates. In desperation, John turned and kicked the gun-hand away from him, and Sarge's horse shied. John used the distraction and scrambled the rest of the way to the loft. He fired down through the floor toward the place Sarge had occupied, but Sarge had leaped from the shying horse onto the ladder. He fired two rounds upward over his shoulder as he climbed. The board John Coates was standing on splintered just an inch from his foot. He sprang to one side and fired again. He tripped on a box and sprawled face down perilously close to the loft's opening over the barnyard.

Sarge arrived at the top of the ladder and saw Coates pick himself up and limp across the opening. From his position, there was nothing behind Coates but blue sky. Sarge fired again and stumbled forward over the same box Coates had encountered. His next shot went wild. He was on his hands and knees when Coates lurched sidewise from the edge of the opening. He looked back toward Sarge with cold eyes, his body silhouetted against the sky. With his left hand, John reached in his belt for Tom's gun. With his right hand, he fired his last round. Sarge rolled to one side. The round threw up a dusting of debris, and John pulled out the second gun and quickly dropped the first into the holster. He moved the six-gun from his left to right hand and squeezed the trigger. Sarge knew he was running low on ammunition. He steadied the grip of his six-gun on the floor and fired once more. His bullet found its target, and Coates doubled over and tripped back a step. It was a step too far. His boot found only air. His surprise was evident as his head tilted back, and his eyes widened. He flailed for a handhold on the barn's wall only inches beyond his grasping fingers. Then his backward flight continued. His hat flew skyward, caught by a gust of wind. For a brief moment, it hung in the air, the only object in Sarge's line of sight against the pale blue sky. A second passed before Sarge heard the thud of John Coates' body hitting the ground. Sarge staggered to the entrance and looked out. He waited, panting as he watched his brother hurry to the still body sprawled in the barnyard. Coates still had one six-gun in hand and, the other lay in the dirt a few feet away. Tom knelt over the body. He shook his head. When Tom rose, he pulled his gun from Coates' left hand and looked up at his brother. He pulled out his bandana and wiped his face. "I think he's dead. You came along at a very good time." He smiled. "This makes twice."

Bronco and Preacher exited Doc's office with Sheriff Beckett. Preacher was shaking his head in disbelief. "I just knew we had that skunk nailed!"

Beckett nodded. "So, did I. The man's got more lives than a black cat."

Bronco interrupted their jawing with a shout. "Look, there's Sarge with Tom." The men waited in mixed bemusement and disgust as the wagon pulled alongside. Sarge's horse was trailing behind.

"Guess what," Bronco said. "That ain't John Coates in the doc's morgue. It's Elwood Clemens." He looked around at the two other men for confirmation and then back to Sarge and Tom.

"Sounds about right," Sarge said. Preacher noticed a bit of humor in his eyes. His friend's lips lifted a bit at the corners.

Beckett leaned forward. "There ain't nothing right about it!" he said, exasperated that Sarge didn't seem to think the news appalling.

Bronco's mouth was open in surprise. He turned toward Preacher as though for counsel.

Sarge looked at his brother and then at the gloomy group of men. "Take a look in the back of the wagon." He frowned, then grinned. "I'm right, sorry to bring you another body, Sheriff."

66

Sunday morning, Miss Maggie took her place at the piano next to the chancel of the Titustown Baptist Church. She looked up on the platform at Preacher and smiled. He was seated behind the pulpit beside Cal Jordan. He was wearing the new suit he had purchased just the day before. His big gap-toothed grin lit the room.

Deacon Cal Jordan rose and walked over to stand beside the pulpit. He looked out at the first row of pews. His wife, Wanda, and two daughters sat close by Miss Emmy and his daughter-in-law, Mrs. Sarah Jordan. The benches were packed. He cleared his throat, and the low hum of many and varied half-volume conversations subsided.

"Today, before we start the worship service, I want to introduce you to an unusual man. For weeks since the end of the war, you all know that our community has been terrorized by a lawless element who placed no value on human life. These individuals, who I will not name in this sacred place, robbed and murdered several of our neighbors. In my case, one of those men badly wounded my uncle, Pappy Jordan, and killed my beloved son, Jimmy, who we buried only a few days ago. One of his kin sheltered the killer and abducted my daughter-in-law." His eyes were shiny. He paused and cleared his throat once again.

"This man," he placed his hand on Preacher's shoulder. "This man solved the mystery of that abduction with his companions, Madison Jones and Bill Brumley. And, led by our Sheriff Ben Beckett, we rescued her from her abductor. This man also saved me from making the biggest mistake of my life. Through his gentle persuasion, he stayed my hand as I contemplated the cold-blooded murder of another human being." There was a renewed hum among the members of the congregation. In the time since they had brought in Elwood Clemens' lifeless body, truths and half-truths had spread concerning his demise. With the confirmed deaths of both men, the stories had redoubled. Cal raised his hand a bit, and when the sound diminished, he continued.

"For better than a year, this church has been absent a minister of the gospel. Reverend Thomas passed away, and we were leaderless. And being leaderless, we did nothing. As a deacon, I am as much at fault for that as anyone." He paused and looked out at the crowd as if accepting their unspoken rebuke.

"I suppose that many, if not all of us, let ourselves get side-tracked by our concerns for loved ones who were gone and in harm's way. In any event, our council of deacons has decided that it is time to rectify that error." An 'Amen' from one of the other deacons setting off to the church's right side interrupted the congregation's hum of voices.

"The man I speak of is sitting here beside me. He is affectionately called Preacher by his friends. His given name is Robert Gracey. He is known by many in Missouri as The Reverend Robert Gracey. The other deacons and I have conversed closely with him about his understanding of the scriptures and his habits. As to his temperament, I can personally testify to that because, as I alluded to before, I am the beneficiary of it." Cal held up his personal Bible and opened it to a marked passage. "I want to read a passage that means so much more to me now than it did just a week ago. This reading is from

John 15:13 and 17. *"Greater love hath no man than this that a man lay down his life for his friends. These things I command you, that ye love one another.* Cal looked up. *"That you love one another."* Cal looked out on the hushed crowd.

"This man stopped me from killing a man not by being willing to lay down his life for him but being ready to lay down his life to protect me from an inner cry for vengeance. The other deacons and I have concluded that in this time, after the trials that we have all faced, we need a man who can awaken us and renew us in the words of the Holy Bible. A man who can rechallenge us to forgive each other daily and help us, with the grace of God, to forgive ourselves." Cal grinned. "Well, I have said more than I meant to. So, my friends, I present the new pastor of the Titustown Baptist Church, the Reverend Robert Gracey." Cal stuck out his hand and shook Preacher's, then joined his wife and daughters in the front pew. Miss Maggie started the applause. Eventually, it swept through the congregation.

Preacher stood, walked to the pulpit, and made a motion for the congregation to rise. "Thank you, brother Jordon. I will try to live up to the praise you have bestowed on me. I can think of no more appropriate new beginning for this church and my ministry here than with prayer. I want to start my time here, witnessing my firm belief that God hears our prayers. As we go forward, I want us to invest ourselves in knowing that we owe our God more than he owes us. To me, that means our primary goal and obligation to our God is to thank Him for our many blessings. Every breath we take, every caress we share, every crop that comes in, every newborn, whether calf, or foal, or human, is a gift from God and deserves our thanks. The Bible says in Thessalonians 5:16-18, *"always rejoice, pray without ceasing, give thanks in all circumstances; for this is the will of God in Christ Jesus for you."*

Preacher tucked his chin to his big chest and prayed. True to his word, his prayer was one of thanks. As he prayed, a flood of reasons to be thankful came into his mind and heart. Twice he halted and swiped away the sweat and tears, but he could not run out of reasons to be grateful as he recalled the need to bind up the community's wounds and renew the hearts of God's people. As he prayed, there were many Amens, occasional sobs, and even some laughter to fill the house as His people finally let go, at least for the moment, of the torments that had hardened their hearts and blinded their eyes. When he finished, the Reverent Robert Gracey looked up and laughed. "My friends, we have been here for an hour, and that is my first sermon! Just so you will want to come back, I promise that I will never preach that long again! And," he grinned, "you won't ever again have to listen to one of my serons standing up."

Bronco, sitting on the back pew, looked over at Sarge and grinned. He realized that he had never heard the remainder of Preacher's story. But, somehow, now, it no longer mattered.

The congregation nodded and laughed, and as Preacher stood at the door shaking hands with his new parishioners, some felt the call to hug the new pastor. His words had pulled them together in their common humanity, and many went home with a little more hope for their individual and collective futures. They knew they would face more trials and tribulations. But, they knew that with His help, they could persevere.

THE END

About the Author

Charles Reed is the author of four other works, *Trouble in Harlon County* (The first novel of The Pursuers Series), *Justice in Harlon County* (The third novel of The Pursuers Series), *Tracks to Harlon County, Twenty-One Tales of Life and Adventure,* and *The Long Caper,* a time travel adventure to 1865 Harlon County,

Charles was born in Saint Louis, Missouri. Because of his father's occupation, he moved often throughout his early years. During that period, he attended twelve schools in four states. When not writing, Charles is an avid reader of biography, history, and historical and mystery fiction,

Charles has run three marathons, three half marathons, numerous *Tulsa Runs* and participated with his bicycle in the *Free-Wheel across Oklahoma* six times. In addition, Charles has traveled in Europe, the Orient, and South America. His first air travel was to Southeast Asia, where he served as an infantryman with the 101 Airborne Division.

CPSIA information can be obtained
at www.ICGtesting.com
Printed in the USA
LVHW020847201121
703857LV00001B/45